BLOOD CRUISE

JAKE BIBLE

SEVERED PRESS
HOBART TASMANIA

BLOOD CRUISE

WWW.SEVEREDPRESS.COM

ISBN: 978-1-925342-77-2

1.

Six levels of security.

Dr. Harold Glouster had insisted on ten, at the very least, but the company he worked for, Oceanic Applied Sciences, had told him six would be sufficient. After all, despite the passive sounding name, they were one of the world's leading defense and weaponry research and development firms. If they could not keep Dr. Glouster's project safe then no one could.

That was the point that was hammered home to Dr. Glouster time and time again when he made his weekly report via video conference to the OAS board.

"It has become too smart for its enclosure," Dr. Glouster sighed as he stared at the eight faces that filled the split screens on his computer monitor. He gave a sidelong glance at the massive tank of saltwater that took up almost the entire room he had been working in for the past eighteen months. "I cannot stress enough—"

"Yes, Doctor, we know," Mathias McDowell, CEO of OAS, interrupted. "And your concerns are noted and being taken seriously. As I have said time and time again."

"Yet you do nothing about it," Dr. Glouster responded. "I stated four weeks ago that I would need a new facility. You did not deliver."

"You are working in the most state of the art bioweapons labs in the world, Doctor Glouster," McDowell snapped. "It is not a simple matter to just move you to a new facility. Your work has specific needs to be considered that would render any outfitting of a new facility useless to future work."

"You mean it is too expensive," Dr. Glouster countered.

"I do," McDowell said, smiling the smile that had had Wired, Forbes, and Vanity Fair magazines scrambling to get him on their covers once OAS went public the previous month. "Do you know why, Doctor? Because I run a company that is in the business of making products that make money. Your projections show that OAS will not see a profit from your product for at least a decade."

"It is not a product, McDowell," Dr. Glouster said. "It is a living creature. I have manipulated its DNA, giving OAS two hundred and four new patents, but it is still a living, thinking, sentient being."

"Sentient?" McDowell asked. "Like a dog or cat, yes?"

"Closer to a primate," Dr. Glouster replied. "Its intelligence tests are off the charts as of yesterday. I do not know how, but it has made considerable strides in complex reasoning as well as applied recall. It is remembering significant amounts of information and using those memories to inform its decisions. Tricks I have used on it in the past, as recent as last month, to try to find its weaknesses are no longer effective. It knows the tricks and is even anticipating them."

"But it can be controlled, yes?" McDowell asks. "Like a dog or a cat?"

"Have you ever tried to control a cat?" Dr. Glouster asked. "I believe you should be looking for a different example."

"Then forget the damn cat!" McDowell shouted. "Can the creature be controlled? Can it be given a mission, complete that mission, and return for further orders? Can it be trained like a dog and be just as obedient? That is what you promised me, Doctor Glouster. You did not promise me an eight-legged sea monkey that is more trouble than it is worth. And believe me when I say that it is worth millions upon millions at this point since you have gone well over budget and over schedule!"

The look on Dr. Glouster's face could not be interpreted as anything but contempt. It was reflected back at him by all eight boxes on the split-screen monitor. The man fought down the urge to tell McDowell to go to hell and walk away from the project. Just walk away from it all and let OAS sort it all out.

But he could not do that to his creation. Not after all of the hard work, the loss, the sacrifices made. Not after what happened to Melanie Hecht. A true tragedy that would have ended any other career. But her death was the project's breakthrough. A terrifying and repulsive breakthrough from any viewpoint, even by McDowell's loose standards of morals, but a breakthrough that rocketed the project forward at an exponential pace.

"Doctor?" McDowell asked, his calm restored that smile of smiles back in place. "Are you hearing what I am saying to you, Doctor?"

"It has become too intelligent," Dr. Glouster stated. "Let me explain why that is a problem."

"There is no need," McDowell said, sighing heavily.

His eyes flitted back and forth and Dr. Glouster could tell he was looking at his own split screen version of the board meeting. Dr. Glouster watched the expressions on the other board members' faces and realized that something far beyond his control was going on.

"What have you done, McDowell?" Dr. Glouster asked. "I would think an explanation of the subject's rapid progress would be of the utmost importance. Is that not why we have these weekly meetings?"

"It was," McDowell said. "But this will be the last meeting. Everything I need to know is in your notes which I have handed to my top people for a full analysis."

"My notes?" Dr. Glouster gasped. "Those are encrypted on a laptop that I do not connect to the internet. You cannot possibly have access to my notes!"

"Yes, yes, I know," McDowell said. "But did you really believe a laptop given to you by OAS would ever be truly private?"

He chuckled and rubbed at his temples.

"Since we are nearing the end of the conversation, I'd like to let you in on a little secret, Doctor. Nothing you have been doing for these past eighteen months has escaped my notice. Nothing. Not even what happened to Dr. Hecht. Which, amusingly enough, you reported as a workplace accident. She slipped and hit her head, Doctor? And somehow her body was lost before it could be transported off ship? How do you lose a human corpse, Doctor? I have made sure protocols are in place to account for every damn paper clip, staple, and roll of toilet paper on that ship. A body does not go missing unless someone wants it to. Even then..."

The split screens were replaced by an autopsy photo of the late Dr. Melanie Hecht, her body bone white and desiccated.

"Surprised? You really shouldn't be, Doctor," McDowell continued. "Dr. Hecht was not a paper clip or roll of toilet paper.

She was an expensive asset that OAS lost due to your negligence. Lucky for us all, her death was the turning point in the project. I was this close to pulling the plug on you, Doctor Glouster." He held up his thumb and forefinger, squeezing them together until they were only a hair's breadth apart, as his image replaced that of Dr. Hecht's corpse. He was the only image on the screen, the splits of the OAS board no longer visible. "And when you get the plugged pulled by me, you never get plugged back in."

He leaned back from the screen and folded his hands behind his head.

"I am sorry, Doctor Glouster, but your request for a larger enclosure, as well as a larger facility all together, has been denied," McDowell said. "I am also sorry to tell you that your services are no longer needed. We have what we need to proceed on our own and your continued refusal to be a part of the OAS team is just not acceptable. Consider your plug pulled."

The screen went blank before Dr. Glouster could respond. He stared at the monitor for exactly two seconds before jumping up from his seat.

Six levels of security.

All of which were designed to protect the ship from outside threats. But Dr. Glouster knew that outside threats were not the problem. It was what was already inside that was the true danger.

2.

"I just want you to be smart and safe," Ben Clow said as he leaned against the door jamb of his daughter's bedroom. "I know your mother will say yes to pretty much anything you ask this weekend, without any thought toward the consequences. It sucks, Tee, but I need you to be the adult while you are over there."

"I got it, Dad," Tanni Hunsaker-Clow replied as she reclined against the mound of pillows on her bed. "I've been to Mom's before, ya know? I am prepared for the complete and total lack of supervision and logic." She looked up from her phone, her fingers pausing from their constant typing. "I'll be sure to make nothing but rational decisions that have been thought through from all angles. I will not let emotion cloud my judgment or inform my choices."

"Don't make fun of me," Ben said. "I haven't been in the game for over four years now."

"I read the blog, Dad," Tanni said. "And you spout some form of that motto at the end of every single entry. Who are you trying to convince? Your readers or yourself?"

"How old are you? Sixteen?" Ben laughed. "The world will be screwed when you actually know what the hell you're talking about."

He sighed and rubbed at his face, the salt and pepper scruff on his cheeks and chin making an audible scratching noise. Ben moved from the door and sat on the edge of Tanni's bed, smiling down at the comforter that still sported oversized, brightly colored flowers.

"Listen. Do me a solid, okay?" Ben asked.

"If you promise never to say do me a solid ever again," Tanni replied.

"Promise," Ben said. "Just look after your sister. Alright? I know you want to sneak off from your mother to go spend time with what's his name."

"Who?" Tanni asked, her eyes going wide.

5

"You know, the guy you've been texting with for the past month," Ben replied. "You think I didn't notice you were sending love texts to some boy? What is his name? Alex?"

Tanni's face went pale and Ben laughed.

"Chill. It's all good," Ben said. "I'm not the dad that wants to buy a shotgun and cram it up his daughter's new boyfriend's butthole. Not that dad, okay? Considering what your mother and I were up to in high school, I have no room to talk. Not to mention the hell your grandfather put me through."

"Pops was a good man," Tanni said, the color returning to her cheeks. "Don't say one bad word about him."

"Your grandfather was a good man," Ben agreed. "He just never thought I was."

"You did end up losing a couple hundred thousand dollars of his money," Tanni said and shrugged. "Can't think why he'd have been pissed at you."

"Who told you that?" Ben asked then shook his head. "Never mind. I know your mother did. But that is in the past. And it's not like he didn't have plenty of money left when he passed away."

"Which is locked in a trust fund for me and the Norms," Tanni said. "Safely out of reach from you or Mom."

"I'm not that bad with money," Ben said. "I used to make a living at money management, you know."

"Playing professional poker is not money management, Dad," Tanni said. "Setting up IRAs and 401ks for middle managers is money management."

"Which is why I have the check book," Maggie Rodriguez-Kimura said as she walked into the room. "And why you have new clothes and get fed every day." The woman leaned down and kissed Ben on the forehead then ruffled his hair. "Isn't he just adorable when he tries to act like he knows what the hell he's talking about?"

"Is adorable the right word?" Tanni grinned.

She pushed off the bed and gave Maggie a big hug.

"Take care of him," Tanni said.

"I always do," Maggie replied, kissing Tanni on the cheek. "But I do agree with your father. Watch over Norma and if you do leave to go hang out with Alex, take her with you. I know it's not sexy fun to have your little sister around when you're with your—" She paused and gave Tanni a serious look. "When you are with your new squeeze, but do not dare leave Norma alone with your mother. She'll end up coming back with a blue Mohawk and inappropriate body parts pierced."

"My mom lives in Olympia, not a circus freak show," Tanni replied then nodded. "But, yeah, I'll make sure that doesn't happen."

"Norma all packed?" Ben asked, giving the two women a confused look.

"Norma is all packed," Maggie said, ignoring the look. "Tee? You ready?"

Tanni pointed to a single backpack. "Yep."

"You don't want to bring more than that?" Maggie asked.

"Nope," Tanni said. "Norma is the one that needs half her room put into suitcases when she leaves the house. Not me."

"You pack that crimson skirt?" Maggie asked. "The one that goes great with your grey sweater?"

"I packed both," Tanni said.

"Good," Maggie said. "You look cute as hell in that outfit. It'll be perfect when you go out."

"I thought we just established that Tanni wasn't going out," Ben said.

"No, we established that Tanni wasn't going out without taking Norma with her," Maggie said. "You can't expect a teenage girl not to go out at all on the weekend, Benjamin. That's just asking for deception."

"I'm the actual parent here, ya know," Ben said. "So why do I feel like I'm the outsider with you two sometimes?"

"Because you're an idiot," Tanni said.

"An idiot with a cute ass," Maggie said.

"Ew. Gross," Tanni laughed.

"Daddy!" a girl screamed from the hallway. Footfalls echoed into the room then ten-year-old Norma Clow came bursting in, her clothes covered in sawdust. "We have a Code Seven Hundred emergency! Jail break! Jail break!"

Then the curly haired redhead was gone, a few specks of sawdust floating to the carpet in her wake.

"I'm guessing there is a guinea pig on the loose," Maggie said, kissing Ben. "I'll let you deal with that while I run back to my place and grab a couple of things for the trip."

"What is over there that isn't here?" Ben asked. "You've been living here full time for a year now."

"There are some items that I haven't brought over," Maggie said. "Personal items."

"She has all her sexy underwear at her apartment," Tanni said. "Not the night on the town underwear, but the underwear that is only on for a minute before it is off."

Ben and Maggie looked at Tanni for a couple of seconds. Maggie smiled and blushed. Ben scowled and blushed.

"Go," Ben said to Maggie. "I'll be over to pick you up by three."

"Sounds good," Maggie said, kissing him again. "Love you."

"Love you too," Ben said.

"DADDY!" Norma screamed from down the hall.

"Jesus," Ben said. "How the hell does a guinea pig manage to escape so much?"

3.

With his back pressed against the tank, his eyes locked onto the many firearms pointed at him, none of which he could identify, Dr. Glouster held up his hands and focused on the man standing a few feet in front of the assault team or whatever it was called.

"I am warning all of you that you are going about this all wrong," Dr. Glouster pleaded. "It will not respond to you. It is only responsive to my commands. You will need me to help you transport it to the next facility."

"I'm afraid that won't be happening, Doc," Miles Wagner, Chief Security Field Officer for OAS said. "However, I have been granted authority to decide your fate. Mr. McDowell made it clear he would like all loose ends tied up neatly. I probably do not have to go into detail as to what that means, do I?"

"No, you do not," Dr. Glouster replied. "You have been ordered to execute me and my staff so that we cannot share our program with any rivals."

"Exactly," Wagner said. "If you were allowed to walk then you could set up shop and start this Dr. Frankenstein crap somewhere else."

"Dr. Frankenstein?" Dr. Glouster asked. "Do you even know what we do here, Mr. Wagner?"

"Not really," Wagner said and shrugged. "But knowing what you do is not my job. I don't get paid to know. I get paid to complete my mission."

The man turned and pointed his automatic rifle at the six men behind him. They didn't have time to even raise an eyebrow before he put a bullet in the middle of each of their foreheads.

Dr. Glouster screamed and fell to the ground, his arms covering his head as he tried to make himself as small as possible. He stared in horror as the assault team collapsed and the blood began to pool and flow across the textured metal of the lab floor. His eyes went to Wagner's back and he tried to say something, but all he could do was stammer out a small squeak and a gasp.

Wagner knelt and checked to make sure each of the men were truly dead. He spun about on one knee and regarded Dr. Glouster once his pulse taking was finished.

"Like I was saying, Doc," Wagner continued as if he hadn't just murdered six men that had trusted him with their lives. "I get paid to complete. Your staff are already dead. That part is completed. Their bodies were long cold before I had my team hack your security codes and step one foot inside this lab. Now I need to complete the rest of my job."

"I…d-d-do not underst-st-stand," Dr. Glouster stammered.

"What part?" Wagner asked, standing and taking a step towards the tank. Dr. Glouster cried out. "Calm down, Doc. I told you I had been granted authority to decide your fate. My new employers are leaving it up to me as to whether you come with, which means giving me your full cooperation, or whether you stay here and I put a bullet in your brain."

Wagner pressed a finger to his ear.

"Lab is clear. Send in the team," he said. "Which will it be?"

Dr. Glouster shook and cowered.

"Doc? That last question was for you?" Wagner said. "Which will it be? You come with and do not even think of being a problem? Or you stay and I add one more body to the count?"

"All dead?" Dr. Glouster asked. "You killed my whole staff?"

"Ship's crew as well," Wagner said. "There isn't a single person left alive on this ship. That's going to change as my new team hops aboard. Their boat should have arrived about the time my old team figured out the hard way that they were fired."

"Why?" Dr. Glouster asked.

"Money," Wagner said. "You think I do this job because I like working for assholes like McDowell? You think I enjoy getting shot at, beat up, or even killing people?"

"Yes," Dr. Glouster said.

"I don't," Wagner responded. "Well, sometimes I do. The part where I'm killing dickheads that think they can shoot at me and live. But the other stuff? Man, I wanted to be a radio DJ when I was a kid. But poor folk like me don't get to do that stuff. We get to enlist and fight and die for our country. Some of us, those that show they have a certain skill set, then get plucked from the grunts and end up training to do things that would make Ted Bundy shiver."

"I do not pity you," Dr. Glouster said. "Whatever your circumstances were before you became the man you are now, those circumstances are no excuse for killing innocent people."

"I hate to break it to you, Doc, but there are no innocents on this ship," Wagner said. "Never were. What did you think you were doing? Making a new kind of guard dog? No way, Jose. You were taking an innocent animal and turning it into a killing machine. You may have been able to wash your guilty hands if it was some shark or something you were adding frickin' laser beams to. But that ain't no shark."

"Mechanical modifications have not been part of this project, Mr. Wagner," Dr. Glouster said. "All of my work has been biological. I have simply enhanced the creature's natural abilities, boosting the ones more suitable to OAS's needs and parameters."

"Too bad OAS won't get to see those needs met," Wagner said. He stepped closer to the tank, his hand resting against the ten-inch thick glass. "It's cold. I thought it would be warm like those tanks at the Chinese restaurants."

"This is a cold water creature," Dr. Glouster said, still cowering on the ground. "It thrives in waters between forty and fifty-four degrees Fahrenheit."

"Fifty-four? That's pretty specific," Wagner said. "It got a name?"

"Excuse me?" Dr. Glouster replied.

"Does. It. Have. A. Name?" Wagner asked slowly.

"No, it does not have a name," Dr. Glouster said. "It is not a pet."

"So you just call it the creature?" Wagner asked.

"Yes," Dr. Glouster said. "I have stayed objective throughout the entire project. To name the creature would be to connect emotionally. That would cloud my judgment and possibly influence my findings."

"Staying objective is always a good idea," Wagner said. "We have that in common. You're a man of science, I'm a man of action. Neither of us have time for emotions to get in the way."

Wagner tapped on the glass.

"Do not do that!" Dr. Glouster shouted as he shot to his feet and grabbed Wagner's arm.

He was spun about so fast that he became dizzy and nearly passed out as Wagner jammed the doctor's arm up behind his back.

"Men of science shouldn't grab men of action," Wagner said. "You lied to me."

"I did no such thing," Dr. Glouster gasped.

"You said you were objective and didn't let emotion get in your way," Wagner said. "That was pretty emotional, Doc, grabbing and shouting at me."

"I did that because it does not like it when people tap on its tank," Dr. Glouster said. "Need I remind you what happened to Dr. Hecht?"

"She died because she tapped on the thing's tank?" Wagner asked. "How? I saw the video of her death. She didn't tap on anything except the clipboard she was holding."

"She'd tapped on the tank two days earlier," Dr. Glouster said. "It reacted negatively and she continued to do it. At the time, I thought nothing of it since the creature's behavior was of interest to the project. How it reacts to simple negative stimuli is essential data."

"Two days earlier? Are you saying this thing remembered what she did and was holding a grudge?" Wagner asked. He let go of Dr. Glouster and took a few steps back from the tank. "Damn. Remind me not to piss it off."

"If I have to remind you, it is already too late," Dr. Glouster said.

The passageway outside the lab was filled with the sound of heavy footfalls. Wagner turned from the tank and smiled at the dozen men that rushed into the room.

"Clean up the bodies," Wagner ordered. "All of them. I want this ship spotless before we sink it. No evidence left behind." He pressed his finger to his ear again. "Cutting crew? Are you in place? Good. I'll tell you when the transfer is to begin. Sit tight."

"Mr. Wagner, I must warn you that transferring the creature is not like moving a goldfish from one bowl to another," Dr. Glouster said. "I would advise you allow me to inspect the new tank you have prepared."

"New tank? No, Doc, I'm bringing this one," Wagner said, pointing at, but for sure not tapping, the glass before him. "This isn't my first extraction of an item of a unique nature. I've learned the hard way that if scientists have something set up a certain way then it's best not to mess with that way."

"You are more intelligent than I would have thought," Dr. Glouster said.

"I should consider that an insult, but I don't," Wagner said. "In fact, I should be mad at myself. I usually like it for people to completely underestimate me. And here I go showing my hand."

4.

"Daddy look!" Norma called from the middle seat of the minivan. "I did it! I did the card trick!"

"Cool, Punkin," Ben replied as he turned onto a residential street. "You'll have to show me when we get to your mom's."

The road was lined with massive fir trees, many at least seventy-five feet tall. They stood guard over the arts and crafts houses that lined the neighborhood known for its bohemian and artistic-inclined residents. Only a mile from Evergreen University, the street was a strange mix of college kids and long-term homeowners. One of the last refuges of the eclectic style Olympia, Washington was known for. A style that was quickly fading away as the ever growing sprawl of Seattle-Tacoma moved south and swallowed the quaintness of everything around Puget Sound.

Ben took another turn then slowed down and looked at the old house that he had spent so many years living in. Both girls were born there. Literally. In the front room in an inflatable pool with a midwife standing by, calling out encouragement while two "shamans" chanted and burned incense over by the wall.

Ben should have known the marriage wouldn't last when one of the "shamans" told him that his aura was poison and he needed to work on his morning cleansing routine. Ben had responded that black coffee and a good, long poo was his morning cleansing routine. The shaman was not amused. Neither was Bobbi.

Bobbi Hunsaker. Always Bobbi Hunsaker. Never Bobbi Clow or even Hunsaker-Clow like the girls were named. Bobbi Hunsaker. Daughter of Matthew and Elizabeth Hunsaker. Of Hunsaker Investments LLC. Puget Sound elite. That Hunsaker.

The woman stood on the porch of the cute bungalow dressed in a flowing skirt and a leather halter top despite the cold Pacific Northwest weather that had set in and wouldn't leave for the next few months. Bobbi waved as Ben pulled into the driveway, but he knew the wave wasn't for him.

"There they are!" Bobbi called out, her arms open wide as the two girls piled out of the minivan. "My beautiful girls!"

Norma hurried across the damp, emerald green lawn to her mother while Tanni held back, her head shaking back and forth.

"What?" Ben asked.

"Leather halter top?" Tanni huffed.

"So?" Ben replied.

"She's vegetarian," Tanni said.

"Be nice," Ben said as he opened the back hatch and started to unload the many suitcases Norma had insisted on bringing. "You know your mother dresses to her own drummer."

"She dresses like she's going to a festival and wants to get laid by some guy in a lame ponytail," Tanni said.

"Don't forget he's shirtless and has a patchwork vest on to go with the lame ponytail," Ben laughed then stopped himself. "Nope. Not going to do this. Your mother has a big heart. Appreciate that. Mine did not."

"Neither does hers," Tanni says. "Grammy Liz hasn't called me in six months. Not since she left for Tuscany with that Gary guy."

"Then feel lucky, sweetheart," Ben said. "Because she's taken the time to email me at least a dozen times to tell me what a horrible man I am and that I don't deserve custody of her grandchildren."

"What? She'd rather me and the Norms live with a convicted felon?" Tanni said.

"It was pot, not murder," Ben said.

"Why do you defend her?" Tanni asked as they walked towards the house. "She blames you for the break up when we all know that it was her wide open legs that split you up."

"Jesus, Tee," Ben said, nearly dropping a suitcase in the wet grass as he struggled to cart them all to the porch. "I don't need to hear you say stuff like that."

"Say stuff like what?" Bobbi asked as they reached the porch.

"Nothing," Tanni said, giving her mother a quick hug and peck on the cheek. "Bye, Dad. Love you."

"Uh, love you too," Ben said as he watched his daughter disappear inside the house. "Thanks for the help."

"You can just set those here," Bobbi said, indicating to a spot on the porch.

"I don't mind bringing them inside," Ben said.

"No, I'd rather you didn't, Ben," Bobbi said, her hand to her chest. "Sometimes it can take a week for me to smudge your negativity from the house. I just don't have it in me to do that this time. The house is mine. You need to learn to separate yourself."

Ben tried to respond several times, but nothing that came to mind would have been something he wanted to pass his lips. Not if there was a chance his daughters could overhear.

"Right. Sure," Ben said finally and set the suitcases down in the exact spot Bobbi had indicated. "Well, nice talking with you, Bobs."

"I hear you have a weekend with Nick planned," Bobbi said, her voice light and airy.

Ben knew that her tone was a complete sham and he waited for the other shoe to drop. When it didn't, he sighed then asked, "How did you hear that?"

"Nick told me," Bobbi said. "We still have dinner regularly, you know. He isn't just your friend, Ben. I have known him almost as long as you."

"Well aware of that, Bobs," Ben said. "Also aware that he was the first man you screwed after our divorce. Taken me a little bit to get over that."

"We screwed before the divorce," Bobbi said. Light and airy and deadly. "After the separation, of course."

"Of course," Ben said. "Listen, as much fun as this is, I better go. Gotta pick up Maggie then head out. As much as you want to ruin the olive branch Nick is extending, it's not going to happen. Screwed my wife or ex-wife, doesn't matter. You've known Nick since high school, but I've known him since we were born. Literally."

"Yes, you two were side by side in that sterile hospital," Bobbi said. "It's unfortunate he was able to shake off that bad beginning and find a spiritual side and you weren't."

"Yeah, you just keep believing that, Bobs," Ben said. "Nice seeing you. Have fun with the girls. I'm sure I'll hear all about it from Tanni's texts."

"Oh, I don't think so," Bobbi said. "This will be an electronics-free time with my daughters. I do not trust those devices. They allow microwaves into my space which disrupts the positive energy I have fought so hard to restore."

"Awesome," Ben said, giving her a thumbs up. "But be sure Tanni has her phone on her if she goes out, okay? The world isn't like when you and I grew up, Bobs."

"No, it is not," Bobbi said in a way that implied it was somehow Ben's fault the world had changed.

He shook his head, waved, and walked back to the minivan.

He was at least six blocks away before he started yelling and pounding the steering wheel. It was another six blocks before he calmed down enough to pick up the phone and call Maggie.

"Hey," he said when she picked up. "Children have been delivered to the Earth Mother and I'm on my way to get you. Ready?"

"Ready," Maggie responded over the phone.

There was a bleeping sound and Ben pulled his phone from his ear. He stared at the screen until a car horn pulled his attention back to the road.

"Hold on," Ben said to Maggie as he pulled the minivan over to the side of the road.

He read the text again and frowned then typed in, "Will do."

"Have you talked with Nick today?" Ben asked as he put the phone back to his ear.

"Talked to Nick?" Maggie responded.

"That's what I just said," Ben laughed. "He just texted me and wanted to make sure I told you to pack extra toiletries, just in case. He forgot to tell you when you talked."

Maggie paused. It wasn't long, but long enough for Ben to worry.

"Yeah, he called me to see what your mood was," Maggie responded. "It was weird, but sweet, in a Nick way."

"Yeah, very weird. Why do we need extra clothes? I didn't pack extra clothes," Ben said. "I'm going to call him right now."

"No, don't do that," Maggie said. "Then he won't trust me anymore. You've told me all about your history, Benjamin. It's best he thinks he has me in his confidence that way we can compare notes later."

"Good call," Ben said. "I should have you start writing for my blog."

"I know zilch about poker and want to keep it that way," Maggie said. "Teaching is good enough for me. Speaking of, I want to enjoy this long weekend and not think of the grades I need to enter until we get back Tuesday night, cool?"

"Cool," Ben said. "No thinking."

"That's not exactly what I said," Maggie laughed. "Now, get off the phone and hurry your ass over here. I need to get my drink on and Nick said he'll have a fully stocked bar waiting for me."

"Did he now? You must have his confidence if he's already promising drinks," Ben said. "See you soon."

5.

Dr. Glouster stood on the main deck of the AOS ship and stared in wonder as the crane lifted the saltwater tank directly out of the center of the ship. It had taken a construction crew two hours to cut through the decks and down to the lab. It had taken another hour to make sure when they cut through the final deck no debris fell onto the tank and damaged it.

Dr. Glouster had warned everyone, especially Wagner, that the creature would take advantage of any damage to its tank. He had learned early on when the creature was still a small adolescent that it could worry away at a small ding or crack on the thick glass until it was able to force an opening.

Two tons of sea water was not easy to clean up.

Neither were the lab assistants the creature had injured before it could be wrangled into a temporary tank while the main one was repaired. And that had been while it was an adolescent. Now, at full size and strength? A man would be torn apart in the blink of an eye.

"Be careful!" Dr. Glouster yelled as the tank was jostled by a hard turn of the crane. "It could be hurt while it hides in its cave."

"You really went all out for that thing's habitat, didn't you, Doc?" Wagner asked as he came up next to Dr. Glouster. "You gave it its own hidey hole and everything."

"It is a shy species and does not like to be disturbed," Dr. Glouster said.

"Then why choose it?" Wagner asked.

"Excuse me?"

"Why choose it for the project? Why not a bloodthirsty shark or even some aggressive type of eel?" Wagner asked. "Seems to me you're going against nature with this project."

"It was chosen for many reasons," Dr. Glouster said. "It is a highly advanced predator, to begin with. But mainly for its intelligence and dexterity. The creature does not have bones so it can squeeze through almost any opening as long as that opening is slightly larger than its beak."

"Yeah, that's freaky," Wagner said. "Never did like the no bones thing. Hey, did you see that YouTube video?"

"I do not watch YouTube," Dr. Glouster said. "I have work to do."

"So do I, Doc," Wagner replied. "Plenty of work. Doesn't mean I don't know how to unwind."

The two men watched the tank as it moved over the short space of open water between the two ships. The one it was being transferred to looked like a retrofitted Navy cruiser. Except the equipment on the main deck, as well as the equipment being used by the crew members, was considerably more high-tech and new looking than anything the US Navy had. Dr. Glouster didn't recognize half the weapons being held by the men standing guard as the tank was centered over a hold hatch and slowly lowered below deck.

With a loud thunk, the massive cables on the crane went slack. There was a lot of shouting from the men and the cables were raised back to the crane as the hold hatch was closed and locked down. Wagner patted Dr. Glouster on the shoulder.

"You never officially answered me, Doc," Wagner said, the pat turning into a grip which became hard as steel for a split second before easing off. "Are you staying or coming with?"

"I would prefer to live, so I will be coming with," Dr. Glouster said. "Plus, without me you run the risk of the creature escaping into the wild. I know its habits and how it thinks. It trusts me, I believe. If there is a problem I am the only person you can rely on to get it under control."

"What if it doesn't want to be under control?" Wagner asked. "What if it decides killing us all is what it really wants?" Wagner patted the semi-automatic rifle slung at his side. "Will this stop it?"

"That depends," Dr. Glouster said.

"On what?"

"On how much ammunition you have," Dr. Glouster said and smiled. "Because you will need a lot to stop the creature if it doesn't want to be stopped."

Wagner began to laugh then saw the look in the doctor's eyes. He swallowed hard and gave the man a serious nod.

"Fair enough, Doc," Wagner said. "Good thing I have a lot of ammunition then, isn't it?"

"Yes," Dr. Glouster said and nodded. "It is."

6.

The ferry docked at the Bainbridge Island Ferry Terminal and Ben waited patiently for the attendant to give him the signal that it was his turn to disembark. He nodded at the man, refrained from honking at a Prius that wouldn't get out of his way, then maneuvered the minivan through the ferry traffic until he was on 305 and heading northwest.

"I don't get why we had to take the ferry over," Maggie said from the passenger's seat, lounging with her feet up on the dash.

She looked perfectly at ease as if they hadn't spent nearly an hour on a rocking ferry being jostled up and down by the less than calm waters of Puget Sound. Ben wasn't so at ease. Not usually one to let nausea get to him, the ferry trip and seeing Nick for the first time in a very long time was doing a number on his digestive system.

"Are you okay, babe?" Maggie asked. "You're looking a little belchy."

"I'm good," Ben said then did belch. "Better after that."

"Why didn't we just take the Narrows Bridge if we're going to Port Angeles?" Maggie asked. "This is kind of a weird way to go."

"We aren't going to Port Angeles," Ben said. "I thought I told you that I got a text from Nick that there was a change in plans."

"No, you did not tell me," Maggie said. She paused for a couple seconds and Ben was about to look over at her when she said, "What change?"

"We're meeting at a marina in Hansville," Ben said.

"Hansville? What the hell is a Hansville?" Maggie asked.

Ben shrugged and shook his head. "Not a clue. Never heard of it until I Googled it. Nick says he has a surprise for us there."

"Nick and a surprise? Great," Maggie said. "What could go wrong?"

"I'm hoping nothing," Ben said. "He has screwed up a lot, but I don't think he'll screw this up. We've been friends our whole lives and I'm going to give him the benefit of the doubt."

"You think this new marina has anything to do with why he told me to pack more clothes?" Maggie asked. "You don't think instead of his family's cruiser we're going to be sailing, do you?" She holds up her hands, fingers splayed. "This mani cost me a month's groceries, Benjamin. I can sail like a pro, but I am not chipping these nails."

"You can sail like a pro?" Ben asked, giving her a surprised look. "I didn't know that."

"Yes, you did," Maggie said. "After our second date, back at my place? I was talking about how my grandfather taught me to sail and we always went out on the Sound in his sloop on his birthday."

"Yeah…our second date? When you wore that v-neck cashmere sweater and no bra?" Ben laughed. "You really thought I was paying attention to a story about your grandpa?"

"I had a bra on," Maggie replied.

"No, you didn't," Ben said. "No bra. Trust me."

Maggie gave him a sly smile. "Okay, maybe I didn't have a bra on."

"See? No bra on you means no brains in me," Ben said. "That's just the rules of life, Mags."

She grabbed his leg and gave it a squeeze. Ben jumped a little, causing the minivan to swerve, and someone behind him honked.

"Really?" Ben shouted. "Bite me and go back to California!"

"This better not be a sailboat," Maggie said. "Even without the issue of my nails, I did not pack for rigging."

"Nick must have needed to bring the cruiser in for something," Ben said.

"Something that the marina in Port Angeles couldn't do?" Maggie asked. "You believe that?"

"No," Ben said. "But I'm giving him the benefit of the doubt. I thought you would too since you guys are so buddy buddy now."

"Not buddy buddy," Maggie said.

The tone in her voice caused Ben to give her a quick look, but her head was turned so he couldn't see her expression as she looked out at the landscape rushing by.

They drove another twenty minutes then turned onto Hansville Rd. Ben smacked his forehead and grinned as they passed a sign.

"Point No Point!" he said. "Duh. I've been to Hansville before. Our families used to picnic out here when we were kids. I totally forgot about this place. Haven't been here in twenty years. I see his game now. He's going for nostalgia points."

"This place mean that much to you two?" Maggie asked.

"It was before my mom died of cancer and his parents got divorced," Ben said. "Things were happy here. God... I can't believe he remembered."

They continued on Hansville Rd., passing old tracts of farm land that were interspersed with wooded estates. Mansions and trailers, a true reflection of the modern economic times. They came to a long curve, passing the post office and an old auto repair shop. The Sound was to their right and Maggie stared out at the dark waters, watching the white caps lift and break, over and over.

"Choppy," she said. "Wind is blowing rough. Look at the flags."

They passed a small row of businesses, many of them closed for the season. Ben glanced to his right and saw flags whipping about and he frowned. The weather didn't look promising at all.

"It could change, depending on where we're headed," Ben said.

"You don't know?" Maggie asked.

"You seem to know as much as I do," Ben said. "Nick kept saying he had a surprise for me."

"For you or for us?" Maggie asked.

"Me," Ben said, giving her a sly smile. "But me is us."

"Is it now?" Maggie smirked. "That's good to hear."

Ben kept the minivan aimed down Twin Spits Rd, but didn't turn left when they came to the sign for Hood Canal Dr. and Coon Bay. Maggie turned in her seat and looked out the back then looked at Ben.

"Isn't Coon Bay the marina area?" Maggie asked.

"See, you know more than I do," Ben said and tapped his GPS. "But he gave me an address that's up this way. Looks like it's a private dock or something."

A couple miles and they turned onto Skunk Bay Rd. Maggie gave Ben a look that clearly said she was not liking the omen of that name. After a quarter mile, they turned onto a private drive then stopped as they faced a heavy iron gate. Ben inched up to a key pad and pressed the intercom button.

"Ben Wa Balls!" a static-filled voice shouted from the small box. "Is that you?"

"Hey, Nick Of Time," Ben said and pointed a finger at Maggie as she started to laugh. "You want to tell me where the hell we are?"

"You are right where you are supposed to be," Nick said as a loud buzz rang out and the gate began to swing inward. "Just keep going straight and you'll run right into me."

"Then don't stand in the road, dumbass," Ben replied. "See ya in a sec."

"Looking forward to it," Nick replied.

"Don't say it," Ben said to Maggie as he drove through the gate.

"Ben Wa Balls?" Maggie laughed. "He actually calls you that?"

"He only called me that to undermine my position with you," Ben said. "Make me look silly so he looks good in your eyes. He's nervous about meeting you. In person. I guess you've already met via text."

"Ha ha ha. That's some deep insight into your friend's psyche there, Ben Wa Balls," Maggie said as she continued laughing. "You get a degree in psychology I don't know about?"

"I know Nick as well as I know myself," Ben said. "Trust me. He's going to make you his new best friend so he has an ally in case the two of us fall into old patterns."

"Old patterns?" Maggie asked. "What kind of old patterns? This isn't going to be a hookers and blow vacation, is it?"

"Jesus, no," Ben replied, taking his turn to laugh. "Nick doesn't have that kind of money anymore. Not after the crap he pulled."

"Are you sure?" Maggie asked as they came out of the tree-lined drive that turned into a staggering view of a massive estate house. "That has to be thirty thousand square feet at least."

"It's not his," Ben said. "Nick has connections, not money. Whatever he has planned, it is financed by favors given and cashed in. Trust me." Ben smiled. "There he is."

Directly in front of them was a small parking area situated in front of a gated dock. In front of that gate was a man with his arms wide open. Nice suit with no tie, slicked back brown hair, and a blindingly white smile, Nick Sheeran walked forward as Ben parked the minivan.

"You are so slumming up this place, dude!" Nick said as Ben hoped out of the van. "You brought a minivan?"

"I own a minivan," Ben said.

"What happened to the Mustang?" Nick asked as he gave Ben a huge hug.

"I became a grownup, dude," Ben replied. "You may have heard of it. It's a natural progression from being a kid."

"Screw that," Nick said. "Being a grown up is boring."

"Really? How would you know?" Ben asked. "Have you tried it?"

Nick's smile faltered slightly then snapped back in place. "I may have had a taste or two these past few years. Wasn't to my liking, my friend. Holy shit." He turned and looked at Maggie as the woman came around the front of the minivan. "Facebook does not do you justice, Miss, uh, Rodriguez? Kimura?"

"Rodriguez-Kimura," Maggie said. "Mexican and Japanese."

"No shit," Nick said. "Those cultures should mix more often if what happens always looks like you."

"I'm taking that as a compliment," Maggie said.

"You should," Nick said and held out his arms. "Come here." He grabbed her up in a huge hug, nearly lifting her off her feet.

"Yeah, let her go, dude," Ben said. He looked down the dock and only saw a speedboat. It was a very, very nice speedboat, worth more than the house he'd lost in the divorce, but not exactly the size for an extended weekend trip. "Nick? Something wrong with your family's cruiser?"

"Huh? What?" Nick asked then turned and looked down the dock. "Oh, that. No, nothing wrong with the rust bucket."

"Hardly a rust bucket," Ben said. "The tile in the head cost more than my minivan."

"Minivan," Nick chuckled. "Dude." He gestured to the dock. "No, that is our ride to our ride."

"Ride to our ride?" Ben asked. "Yeah, we're out of here."

"Whoa! Hold the hell on, man!" Nick said. "What are you talking about?"

"I am talking about a boat that looks like it costs close to a hundred thousand dollars that you say is taking us to our actual ride," Ben said. "Which means the actual ride costs a lot more than that boat there. No way you have access to anything worth that much unless you are pulling a scam."

"No scam," Nick said. "I promise. I own that boat and the one we will be staying on the next few days. I'll show you the papers as soon as we are on board. I promise. Swear on my soul."

"You don't own your soul, dude," Ben said. "You wagered it, and lost it, to Paulo Marquez in 1997, remember?"

"Yeah, I remember," Nick said. "Wakes me up at night sometimes."

"You wagered your soul?" Maggie asked. "In a poker game?"

"Poker? Hell no," Nick said. "Nobody would allow a stupid wager like that at the table. No, I wagered it over a woman."

"Of course you did," Maggie said. "And I'm sure it's a great story, but my nipples are about to freeze off. Can we grab our bags and get going?"

"My bad!" Nick laughed. "Five minutes and I'm already a shitty host. Sorry. I'll grab a cart."

He hurried over to a small shed by the dock gate and yanked the door open. With cart in hand, and whistling a tune that sounded like a mash-up of Sweet Caroline and 99 Problems, Nick wheeled the cart to the back of the minivan and pulled open the hatch. He loaded up the bags, shut the hatch and then bowed low.

"What do you have in your suitcase?" Nick laughed as he smiled at Maggie. "Pretty sure lingerie isn't that heavy."

"Pretty sure what's in my suitcase isn't your business," Maggie said, smiling back.

"Saucy," Nick said.

"Where should I move the van?" Ben asked.

"Leave the keys," Nick said. "I have a guy coming to move your car. Uh, I mean, *minivan*." He snickered. "We won't be coming back here. I'll drop you guys off closer to Olympia. When we get back."

"You know I have alarm bells going off, right?" Ben said, offering to take the cart but being refused as Nick slapped his hand away.

"Oh, I know, brother," Nick said. "You gotta learn to trust more."

He started whistling again, rolled the cart to the gate, punched in a code, and pushed the gate open.

"I have to learn to trust more," Ben said to Maggie. She didn't respond, her eyes studying the speedboat. "Hello?"

"Huh? Sorry," Maggie said. "It's a nice boat."

"I bet the one we're staying on is a million times nicer," Ben said. "Literally. Nick may not have much of his own money, but the man has a knack for getting others to let him use theirs."

"He said he owned the boat," Maggie said.

"Nick says a lot of things," Ben replied then gestured and bowed. "After you."

Maggie gave him a playful look then walked through the gate and onto the dock where Nick was waiting for them. Ben gave Nick a wary eye as they passed. The man, following right behind with the luggage-laden cart, just smiled and kept on whistling.

7.

"Tank is secure, sir," a man said as he stepped onto the bridge. "No sign of the creature, though. Should we be worried?"

"Should we, Doc?" Wagner asked Dr. Glouster. "You said it was naturally shy, but you'd think we'd have a glimpse by now." Wagner scratched at his chin. "Please tell me I didn't kill a ship full of people over a diversion."

"The creature is in the tank," Dr. Glouster said. "I will be happy to show you, if you'd like."

"By show me, you mean you'll coax it out into the open?" Wagner laughed. "Not shove me in the tank so the thing eats me, right? Because that's not how I plan on going out."

"Do any of us get to plan our leaving this world?" Dr. Glouster asked.

"More than you think," Wagner said. "Come on, Doc. Time to see proof of purchase."

Dr. Glouster gave the man a strained smile and nodded.

It took them a long while to navigate down the decks, through the passageways, and past the crew, the majority of which were heavily armed, before they came to a door that was certainly unlike the others.

"It looks like a vault," Dr. Glouster said.

"It is a vault," Wagner responded. "This ship was originally designed by the US government to transport important, sensitive cargo. NCDC gave it a few upgrades and offered it to me to use if needed. I figured this was the perfect op for it."

"NCDC?" Dr. Glouster asked.

"What? Oh, yes, my employers," Wagner said as he keyed in a code and then spun the huge wheel in the center of the vault door. "I didn't mention that?"

"New Century Defense Corp?" Dr. Glouster asked. "I should have known Agnes was behind this."

"Agnes? Huh, sounds like you have history with NCDC's CEO," Wagner said as he pulled the door open. "Step back, Doc. This door is heavy and I'd hate for you to stub your toe."

A ring of armed men circled the massive tank that filled the vault almost to the walls on each side. Dr. Glouster looked up and was not surprised to see a barred hatch in the ceiling where they had lowered the tank through. He studied the walls of the vault, noticing the complete and total lack of seams, vents, or any signs of how the space was put together.

"A single, solid piece of metal," Wagner said before Dr. Glouster could ask. "Micro holes are everywhere for ventilation. Power is through surface conduction. No conduits."

"Then how did you plug in the tank?" Dr. Glouster asked.

"Oh, I had the adapters ready for months, Doc," Wagner said. "Getting information on the creature wasn't easy, but finding out the schematics to the tank was. It's why I jumped ship." He laughed at his own pun. "OAS is sloppy. NCDC is not. The team that designed this vault stopped breathing the second they said the job was done."

"You have no problem with murder, do you?" Dr. Glouster asked. "All of the needless death and blood? For what? Profit?"

"You're getting boring, Doc," Wagner said. "How about you knock off the holier than thou crap and show me the goods?"

Dr. Glouster began to respond then shook his head and stepped towards the tank. One of the guards handed him a tablet and Dr. Glouster looked surprised then swiped the screen to see a familiar interface.

"I see you had no problem recreating the software interface," Dr. Glouster said.

"Like I said, Doc, OAS is sloppy," Wagner said and shrugged. "I copied your tablet exactly. Except for the tracking software embedded. That I left off so OAS can't find us. Otherwise, that tablet is basically the same as the one I made you leave behind."

Dr. Glouster studied the tablet for a minute and made sure it was the exact interface he needed. As far as he could tell, it was a perfect duplicate of the one he had used on the old ship.

He tapped at the screen a few times and the water darkened considerably.

"That doesn't make it easier to see, Doc," Wagner warned. "You're getting more boring."

"I have made it so the inside of the tank is reflective and no longer showing us out here," Dr. Glouster said. "I have also darkened the interior since the creature prefers to be more active in the evenings. It is a natural state for its species."

"Good for you," Wagner said. "So where is it?"

"Just wait," Dr. Glouster said. "It will come out. This is the normal protocol during feeding time. It will expect to be fed and should appear any second now."

The interior of the saltwater tank held a perfect replica of the ancient volcanic rock that made up much of the Pacific Northwest coast line. Plenty of hiding places for a sea creature that preferred to stay out of sight.

After a couple of minutes, and some low grumbling from Wagner, there was the hint of movement at the back of the tank. Dr. Glouster continued to tap at the tablet then frowned.

"The food chute?" Dr. Glouster asked. "You didn't connect the food chute?"

"Food chute?" Wagner asked. "That wasn't in the schematics."

"You didn't think that would be an issue?" Dr. Glouster snapped. "That maybe we would need to feed the creature?"

"I don't know, Doc," Wagner said. "I figured you opened the top and tossed in some canned tuna or something."

"You are well aware it does not eat canned tuna," Dr. Glouster said.

"Yeah, I'm well aware of that. I'm just messing with you," Wagner said. "We couldn't accommodate a food chute in this vault. You're going to have to go all Sea World and throw its meal in from above."

He snapped his fingers and two of the guards hurried from the vault. They returned in a couple of minutes with a cage that held a live goat. The goat bleated and complained as the guards wheeled the cage closer to the tank, its animal instinct telling it that things were not as they should be.

"I have never fed it goats before," Dr. Glouster said. "Only pigs."

"Yeah, I know," Wagner said and frowned. "And this is the one detail I'll admit I screwed up. But, unfortunately, I couldn't supervise this detail myself and had to rely on others to get it done. Looks like some dipshit thinks a goat is the same as a pig."

"A goat is not the same as a pig," Dr. Glouster snapped. "Pigs blood is very similar to human blood. Goat's blood is not. I certainly hope the creature does not get offended at the meal offered to it. I have been very, very careful to maintain the proper diet since it is crucial to the overall mission of this project."

"I've got goat," Wagner said. That was all he said no matter how much Dr. Glouster glared.

"Fine," Dr. Glouster huffed. "Goat will have to do."

"Good to hear it," Wagner said. "Now, where is the thing?"

"You are looking right at it," Dr. Glouster said.

"Yeah, I don't see shit," Wagner replied. "Thought I saw something in the back, but I don't see anything but rocks right now."

"You believe you see rocks," Dr. Glouster said. "Which is exactly as it should be. The creature is up against the glass on the bottom left of the tank."

"Bullshit," Wagner said. "I've got good eyes, Doc. Trained eyes. Eyes that notice things a freakin' hawk would overlook. There is nothing…there…"

As the guards hooked cables to the top of the goat cage and it was raised into the air, there was a brief shimmer and flash from the spot Dr. Glouster had indicated. Wagner stepped forward, but Dr. Glouster placed a hand on his arm. The man glared at the hand, glared at Dr. Glouster, but the hand remained in place.

"Do not present yourself as an optional target," Dr. Glouster said, turning to the other men in the vault. "That goes for all of you, as well. Remain still as the cage is lowered into the tank."

"Thought you said it wouldn't see us?" Wagner asked.

"There are more senses than sight," Dr. Glouster replied.

The cage hung over the tank then was slowly lowered until it rested on the top. Dr. Glouster took a deep breath and tapped at the tablet. The sound of something sliding open echoed in the vault and the bottom of the goat cage opened up. The goat fell screaming into the tank and was lost from sight.

"Where the hell did it go?" Wagner asked. "Where the hell is the goat?"

"The creature took it," Dr. Glouster said as the empty cage was swung out and away, then lowered, the bottom snapping back in place as it touched down on the vault floor. "Look closely and you will catch glimpses as it feeds."

"How the hell can it hide a goat?" Wagner asked.

"The creature's natural ability to mimic its surroundings means that anything wrapped up in its arms will be almost impossible to detect," Dr. Glouster said.

"That goat was four feet tall, Doc," Wagner said. "Your creature would need to be what, twenty feet long to hide something that size?"

"The creature's mantle is eight feet long by four feet wide with an arm span of thirty-eight feet," Dr. Glouster said proudly. "As far as we, I mean, as far as I can estimate, it weighs close to three hundred pounds. Hiding a goat of that size is not an issue. Especially once you consider the size of the web between the arms. It could envelop you, Mr. Wagner, and no one would even know."

There was some thrashing in the water and Wagner took a couple of steps back. Dr. Glouster tapped at his tablet then looked up in alarm.

"The hatch is not locked!" Dr. Glouster shouted. "Why won't it lock?"

"Your tank, Doc," Wagner said, taking another step back. "You lock it."

"Your damn interface!" Dr. Glouster shouted as he waved the tablet at Wagner. "I never had this issue in my own lab!"

"Lock it down!" Wagner shouted as he pointed at three of the guards. "Get your asses up there and make sure that hatch is secure! Now!"

The three guards stared at the tank, none moving. Wagner withdrew a pistol from the holster on his hip, stepped up to one of the guards, and placed the muzzle against the man's temple.

"Who do you fear most? That thing or me?" Wagner asked. "Get up there now."

The other two guards scrambled to a ladder propped against the wall and set it up against the tank. The third guard waited until

Wagner had removed the pistol before hustling over to the ladder and joining his comrades.

The first man to the top screamed and disappeared instantly.

"Oh God," Dr. Glouster said. "The hatch is fully open."

"Shit," Wagner cursed. "Lock it the hell down now!"

The two other guards scrambled to the center of the tank and dove at the hatch. The first man to reach it was able to pull it halfway across before he was snatched away, lost in the murky waters of the tank. The last guard left grabbed the hatch and slammed it closed. The hatch bent upwards suddenly and the man was lifted a foot in the air. He screamed like a teenager, his voice cracking with pure fear.

"Get up there and help him!" Wagner ordered.

The remainder of the guards climbed the ladder and all put their weight on the hatch, pulling it back to keep it closed, while Dr. Glouster furiously tapped at his tablet.

"Doc? Making any progress?" Wagner asked, his pistol still out and pointed directly at the tank.

"I am trying, Mr. Wagner," Dr. Glouster said.

A man's face was pressed against the glass, his dead eyes bulging in their sockets. The head was pulled back into the shadows then thrust forward with enough force to shatter the skull, sending blood and brains leaking out into the tank's water. Dark clouds floated up from the crushed head and Wagner glared.

"That was Henricksen," Wagner said. "He was a good man."

"I highly doubt any of your men could be described as good considering the line of work they are in," Dr. Glouster said.

"What did I say about the holier than thou crap, Doc?" Wagner snarled. "Keep it to yourself."

There was a loud whirring and a distinctive thunk then click. Dr. Glouster let out a long breath and lowered the tablet to his side.

"It is locked down and secure," Dr. Glouster said. "I had to reroute two systems and override your security protocol to do it, but it is done. The creature will not be able to harm anyone else."

"That's good to hear," Wagner said, letting out his own long breath. "Now, what do we do about the bodies in the tank?"

"The creature will take care of them," Dr. Glouster said. "While it primarily drinks blood, it will also strip the bones of the flesh and eat that as well. It may even pulverize the bones if it gets bored. Their uniforms are another issue. You will need to figure out how to remove them so they do not clog the filtration system. I'll leave it to you to come up with a solution."

"Nope," Wagner said, holstering his pistol and clamping a hand on Dr. Glouster's shoulder. "You'll figure it out. I didn't spare your life so I end up doing the janitorial work, Doc. You can direct my men how you need, but you don't leave this vault until all the bugs are worked out."

Wagner walked to the door and patted the huge locking mechanism.

"This room may be nearly impenetrable, but that thing in there is not a natural part of this world," Wagner said. "Which means there are variables. You will remove as many variables as humanly possible." He smiled. "Then you'll remove the rest that aren't humanly possible. Are we understood, Doc?"

"Yes, Mr. Wagner," Dr. Glouster replied. "And no need for threats. If the creature gets out of the tank and ends up loose on this ship then I am in as much danger as you are. It is in all of our best interests that I fix the problems you have created."

Wagner started to respond to the barb, but only shook his head and left the vault, leaving Dr. Glouster with a group of guards that looked too terrified to move from their spots on top of the massive tank, hands glued to the hatch's handle.

8.

"Benjamin," Maggie said as she pointed at the yacht in front of the speedboat. It grew larger and larger as they got closer and closer. "What is that?"

"Half of the gross domestic product of any decent-sized country," Ben said then tapped Nick on the shoulder. "No way that's yours, Nick. Want to tell me how you can possibly afford that thing?"

"What that really is, to answer the pretty lady's question first, is a Baglietto 65M Motor Yacht. She's called the Lucky Sucker, which is about as perfect as it gets," Nick said as he slowed the speedboat down and steered it towards the aft end of the huge yacht that waited for them in the Sound. "And to answer *your* question, Benny Boy, I *can't* afford it. The upkeep and maintenance alone is more than my trust fund allowance for half a year. Don't get me started on the crew's salaries."

"Trust fund?" Maggie asked.

"Yeah, I have one," Nick shrugged. "But it only covers the lease on the duplex in San Francisco and the condo here in Queen Anne. With just enough left over for some nights out on the town. Did you know I learned how to cook, Benny Boy? Had to or I'd starve."

"You could get a job," Maggie said.

"Whoa there, no need to get offensive," Nick laughed. "Jobs are for the loser masses and the noble few. I belong to neither of those categories. I applaud your dedication as a, uh, teacher, Maggie, but I don't even have a bachelor's degree. Neither does my boy here. Straight outta high school and into the real world was how we attacked things."

"I wouldn't call being rounders the real world," Ben said. "Not seeing sunlight for five days straight doesn't exactly count as real, Nick."

"You had to support that brand new baby somehow," Nick shrugged. "That was pretty real."

"What the hell?" Maggie whispered as a portion of the yacht's hull slid open wide enough for Nick to expertly guide the speedboat inside.

Florescent lights turned on as soon as the tip of the bow was in. More flickered to life as Nick cut the engine and two deck hands jumped aboard and began to tie the boat down. It was lifted a few feet in the air and the hull behind them slid closed. There was the sound of loud pumps and the water under the boat was quickly drained out.

"After you," Nick said, pointing to the hand being offered to Maggie by one of the crew members. "That's Carl."

"Dennis," the man said. "He calls us all Carl."

"Jesus," Ben said. "You can't learn their names, Nick?"

"No need," Nick replied. "Like I said, I can't afford this thing. I'm selling it ASAP, dude, so no need to learn anyone's names."

"If you can't afford it then why did you buy it?" Maggie asked, smiling at Dennis as he helped her onto the short platform next to the boat.

"Buy it? I'd never buy this thing," Nick said. He gave Ben a huge grin. "I won it. Fair and square."

"Fair *and* square?" Ben asked. "Those words never apply to how you play cards."

"Not cards," Nick said. "Russian roulette."

Ben nearly stumbled and fell from the platform as Dennis helped him up as well. He turned and looked over at Nick as the man jumped effortlessly next to him.

"Have you lost your mind?" Ben asked.

"Me? Nope. But the guy that lost to me did," Nick said. He spread his arms wide, which other than his blindingly bright smile, seemed to be his trademark feature. "Was my luck good or what? Told you the name fits."

Maggie shook her head. "Can we get the bags? I want to change out of these damp clothes."

"Let me show you to your cabin, my good friends," Nick said. "The Carls will get your bags. Although, I think we should toss Ben's overboard. I know he only brought jeans and t-shirts. That just won't do on such a beautiful vessel as this."

"So you want me to walk around the ship naked for the next couple of days?" Ben asked. "I know you're a little loose on your sexual preferences, but I have no plan to let you ogle my junk on my vacation."

"No ogling will occur because I have outfitted your cabin with some of the finest suits that money can buy," Nick said. "Only the best for my buddy."

"Suits? Plural?" Maggie asked. "Was I supposed to bring dresses? I only brought one. Everything else is sweaters and pants."

"Did you think I'd leave you out, Ms. Rodriguez-Kimura?" Nick said, looking hurt. He put his hands to his chest. "I'm going to have to change your perception of me, I can see."

"Knock it off, Nick," Ben said. "Show us to our cabin so we can change. Then we're going to sit down and you're going to tell us exactly what the bloody hell is going on."

"Bloody hell?" Nick laughed and gave Maggie a wink. "Uh-oh, Benny Boy must be really irritated with me if he's pulling out the Brit slang."

He put an arm around Ben's shoulders and one around Maggie's.

"Come on, guys, relax," he said. "I promise that you are about to have the time of your life. Trust me."

9.

There was a knock at the door and Wagner sighed. He pushed the plate of food across his desk and leaned back.

"Enter," he said.

The door opened and a guard ushered Dr. Glouster inside.

"How goes the work on keeping that thing from eating more of my men?" Wagner asked.

"Not as well as I would like," Dr. Glouster said, standing in front of the desk. "This ship's systems are not compatible with the systems I have in place in the tank. You thought you did your homework, Mr. Wagner, but you did not."

"Doc, listen, the only reason I left you alive and brought you with me is because you said you could control that thing," Wagner said. He opened a drawer, pulled out a pistol, and set it next to the plate of food. "If you can't control it then you are dead weight."

"I didn't say I couldn't control it, Mr. Wagner," Dr. Glouster said. "I said the ship's systems are not compatible with the tank's systems. I believe I know a way to make them compatible. But I will need some time and a few of your best techs."

"Techs I have plenty of," Wagner said. "Time I don't. We will reach our destination in three days. Then I hand off that tank and it's not my problem. What is my problem is that thing killing my men. I need it fixed now. Not in three days, but *now*. Can you do that or not, Doc?"

"No," Dr. Glouster replied. He was smiling. "But fixing it isn't the problem. Your men being killed is. I suggest we look at this another way."

"And what way is that?" Wagner asked.

"I suggest we leave the tank open," Dr. Glouster said. "That vault is more than able to hold the creature. To feed it, we open the top hatch in the vault and drop down the food. The creature will remain in its tank because it must in order to survive. While it is fast, it cannot scale four decks fast enough to get out. I assume you can open the inner hatch remotely?"

"I can," Wagner said and smiled. "Good plan, Doc. We open the top hatch, drop in some goats, close the top hatch, then open the vault hatch and let the barnyard slaughter begin."

"Precisely," Dr. Glouster said.

"You figure out how to get those uniforms out of the tank yet?" Wagner asked.

"I have a solution, yes," Dr. Glouster said. "Which is why I am here."

"Oh?" Wagner replied, surprised. "The improvised feeding chute wasn't the real reason?"

"It was one reason," Dr. Glouster said. "But that was an easy fix compared to the issue of removing your men's clothing before it clogs up the filtration system."

"Spill it, Doc," Wagner said. "I'm all ears."

"I will need a distraction," Dr. Glouster said. "We will need to lure the creature from the tank so one of your men can go in and remove the clothing. Once that is accomplished, we will need to lure the creature back into the tank. That part should not be hard as the creature prefers it in the tank. It is its safe place."

"Safe place?" Wagner laughed. "This thing sounds like a spoiled college freshmen with trigger issues. Safe place, my ass."

Dr. Glouster coughed softly and waited. Wagner looked the man straight in the eyes then shook his head.

"No," Wagner said.

"Excuse me?" Dr. Glouster asked, his turn to sound surprised. "Did you say no?"

"I did, Doc," Wagner said. "I'm not risking more of my men. Do we really need the filtration system if we're leaving the tank open? Can't it get air from there?"

"You killed a lot of goldfish as a kid, didn't you?" Dr. Glouster glared.

"I killed all kinds of things as a kid, Doc," Wagner replied. "It's why I do what I do."

"The filtration system is already compromised," Dr. Glouster said. "If we do not clean it out soon then the entire environmental system will collapse and the creature will have maybe twenty-four hours before it dies from the toxicity levels that will build up in the tank. As much as I have enhanced it, it is still a living being and susceptible to harm from a toxic environment."

"Then what freakin' use is it?" Wagner barked. "The whole world is a toxic environment! The thing needs to toughen up if it's going to do the jobs it's been built to do!"

Dr. Glouster took a couple of steps back. He composed himself then stepped forward to his previous position.

"Mr. Wagner, how will it look to NCDC if you allow the creature to die on your watch?" Dr. Glouster asked. "Will they care that you refused to risk your men's lives? Did they hire you to keep your men safe or did they hire you to deliver an asset that is worth millions? Possibly billions if it is fully successful and I am able to recreate the process on a larger scale."

"Those are good questions, Doc," Wagner said. "And we both know the answers to them."

Wagner took a deep breath and held it. He let it out slowly through his nose, creating a whistling effect that visibly annoyed Dr. Glouster.

"How many men do you need?" Wagner asked.

"At least four," Dr. Glouster said. "Two to lure it out of the tank and two to go in and clean the filtration system. It shouldn't take more than five minutes. But it would be advisable to have several more outside the vault. Just in case."

"Just in case. Right," Wagner said with a distrustful smirk. "Why don't we just tranq it? I know you've done that before."

"The move has put the creature under great stress," Dr. Glouster said. "If I were to use tranquilizers then there would be a considerable risk of the creature dying. Its body cannot handle the amount needed to incapacitate it."

"You've got an answer for everything, don't you, Doc?" Wagner said. His eyes were cold, but Dr. Glouster met them.

"I am supposed to have an answer for everything," Dr. Glouster said. "It is why I am paid what I am paid. Or was. I doubt I'll be paid the same once you hand me over to NCDC."

"Not my problem," Wagner said and picked up the pistol from the desk. Dr. Glouster stiffened. Wagner's smiled widened. "Relax." He placed the pistol in the desk drawer and pulled the plate of food back to him. "Anything else?"

"No," Dr. Glouster said. "I'll get started right away. Please inform your men that I will be directing them and they need to listen to my orders. If they do not listen, and hesitate in the slightest, they will not make it."

"Of course," Wagner said and nodded at the door. "Keep me posted, Doc."

Once the doctor had left, Wagner pushed his food away again and opened a different drawer. He pulled out a satellite phone and quickly dialed a number.

"This is Wagner. I need to speak to Ms. Marion," Wagner said. "Yeah, yeah, I'll hold."

He tapped his fingers on the desk as he waited. Several minutes went by and Wagner began to get impatient. His annoyance level rose to the point where he almost hung up.

"Mr. Wagner? Is everything alright?" a woman's smooth, almost soothing voice asked on the other end of the phone. "I wasn't expecting a call from you so soon."

"I think we have a problem with Dr. Glouster," Wagner said.

"No hello?" the woman asked.

"What? Oh, right, sorry. Hello, Ms. Marion," Wagner said.

"I thought you had handled the issue of Dr. Glouster by allowing him to think you spared his life in exchange for his help," Ms. Marion said. "Is he not helping?"

"He is, but I don't trust the guy," Wagner said. "We've had a couple of hiccups already. How close are your lab people to learning the process for making another creature like this?"

"Close, but not close enough," Ms. Marion said. "I would prefer you keep Dr. Glouster alive long enough for us to interrogate him and make sure we have all the nuances of the process in hand. Can you do that for me, Mr. Wagner? Can you use your skills to keep one man alive? I know you prefer to kill, and you will get to kill Dr. Glouster, but for now I need you to do the opposite."

"Yeah, I can keep the guy alive," Wagner said. "But if I catch a sniff of him trying something, I will not hesitate to feed him to his own creation."

"Try something? Such as?" Ms. Marion asked.

"I don't know," Wagner said. "But I think the project advanced further than I thought. Those hiccups we had today looked like accidents, but I'm not so sure anymore."

"You think the doctor has control of the creature?" Ms. Marion asked.

"I think the two of them have a relationship of some kind," Wagner said. He laughed at his words. "I know how that sounds, but think of it like a dog and his master."

"That is how I think of most things, Mr. Wagner," Ms. Marion said. "And like a good dog, I expect you to protect the project and make sure it is not compromised." There was silence for a couple of seconds. "If you know for sure that Dr. Glouster will prevent you from accomplishing those goals then I authorize his sacrifice. It will put us behind, since I am not confident we have all of his files, but it is better than him sabotaging the work."

"That's all I needed to hear," Wagner said. "I will do everything I can to keep things under control and exactly as planned. But it makes me rest easy knowing I have the option of removing Dr. Glouster from the equation."

"Is there anything else, Mr. Wagner?" Ms. Marion asked.

"No, ma'am," Wagner replied. "Next time you hear from me we will be about to arrive at the NCDC facility."

"And that is all *I* needed to hear, Mr. Wagner. Goodbye."

"Yeah, good—" Wagner started to respond, but the line was dead in his hand before he got the first word out. "Bitch."

10.

"Holy son of a…" Maggie trailed off as she stared at the size of their cabin.

Ben wrapped his arms around her from behind and kissed her neck.

"I hope you're talking about that bed," Ben said. "Because we could do some serious damage in that bed. It's like a super king or something."

"It's a normal king," Maggie said, turning herself in his arms and giving him a long kiss. "But, Mr. Horny, I was talking about the whole room. Did you notice the wet bar?"

"I did," Ben said. "Want me to fix you a drink?"

"Yes," Maggie said as she started to slip out of her clothes. "Bring it to me in the bathroom. I'm going to shower, change, and get ready for dinner."

"I like the sound of that," Ben said.

"It's just a shower," Maggie said as she unhooked her bra and tossed it at him. "We'll have plenty of time for fun later."

"Want me to bring you your clothes?" Ben asked.

"No," Maggie said quickly. Ben frowned. "What? Let a girl have her secrets. No peeking in my suitcase."

"Okay, okay," Ben said, hands up in defeat.

Maggie smiled at him then stepped into the bathroom. She started to close the door and stopped in mid-movement.

"Oh. My. GOD!" she cried out. "There's a tub in here bigger than your minivan!"

"And that tub will get some use tonight too," Ben said as he went to the wall and popped open one of the closet doors. He stared at what was inside and then shook his head over and over, faster and faster until his face was red with anger. "That son of a bitch. That stupid son of a bitch."

He grabbed out a crimson silk shirt and stomped into the bathroom.

There was already steam filling the room as Maggie stepped into the shower stall and sighed.

"On second thought," she said as she saw Ben come in. "Maybe you should join me."

When Ben didn't answer, she wiped the condensation from the shower glass and frowned.

"What are you holding" she asked "Benjamin? What is wrong?"

"It's a crimson silk shirt," Ben nearly snarled.

"Okay... Is that bad?" Maggie asked. "You like crimson, don't you? I wear it all the time and you always compliment me on it."

"Yes, I do like it," Ben said. "But I don't wear it. Not anymore."

"Not anymore? What does that mean?" Maggie asked.

Ben stomped out of the bathroom as Maggie called after him. With the shirt clutched in his fist, he yanked open the cabin door and stormed out into the passageway. He turned to the right and blindly started rushing through the ship.

Upstairs, down stairs, around corner after corner. He found two media rooms, a small ballroom, a full bar done up to look like an Irish pub, a billiards room which confused the hell out of him, a formal dining room, a not-so-formal dining room, a solarium maybe (he wasn't sure), and finally the steps that led up to the bridge.

"You!" Ben roared as he threw the shirt in Nick's face. "You son of a bitch!"

"Dude, chill," Nick said, tossing the shirt aside. "What is the problem? You like crimson. You love silk."

"You know exactly what the problem is!" Ben shouted as he got up in Nick's face.

A man in nautical dress standing by the wheel moved towards the two, but Nick held up a hand and he stopped.

"Ben, I'd like you to meet Captain Marcus Staggs," Nick said, pushing Ben back a couple feet. "He's the guy that keeps us from crashing into rocks and shit."

"Not that there are many rocks out in international waters," Captain Staggs replied. "It's good to meet you, Mr. Clow."

"International waters?" Ben asked. "Why would we possibly need to go out into international waters, Nick? Would it have to do with why my closet is filled with crimson silk shirts? Shirts you know I always wore at the table?"

"Yeah, I was going to break the news to him at dinner, Staggs," Nick said to the captain. "But I probably should have told you that." Nick reached out and took Ben by the elbow. "Let's go have a drink, dude. We could both use one."

Ben yanked his elbow free and pulled his arm back like he was going to hit Nick. Nick just stood there, ready to take the hit. After a couple of seconds, Ben calmed down and shook his head.

"Screw you, Nick," Ben said as he turned and stormed off. He stomped down the stairs. "Turn this boat around! We are going home!"

Captain Staggs looked at Nick. Nick shook his head and rolled his eyes.

"We aren't going home," Nick said.

"Sir, I can't keep a man here against his will," Captain Staggs said. "That is kidnapping. I'd not only lose any chance of staying on this ship when you sell it, but I would probably go to jail."

"No one is going to jail and I already promised you that part of any sales agreement is for you to stay on the ship," Nick said. "It's all good. Ben gets a little heated sometimes. We have a long history and it's complicated."

A door behind them on the opposite side was flung open and Ben stepped back onto the bridge.

"What? How the hell?" he glared at Nick. "Did MC Escher design this stupid boat?"

"Maybe. And it's a yacht." Nick smiled. "Come on, dude. Let's have that drink and then I'll show you how to get back to your cabin. You can tell everything to Maggie and see what she thinks. If she agrees that I'm a son of a bitch and that you two should go home then I'll have Captain Staggs turn this baby around and that's what will happen. You will go home. But just hear me out, alright?"

"Why, Nick?" Ben asked, some of his anger gone. He looked more exhausted than enraged. "From the second I saw you today this has all been wrong. I could feel it in my gut before I got out of the car."

"Minivan," Nick said and smirked. "And if you hear me out and decide to stay then you won't be driving a minivan anymore. You'll be driving any damn car you want. Maggie won't have to work as a teacher and be treated like crap all day. Your kids will be set for life."

"My kids already are set for life," Ben said. "Thanks to Bobbi's parents."

"But what about yours and Maggie's kids, man?" Nick asked. "She's only thirty. You're only thirty-five. Those are baby-making years nowadays. You think Maggie doesn't want one of her own? Or a couple of her own? How the hell will you afford them on her salary and the crap money you make from your blog?"

"I don't make crap money," Ben said.

"Really?" Nick asked.

"Shut up," Ben said. He looked at Captain Staggs. "What do you think?"

"Huh? What?" Captain Staggs asked. "No offense, Mr. Clow, but I don't know you well enough to offer advice."

"Yeah, but you're a captain," Ben said. "You make life-saving decisions all the time. I write a blog on professional poker. What the hell do I know?"

"The first step is admitting it, dude," Nick said then held up his hands. "Sorry. Too soon."

"The ship is worth approximately sixty-five million," Captain Staggs said. "I will be getting five percent of that, as Mr. Sheeran has promised, and I believe he mentioned that you would be getting thirty percent. So you have to ask yourself if thirty percent of sixty-five million is worth the trouble, Mr. Clow."

"But worth the trouble of what?" Ben asked, turning his attention back on Nick. "What are you up to?"

"Drinks," Nick said, slowly, cautiously putting his arm around Ben's shoulders. "Let's calm your grrrr down then I explain the plan. Cool?"

"Not cool," Ben said. "Way not cool. But I am going to let you explain. Then I'm going to let you explain to Maggie. You have to sell her, not me."

"Benny Boy, dude, the only thing I hope that gets sold is this damn money pit," Nick said. "Honestly. That is what this is all about. Now, come on, I'll show you how to get to the bar. Or one of them. There are a few. That is important information to have. Trust me."

11.

Dr. Glouster looked at the two men in front of him. He glanced past them at the vault door and nodded.

"Are you clear on the exact plans?" Dr. Glouster asked the men. "To deviate would mean great risk to yourselves and this ship. As soon as this vault opens, I will open the tank's hatch and you will lure the creature out. It will suspect a trap which is why we will keep this vault door open. It cannot resist the urge to escape."

"Seems like a stupid risk," one of the men said. "What happens if the thing gets out?"

"The same thing that happened to your comrades," Dr. Glouster said. "Only ship wide." Dr. Glouster looked up and down the passageway at the dozens of men in each direction. "It is why these men are in place. If you fail at containing the creature then they will be forced to do your job for you."

"If we fail then that means we're dead," the second man said. "I really don't feel like getting killed by sushi."

"Cute," Dr. Glouster said, glaring. "But your joke tells me you do not take this seriously. Perhaps you need to be replaced?"

"No, no, we can handle this," the first man replied, patting the long baton in his hand. "You're sure it will stay back if we spark these up?"

"I am positive," Dr. Glouster said. "It fears electricity, fire, extreme heat of any kind. Due to the creature's nervous system not being centralized, and spread throughout its body, especially its appendages, its legs are extremely sensitive. It knows what electric shocks feel like. It will avoid them at all cost."

"You got this thing pretty trained up, doctor," the second man stated. "Why not tell it to sit and stay?"

"It is a wild creature, despite its time in captivity and its conditioning," Dr. Glouster said. "It will no more obey my commands than a stray mutt you'd find in an alley."

"Give a stray a hot dog and it'll do whatever you tell it to do," the first man laughed.

"Yes, but you would be the hot dog in this scenario," Dr. Glouster said. "How do you feel about your analogy now?"

"I'm not getting paid to feel," the first man replied.

"But getting paid triple like Wagner said won't matter if we end up as fish food," the second man said.

"It is not a fish," Dr. Glouster snapped. "It is in the mollusk family."

"Mollusk? That thing's a giant clam?" the first man asked and lifted his shock baton. "Then what we need is a bucket of garlic butter and a flame thrower, not these joy buzzers."

"Once the creature is out of its tank and focused on you then your teammates will drop down from above, enter the tank, and clean the filtration system," Dr. Glouster said, ignoring the joke. "I have briefed them thoroughly, so it should only take about five minutes for them to complete their tasks. Once they are done, and clear of the vault, then you will drive the creature back with the shock batons and force it into the tank. You leave quickly, we lock it down, and then you will not have to deal with the creature again. It will all be automated from there. Understood?"

"I understood the plan the first six times, man," the first man replied.

"Let's get this over with," the second man said.

"Yes," Dr. Glouster said as he motioned to the vault door. "Let's."

12.

Bourbon in hand, Ben walked around the oval table, his eyes studying the felt surface. There were eight places to sit, all identical, with inlaid trays for chips on the table as well as a small platform next to each seat for food and drink. Ben took a sip of his bourbon and shook his head.

"Who are the marks?" Ben asked.

"No marks, Benny Boy," Nick said. "I already told you that. This will be a straight game."

"No scam, no hustle?" Ben laughed. "Nick, brother, I know you. You don't play straight games. You're a cheater and cheaters always cheat."

"I didn't cheat that much," Nick said. "Only when I absolutely had to. We all can't be poker savants like you, Benny Boy."

"I savanted my way into almost getting killed," Ben said. "Mostly because of my association with you." Ben looked around the room. A bartender stood behind an ornate wooden bar and smiled at Ben. "All the crew in on the job?"

"There is no job," Nick almost snapped. He took a deep breath. "No job, no scam, no con, no marks. Straight poker. This will be a clean game, trust me."

Ben raised his eyebrows and Nick sighed.

"I know, I know, you have zero reason to trust me after Mazatlan," Nick said. "But, come on, Benny! That shit was way out of hand before we walked in that room! What went down wasn't my fault!"

Ben's eyebrows remained raised.

"Mostly," Nick admitted. "It mostly wasn't my fault."

"I wasn't thinking of Mazatlan," Ben said and the air between them dropped about twenty degrees.

Nick held up a finger. "Don't go there. Just don't."

"Fine. I won't." Ben rubbed at his face and calmed down. "The only reason you are holding this game is because you want one of the players to buy this boat off you?" Ben asked. "That's it. You're throwing a poker party to do that? Why not just have a dinner party or bring in strippers?"

"First, some of the guests would not respond to strippers," Nick said.

"Who doesn't respond to strippers?" Ben asked.

"What's this about strippers?" Maggie asked as she walked into the game room. "It just took me thirty minutes to look like this. There is no way I'm stripping it off for anyone. Except for Benjamin. Later."

She was dressed in a sleeveless, black dress that fit her perfectly. The material had a shine to it when it caught the light just right. It hugged her hips nicely without being too provocative, allowing any admirers a chance to fill in the blanks with their own imaginations. Maggie smiled at the men, waited, then quickly frowned.

"No compliments? Really?" she asked.

"Sorry, sorry," Ben responded as he crossed the room and kissed her. "You look stunning. Which is why I stood there like a slack-jawed moron."

"You're always a slack-jawed moron," Maggie joked. "So next time make sure you use your words." She looked at Nick. "What's this about strippers?"

"No strippers," Nick insisted. "And you do look stunning. My girl knows how to nail measurements. I knew she would. Been using her for years with my on again, off again lady friends. She hasn't failed yet."

"You buy dresses for a lot of women without them trying them on first?" Maggie asked. "Big risk. One wrong fit on the butt and you can kiss the romance goodbye."

"I learned that mistake," Nick said. "Like I said, my girl knows how to nail measurements."

"Nick was filling me in on why we're actually here," Ben said. "It looks like I'm supposed to play some poker so he can sell this boat."

"Dude, stop calling it a boat," Nick said. "It's a yacht. Boats don't cost sixty-five million."

"I'm sorry, what?" Maggie gasped. "Did you say this cost sixty-five million? As in dollars? Sixty-five million dollars?"

"Yeah," Nick said, grinning. "Impressed?"

"Sickened, actually," Maggie said. "Do you know how many teachers that could pay? How many teaching assistants? How many new books and furniture for needy schools that could buy?"

"Nope," Nick said. "And why would that matter to you?"

"Why wouldn't it matter?" Ben asked. "She's a teacher."

"Right, right," Nick said. "Sorry. The whole public school morass isn't exactly my thing. But if it's totally your thing then you can buy all the books and new desks you want with your share. That's up to you and Benny Boy here."

"My share?" Maggie asked Ben.

"Our share," Ben said. "We're here to sell this boat."

"Yacht," Nick corrected. "Yacht. The people that will be arriving soon don't buy boats. They buy yachts. Yachts, yachts, yachts."

"I thought you said you were here to play poker?" Maggie asked, her eyes narrowing.

"May I fix you a drink, ma'am?" the bartender asked.

"Pimm's Cup," Maggie said. "Don't skimp on the Pimm's."

"Yes, ma'am," the bartender said and smiled as he got to work.

"Nick wants me to entertain his guest with a game of poker," Ben said. "While he butters them up and tries to unload this yacht on one of them."

"With any luck, there might be a bidding war and I'll get full asking price," Nick said.

"How's your luck lately?" Maggie asked.

"It stuck me with this thing," Nick said. "So, it sucks."

"Why poker? Why Ben?" Maggie asked.

"Yes, Nick, why poker? Why me?" Ben asked, sipping his bourbon. Maggie took the glass from him and took a drink. She frowned and coughed. Ben laughed and took the glass back. "Bourbon, babe, you should have asked first."

"I hate bourbon," Maggie said when her coughing fit was over.

"This should help," the bartender said as he brought her a highball glass of amber liquid over ice with a slice of cucumber floating on top. "Please let me know if that is to your liking."

She took a sip and smiled. "It is to my liking. I didn't catch your name. I'm Maggie."

"Manny Ruiz," the bartender replied.

"Reece?" Maggie asked.

"Ruiz," Manny clarified. "But it is pronounced like Reece, yes. My family has been in Seattle for eight generations, so the pronunciation has become anglicized."

"Haven't we all," Nick said. "I don't know what that means. Thanks, Manny."

There was a slight vibration and a far-off noise. Nick stiffened and shot a worried look at Ben.

"I need to know if you are in," Nick said. "And I kind of need to know now. That's the chopper."

"Chopper?" Ben asked. "You can land a chopper on this thing?"

"For sixty-five million this yacht should transform into a chopper," Maggie said. "And fly itself."

"Benny Boy? Come on. Don't leave me hanging here," Nick said. "Thirty percent of sixty-five million is a sweet, sweet cut."

Maggie choked on a swallow of her Pimm's Cup. She grabbed Ben's arm in an iron grip.

"Ow," he said as he pulled her hand away.

"I'm sorry, did he say we get thirty percent of sixty-five million?" Maggie asked. "Is that what he meant by me buying all the desks and supplies I wanted for school?"

"That's what he meant," Ben said.

"Yeah, he's in. I'm making the call for him," Maggie said. "As long as nothing illegal is happening."

"Nothing illegal," Nick said. "I promise."

"Then why are we out in international waters?" Ben asked.

There was a soft tone and Captain Staggs's voice came out of a speaker set into the ceiling.

"Mr. Sheeran? The guests have arrived," Captain Staggs said. "I will go greet them myself. Will you be joining me?"

"Yeah, Staggs, I'll be right there," Nick said. He looked at Ben. "Come on, man. Please?"

"Answer my question first," Ben said.

"We're in international waters because some of the guests may or may not be on certain lists that may or may not make US law enforcement nervous," Nick said, holding up his hands before the protests could begin. "Not terrorists. Maybe a drug lord and possibly a multi-national crime boss. Or two. They do legit stuff, though, too. That I know of. I try not to pry. Also, if I make the sale here in international waters then I don't get hit with US taxes."

"You'll still have to declare the money," Maggie said.

"You have no idea the circles I run in," Nick said and smiled. "I have an army of people that I can call in a moment's notice that can make sixty-five million disappear. Like that."

"It's true," Ben said. "And it's legal. It's why there's no middle class in America anymore."

"Boo hoo," Nick said. "Benny Boy?"

"Nothing illegal," Ben said.

"Nothing illegal," Nick said. "I even made a no guns policy. There isn't a firearm on this yacht, so things can't get out of hand if the game gets heated."

"Again, why me?" Ben asked. "You know plenty of pros that would play this game for less than thirty percent."

"Would you believe me if I said the guests are fans of your blog?" Nick asked.

"No," Ben said.

"Then you are selling yourself short, because they are," Nick said. "You'd be surprised by the fan base you have in the underworld. Mazatlan was a cluster, but it also kind of made you a legend, dude. I'm just cashing in on that."

"Why am I not surprised?" Ben sighed. "Okay, I'm in."

"Thirty percent of sixty-five million is almost twenty million dollars," Maggie said. "Twenty million! There is no way you are passing that up."

"You know nothing about this world, Mags," Ben said sharply. "Do not even assume you do. Assumptions are very dangerous."

Maggie looked at Ben for a second then cocked a hip and smiled.

"Not a fan of the condescending tone, but this badass attitude is pretty sexy," Maggie said as she took Ben's hand. "Let's go get you dressed so you can wow your new fans and we can get rich."

"Thanks, Maggie," Nick said. "And thank you, Ben."

"Screw me on this and drug lords will be the least of your worries," Ben said. "I still know how to use a knife."

"I know, I know," Nick said.

"You know how to use a knife?" Maggie asked. "Who is this man of mystery next to me?"

The two left and Nick looked over at Manny.

"You ready?" Nick asked.

"Everything is set, Sheeran," Manny said. "We'll make a great impression. Don't you worry."

"Mr. Sheeran?" Captain Staggs called over the intercom.

"I'm on my way!" Nick shouted. "I'm on my way!"

13.

Claxons rang out and Wagner slammed his fist against his desk. He pressed his finger to his ear and switched on his com. He instantly heard the voices of panicked men. Then gunfire and screaming.

"That son of a bitch," Wagner snarled as he jumped up from his desk and ran to the door of his quarters.

He threw open the door and was immediately greeted by six men, one of them holding out an HK MP7A1 submachine gun. Wagner looked at the weapon and frowned.

"That bad?" he asked the man that handed him the gun.

"Yes, sir," the man replied. The man pressed his finger to his own ear. "The creature is still contained in the vault, but it sounds like we have multiple casualties. The doctor may be one of them."

"I can hear the reports," Wagner snapped. He pointed at two of the men. "You make sure the bridge and engine rooms are locked down. This ship does not stop for any reason." He pointed at two more. "You also make sure every single hatch is sealed. This thing does not get above decks, understood? If that means we are trapped down here with it then that means we are trapped down here with it."

"Sir, lockdown is automated," one of the men said. "You can activate it with your—"

"Did I say for you to argue with me?" Wagner roared at the man. "I know I can activate it! I already have! I want the two of you to verify that all hatches are sealed! With your own two eyes! Do you think I've made it this far in this business because I have put my trust in automated systems? GO!"

The two men took off one way while the other two took off another way. Wagner stared hard at the last two men standing before him.

"You two are with me," he said. "Watch our six. Watch the side passages. Watch the vents. Watch everything. If the creature gets loose on this ship it's not going to attack head on, but from our blindsides. I do not want to have a blindside, so eyes open!"

"Yes, sir!" the men replied.

"On me," Wagner ordered as he started running down the passageway to the stairs that led deeper into the ship.

14.

Two things caught Nick's attention as he stepped out onto the what was normally a sun deck, but had been converted to a helipad by the previous owner: the clouds in the night sky hung heavy and black, and many of the people that stepped off the huge Eurocopter EC 175 had not been invited and were for sure armed.

"Welcome!" Nick called out as the rotors on the chopper powered down. "Thank you all for coming! I know most of you, but for those that I don't, I'm Nick Sheeran and this is my humble home!"

"Your home?" a tall, skinny woman asked. "You live here? How cute."

Her voice had a heavy Russian accent that explained the thick blonde hair that framed her sharp angled face. Gorgeous in an off putting way, the woman carried herself like she was used to working hard and being rewarded generously for that hard work.

"Ms. Romanski," Nick bowed. "It is an honor to have you here."

"The honor is mine, Mr. Sheeran," Evgeniya Romanski said. "And I was only playing about this being your home."

"Maybe it'll become your home?" Nick grinned.

"Do not push it, Mr. Sheeran," she replied. "And call me Niya, please."

"I'm Nick, Niya," Nick said as he took her hand and kissed it. He turned to the other guests. "Oh, I know these three! Carlos, Jessica, Lane. It is great to see you."

A short man with dark, pockmarked skin flipped Nick off then laughed.

"I'm only here because of your friend, Nicky," Carlos Whittier said. "I do not need another yacht."

"You're right," Nick said. "You don't. But, you do need this yacht. You can get rid of those pieces of crap you have docked in Baja. They are nothing compared to the Lucky Sucker."

"Horrible name," Jessica Holstein said.

Short, with close-cut brown hair and fine, delicate features, Jessica was almost the opposite of Niya. She moved with the grace of a dancer, and would have looked completely at ease in any ballet company in the world, except for the long scar that went from one side of her jaw, down across her neck, and back up to the other side of her jaw.

"If I buy this thing, I'll be changing the name instantly," Jessica said, giving Nick a quick hug and a kiss on both cheeks. "How does Naughty Nicholas sound?"

"Like I should be honored and insulted at the same time," Nick chuckled. "Lane!"

"No," Lane Garfield said and pushed past Nick. "I'm here to play cards and meet Ben Clow. He is here, right Sheeran? This isn't another one of your bloody bait and switch capers, is it?"

"Dude, one bad condo deal and you still give me shit?" Nick asked, looking offended. "Come on, man, we both know that wasn't my fault."

"Wasn't mine, either, mate," Lane said. "So there we stand."

"Okay, okay, I'm sorry," Nick said. "I should have researched that Zeus guy better."

"Zeus? You did business with a guy named Zeus?" Jessica laughed. "You two deserved to get screwed."

"Bite me, Jessie," Lane said. Average height with thinning brown hair and bright gold eyes, Lane Garfield spoke with a refined British accent that was obviously an artificial cultivation hiding his obvious working class history. He hooked a thumb over his shoulder at the man standing behind him. And the armed men behind the man. "Thought you said no bodyguards and no firearms? Grumpy here brought both."

"Yes, I did say that," Nick said as he turned to the last of the guests and the man's entourage. "Mr. Giraldi, I am pleased you could make it. But I am afraid I do not have room for your men here. Perhaps they could return to shore with the helicopter? I'd feel a lot better if they did."

"No," Tony Giraldi replied. "Not until they have swept this boat to my satisfaction. I don't know you, Sheeran, which means I don't trust you. No offense, but putting my life in the hands of a stranger isn't exactly how I have become the successful man I am."

"I do not know him yet I did not arrive with a small army," Niya said. "I thought the Italians had more balls than this, Giraldi."

"You want to see my balls, Romanski?" Tony snapped.

"You two know each other," Nick said cautiously. "Great."

"We have had dealings," Niya said. "They have been pleasant in the past. I am sure Giraldi would like to keep our dealings that way."

"Pleasant dealings?" Tony laughed as he licked his lips. "I guess you can call them that."

The man was tall and large. Not fat, but certainly heavy and muscular. His accent was a mix of many European countries, but heavier on the Italian side. His black hair was surprisingly long and hung down to his shoulders. The man's eyes were black pinpricks behind prominent cheekbones and skin that was a healthy tan.

"Mr. Giraldi, I'm not trying to be rude, but when you accepted my invitation you did agree to my terms," Nick said. "Again, no offense, but I have had one too many run-ins with hired guns. I am going to have to insist that your men return with the helicopter."

"Tell you what, Sheeran," Tony said. "You let my guys sweep this boat—"

"It's a yacht," Nick muttered.

"—and if they find it's safe then I'll send them back with your rented chopper," Tony continued, ignoring the interruption. "Capisce?"

"Did he really say capisce?" Lane asked. "Christ. What a bloody stereotype."

"What was that?" Tony asked. "You say something?"

"I said what a bloody stereotype," Lane replied, his voice loud and abrasive. "Friggin' Cosa Nostra saying capisce. It's like a bad Coppola movie."

"Are there good Coppola movies?" Jessica asked. "I'm not a fan. Never did get the Godfather thing. Thugs and morons in that movie."

Tony eyed the two then smiled. "You have a problem with the Godfather?"

"She does, mate," Lane said. "I enjoyed them. Even the third one."

"Of course you did," Jessica said, punching Lane on the shoulder.

"Must we?" Niya asked.

"Yeah, come on," Carlos said as he stood there tapping his four thousand dollar loafers. He nodded his chin skyward. "Gonna get nasty soon and I'm already freezing my butt off. Can we go inside and meet this blogger or what? I'm here to play cards and laugh at Nick as he tries to sell me a yacht."

"Thank you, Carlos," Nick said. "And it is a very nice yacht. As you'll all see." He turned back to Tony. "Tell you what. Have your guys bring in everyone's luggage and then they can sweep the yacht. Might as well be useful for something. The second they are done sweeping then they are back on the chopper and out of here. You cool with that, Mr. Giraldi?"

Tony kind of shrugged. "That might work. But I'm trusting my men. Any of them feel like you're going to pull something and I'm on that chopper with them."

"That's cool by me," Nick said. "I don't want anyone here that doesn't want to be here. Now, can we go inside? I want you all to meet Ben and get comfortable. I have an amazing dinner planned, top shelf drinks, and then some quality card playing."

"I can show them below," Captain Staggs said. "If you would like, Mr. Sheeran."

"Thanks, Staggs," Nick said.

"Will you be playing with us, Mr. Sheeran?" Niya asked.

"No, no, not me," Nick said. "I'm off the cards. Just think of me as your humble host for the week."

"Humble," Lane snorted as he walked past Nick and slapped him on the back. "That is never a word I'd use to describe you, mate."

"You can say that twice," Jessica said, following closely behind Lane.

Nick just smiled as everyone filtered in through the hatch that led to the decks below. He stepped out of the way of the large men that trailed Tony, giving them all his best and most welcoming smile. The second they were gone the smile fell away and he turned to look at the thickening cloud bank that grew ever closer. He walked quickly over to the chopper and pulled open the pilot's door.

"This weather going to be a problem?" he asked.

"Not if I can take off in the next fifteen minutes," the pilot said. "I can't get stuck here. I have another job tonight and two tomorrow morning."

"Okay. Great," Nick said. "I'll hurry the lugs along and get them back on your chopper before that."

"I'm not waiting," the pilot said and pointed to a digital clock on his instrument panel. "Fifteen minutes and I'm gone. No warning."

"Right, sure, I get it," Nick said. "Fifteen minutes."

Nick gave him a thumbs up then shut the door. He hurried to the hatch and yanked it open, sweat beading on his forehead despite the cold wind that blew off the water.

15.

Wagner didn't know what was worse, the deafening bark of automatic gunfire confined to the enclosed passageway or the screams of the men dying. When he rounded a corner and saw what waited for him, he knew his answer.

"Mother of God..." he said as he watched a man get snagged from the passageway and yanked towards the vault.

Towards the vault. Not inside it. The man's legs caught the edge of the opening, one continuing to go inside while the other bent at an angle it wasn't supposed to until it ripped from his pelvis with a popping sound that overrode the gunfire. More than a couple of battle-hardened veterans turned and threw up as the man's leg tumbled across the floor while the rest of him was lost from sight.

The vomit only added to the gore and mess that coated almost every inch of the passageway. Wagner had to swallow a few times to keep his own gorge down and he'd spent a year in the Congo trailing the ravages of one of the area's most ruthless warlords. The sense memories from that horrid time came rushing back to him and he had to fight to regain his composure.

"Report!" Wagner shouted into the com once he knew he wasn't going to add his sick to the mess. "Who has eyes on this thing?"

"It is out of its tank, sir!" someone responded.

"No shit!" Wagner yelled. "I guessed that! Give me details, asshead!"

"Fifteen dead! Twenty wounded!" the voice yelled. "Every tech that was working in there is shredded, sir! SHREDDED!"

"Calm the hell down!" Wagner yelled as he pointed for one of his men to get close to the vault and put eyes on the situation.

The man stared at Wagner for a few seconds then took a deep breath and nodded.

"Who is this?" Wagner asked.

"Nunez, sir!" the man on the com replied. "I'm with ten others two decks above! We're keeping it from crawling up into the rest of the ship!"

"Keeping it? How?" Wagner asked.

The man he'd sent ahead got to the edge of the vault, pointed at four others that were busy firing wildly into the vault to stop, then peeked his head around as fast as possible to get a view of inside the vault. His body slumped to the floor in an instant. The head was no longer attached.

"Sir, you need to pull everyone back!" Nunez yelled. "It's feeding off the blood and I swear to God it's getting bigger!"

"Bullshit!" Wagner shouted. "I know this project and rapid growth was not part of it!"

"It is now!" Nunez cried. "Oh, crap! Crap, crap, crap!"

The sound of gunfire filled Wagner's ear and he cut his com. He yanked a small tablet from his belt and began tapping at it, bringing up the security systems for the ship.

"Why do they have the hatches open?" he snarled. "They shouldn't have been opened yet."

He kept tapping and realized he was frozen out of the vault's controls, including the hatches above it on each deck. He almost threw the tablet against the wall, but tucked it back into his belt instead, checked his MP7, then pointed at the last man with him.

"Stay by my side," Wagner ordered. "We'll get to the vault and distract it long enough so I can get a look inside."

"Distract it? How?" the man asked, his face white with fear.

"Throw food at it," Wagner said, a psychotic light filling his eyes.

Wagner rushed down the passageway, got to the edge of the vault, and kept going. He fell to the floor, sliding feet first in the blood and gore, and cleared the vault opening in a split second. In that split second, he caught a glimpse of what was inside the vault.

Death.

Blood-coated death.

Wagner slowed his slide and got to his feet. Just before a tentacle shot out from the vault and slapped the floor where he'd been only a moment before. He jumped back, tripping over a severed arm, and fell hard on his ass. He then realized that the man that was supposed to be following right behind him was no longer in the passageway.

"Stupid coward," Wagner said. He looked around at the couple of men that were still there, the men that had been fighting the whole time, and he gave them a nod. "Grab up all the body parts you can."

The men's eyes went wide.

"You want us to what, sir?" one asked.

"Start grabbing up body parts," Wagner said. "We're going to toss them into the vault as fast as possible and hope the thing goes for them instead of us."

"Instead of us?" another man asked. "You mean we're going in there?"

"No way," a third man said.

Wagner shot him in the face.

"You're useless if you can't follow orders," Wagner said. "Anyone else want to be useless?"

They shook their heads back and forth quickly.

"Didn't think so," Wagner said. "Now grab up body parts. As much as you can hold while still maintaining control of your weapons. We throw and go. No hesitating."

Then men nodded and looked about the passageway. Finding body parts would not be a problem.

16.

Beads of condensation rolled down the side of the glass and Nick rubbed at them with his finger while he leaned against the bar and watched as his guests chatted and laughed. The bar wasn't the same one in the game room, but a different one a deck higher. It was the Irish pub bar, yet Manny was still the bartender, having moved as the party moved. Nick looked up from his glass and across the bar. Manny gave him a quick nod.

"They are working their way back up," Manny informed Nick. "Ashley just said they cleared the lower deck and are on the main deck. They'll be here on the upper deck in minutes."

Nick checked his watch and shook his head.

"Doesn't matter," he said. Almost on cue there was the far-off sound of an engine revving and the distinct whump whump whump of helicopter rotors.

Nick could tell the others heard the helicopter as well. Some of them shifted uncomfortably as they glanced at Tony Giraldi while others shot looks in his direction. One of those looks was from Ben, but Nick gave him a quick smile to say things were in hand. Ben rolled his eyes in obvious disbelief.

"What's gone wrong already?" Ben asked, when he was able to slip away from a conversation he was having with Jessica and Maggie. The two women seemed to hit it off, so they barely noticed as he made his way over to the bar. "You have that look you get when you eat too much dairy."

"Yeah, I bet I do," Nick said. "I feel like I'm going to shit my pants."

"Spill it," Ben said.

"Not now," Nick said. "And not here. After dinner before the game starts."

"Mr. Sheeran?" Manny said. "Dinner is ready in the main dining room."

"Good," Nick said. "Thanks, Manny."

Nick clapped his hands.

"Ladies and gentlemen," he said, a huge smile on his face. "Dinner's ready. If you'll follow me, we'll head up to the fly deck. Feel free to bring your drinks with, but I can assure you there is a fully stocked bar in the dining room. And Manny will be along shortly to fix new cocktails as needed."

"Shortly?" Lane asked. "Shouldn't he be there already? When I sit down, I better have a very dry martini waiting for me."

"Once he cleans up in here, he'll join us," Nick says. "Not to worry though, I've had the chef open two bottles of 2006 Screaming Eagle Napa Valley Cabernet Sauvignon and three bottles of 2003 Jean-Louis Chave Cuvée Cathelin Hermitage."

"Two reds?" Carlos asked. "No white?"

"I believe four bottles of Krug Private Cuvée champagne will do," Nick said.

"Couldn't splurge for the Moet, Mr. Sheeran?" Niya asked. "How unfortunate."

"We'll break out the Dom Perignon later," Nick said. "If you will all follow me?"

"I would prefer to wait for my men," Tony said. "No offense, but I don't eat a stranger's food without it being tasted first."

"Jesus," Ben said quietly. "Medici, much?"

"Excuse me?" Tony asked. "What do you mean by that?"

"The Medici family was a well known—" Ben began.

"I know who the damn Medicis are," Tony growled. "But why did you say it? Because I'm Italian? Is that it? I'm just a stereotype that wears gold chains and tracksuits when I hang around my house waiting for my goomah to call while my wife makes pasta and gravy?"

"Uh, no, I said it because the Medicis were famous for losing food tasters due to attempted poisonings by their rivals," Ben said. "But if you'd rather be a stereotype then who am I to stop you, *Tony*?"

"Guys, come on, chill," Nick said, getting between the two men. "We're all friends here."

"No, we are not," Tony said, tapping Nick in the chest. "You, I know, but barely. I don't consider you a friend on any level, Sheeran. An acquaintance, yes, but not a friend. The poker blogger? Please. He's an amusement. A sideshow freak you trotted out to wow us while you try to unload this money pit."

Maggie snickered. Everyone looked at her and the small smile on her face slipped away. Jessica took the drink from her hand and flipped the men off.

"We're going to dinner," Jessica said. "You guys need a ruler to measure your pencil dicks or will a cocktail toothpick be enough?" She glared at them all. "More than enough, is my guess."

"Yep," Lane said. "Dinner sounds bloody great. Niya?"

"Thank you," Niya said as she took Lane's arm.

Carlos sat at the bar and tipped his glass. "I want to see how this plays out."

"It plays out with some delicious lobster bisque," Nick said. "Let's eat."

"Let's," Tony said, glaring at Ben. "Can't wait to tear into some fresh meat."

He stalked off and Carlos sighed then followed behind.

"The first course is bisque! That's a soup!" Ben called after Tony. "What are you going to tear into? The spoon?"

"Dude," Nick hissed, taking the glass of bourbon from Ben's hand and setting it on the bar. "How many have you had?"

"I don't know," Ben said. "Three?"

"Six," Manny said as he wiped down the bar and tossed the rag in the small sink underneath. "That I know of."

"Shit," Nick said. "Are you stress drinking? I'm bankrolling you, man. You can't lose even if you lose. So relax."

Ben gave Nick a crooked smile then the smile straightened out and Ben cleared his throat.

"I've been dumping them while no one was looking," Ben said. "I've had maybe a shot's worth all evening. Just sizing up the competition and giving them a little false confidence."

"These aren't marks, Ben," Nick said. "I thought I was clear on that. I just need you to play a straight game. Tonight isn't about the cards, it's about selling this damn thing. And I won't be able to sell it if you piss off my potential buyers."

"Really?" Ben asked. "How about if I piss off your main potential buyer, start beating his ass at cards, then let him take me down so he celebrates by buying your boat? How does that sound? Or would you rather I play it straight?"

Nick started to answer, but only laughed.

"I'm heading to the dining room," Manny said, a smirk on his face as he looked at Ben. "Would you care for me to fix you another bourbon, Mr. Clow? Perhaps of the apple juice variety?"

"The what variety?" Ben asked.

"Apple juice is the same color as bourbon," Manny said. "If I add a dot of vegetable oil to it then the liquid will stick to the sides and look just like real bourbon. Since you plan on letting the man win at cards, keeping up the illusion that you are drinking wouldn't exactly be conning him. Just makes the ruse more believable."

"Uh…yeah, sure," Ben said. "That would be great. But, um, how does apple juice with vegetable oil taste?"

"Like apple juice with vegetable oil," Manny said. "That is the downside to the plan."

"How about no plan? No ruse, no illusion, just cards," Nick said. "I have enough bullshit to deal with considering…"

He trailed off, sighed, took a deep breath, grabbed his own drink, downed it, and slapped Ben on the shoulder.

"You know what? Screw it," Nick said. "Take the asshole for everything he has."

"You sure?" Ben asked. "He's going to be pissed."

"He's also going to want to win at something," Nick said. "So when the others start making offers on this yacht, Giraldi's going to top them each time. I may actually get more than asking price if you piss him off enough."

"But not so much that he kills you," Manny said as he walked from the bar. "I'll be mixing drinks in the dining room then move on to make sure all is set in the game room." He glanced over his shoulder at Nick. "Don't forget your timetable, Mr. Sheeran. The guests do have some place to be tomorrow."

"Yeah, yeah, thanks, Manny," Nick said. "Go fix some drinks, will ya? Let me handle the guests."

"That was weird," Ben said after Manny had gone.

"Huh, what?" Nick asked as he rubbed at his face and started to leave the barroom. "What was weird?"

"You not chewing him a new one," Ben said. "The Nick I know would have made a bartender swim home for talking like that."

"Like what?" Ben asked.

"Like he can tell you what to do," Ben said. "Not that I'm taking your side." He studied Nick for a moment. "Are you okay? How many drinks have *you* had?"

"Not enough," Nick said and patted Ben on the shoulder. "Come on. Let's make nice at dinner then play some cards."

"You're playing?" Ben asked.

"I think I might," Nick said. "It'll help settle my mind."

"Really?" Ben asked. "What's going on with you?"

"Nothing," Nick replied quickly. "I just have to make this all work. It's a lot of pressure. Can you do me a favor and take it easy? I like your thinking, but try not to be hard-case Benny tonight, alright?"

"Works for me," Ben said.

17.

"We have one hatch closed, sir," Nunez called over the com. "We had to do it manually since we're locked out of the systems."

"Good," Wagner said as he inched closer to the vault. The passageway was almost clear of body parts after he and his men had thrown them inside, desperate to keep the creature occupied long enough so he could get a look at the thing and what he was up against.

He got a look. It did not make him happy. It made him decide that going in full bore was not the best strategy.

"Where's my fire crew?" Wagner asked. "I need flames down here now so we can keep this thing inside the vault."

"Fire crew is stuck one deck above you, sir," Nunez replied. "All deck hatches have been locked down per security protocol. They can't get through to you."

"Then unlock the hatches!" Wagner barked. He quieted down and shook his head. "You can't because we're locked out of the systems. Sorry."

"Have you gotten a look at the creature, sir?" Nunez asked.

"I have," Wagner said, "and you're right. The damn thing is growing. Did anyone get eyes on Dr. Glouster? Do we know where he is? I have a few questions about some obvious modifications he's made to the project without anyone knowing."

"No sign of the doctor, sir," Nunez said. "But he has to still be in the vault. I don't know if he's alive or dead, though."

"Time to find out," Wagner said as he took a couple of deep breaths, got into a tight crouch, and crept around the vault door and inside the space itself, staying as small a target as possible.

The room dripped with blood. Offal littered the floor along with bones that looked picked clean. Clothing was piled up in one corner with weapons in another. The weapons looked like they'd been jammed into a blender, their metal barrels and grips warped and twisted into useless chunks of steel.

The creature was nowhere to be seen. Not a trace of the huge beast.

Wagner held up a hand and motioned forward with two fingers. He pointed left then right and two men crept in past him, each taking a different side of the vault. Wagner kept his eyes locked onto the tank that stood in the middle, its water a murky rust color. More than a couple of limbs floated in the saltwater, bobbing up and down with the motion of the ship.

Wagner brought his MP7 up and took aim, his eyes sighting down the snub-nosed barrel. His finger touched the trigger lightly and he prepared to squeeze.

"I wouldn't," Dr. Glouster said from the far corner of the vault, a tablet in his hands, a sneer on his face. "You of all people know how thick that glass is."

"Armor piercing," Wagner said, his aim switching instantly to the doctor. "I know what I'm up against, Doc."

"I do not think you do," Dr. Glouster said. "None of you do. Not NCDC, not Ms. Marion, not any of these men here. Not even OAS or McDowell. I have made sure of that."

"How big is it now?" Wagner asked, his eyes darting from Dr. Glouster to the tank and back. "Is that shadow in there the creature? Hard to tell with all the blood."

"All the blood," Dr. Glouster whispered. He cleared his throat and spoke up. "Yes. The blood. That I hadn't planned on. I knew the creature would have an increased appetite due to its enhancements, but I did not think it would have such a hunger for the sanguine fluid. Of course, the moment I realized it did, I took full advantage of the benefits of such a diet."

"Benefits?" Wagner asked. There was a shifting of the shadow and Wagner brought his MP7 back to bear on the tank. "Benefits like rapid growth?"

"Amongst other attributes," Dr. Glouster said. "You see, Mr. Wagner, *Enteroctopus dofleini*, is an amazing species. It's genetic structure is incredible. Did you know that many species of octopuses can actually change their genetic structure within one generation? One generation! I was able to tap into this miracle of evolution and speed up the process, allowing my creature to adapt within its own lifetime."

"Your creature?" Wagner asked.

"Yes, Mr. Wagner, my creature," Dr. Glouster said. "Did you think I would create such a marvel and allow it to be sold to the highest bidder? Leaving me to begin all over again with some new project that is decided by the whims of shareholders and moronic CEOs? I think not, Mr. Wagner. I think not. I put plans in place long ago to make sure my work would be privately secured."

Dr. Glouster tapped at the tablet and the tank's water churned and swirled as three huge tentacles broke the surface and slid over the glass. Two of the tentacles moved in opposite directions, each heading for one of Wagner's men. The third hovered in the air, undulating slowly as Dr. Glouster began speaking again.

The doctor held up his tablet and smiled.

"This is the only modification that I have made to my creature that is not natural," Dr. Glouster said. "While it means I do not have a specifically pure biological product, it does allow me an immense amount of control. See?"

Before Wagner's men could react, the two tentacles grabbed them, lifting them up high and then bringing them down to the floor in the blink of an eye. The men didn't even have time to scream before they were cracked open like walnuts hitting hard pavement. Fresh blood was added to the coagulating gore that slicked every inch of the vault.

Wagner aimed at Dr. Glouster, but before he could pull the trigger, his weapon was yanked from his hands and thrown against the wall, shattering on impact. Wagner's men's bodies were pulled into the tank and the water's murk increased.

Wagner stared then regarded the doctor.

"I gave you the keys when I handed you that tablet, didn't I?" he asked.

"No, Mr. Wagner, I already had the key," Dr. Glouster replied as he reached into his pocket and produced a USB drive. "Your men were looking for weapons when they patted me down. They had no clue that eighteen gigabytes on a piece of plastic and metal was more dangerous than any gun could ever be."

"Your mods are on that?" Wagner asked.

"Yes," Dr. Glouster said as he held up his tablet.

Wagner narrowed his eyes, turning back to the tank.

"Why not have it kill me as well?" Wagner asked.

"I could, I could," Dr. Glouster said. "But I need you. For now."

"Need me?" Wagner asked. "Can't see why."

"Can't you?" Dr. Glouster asked. "Mr. Wagner, I am a scientist, not a sailor. You are in charge of this ship which means you can give the orders to turn us in the direction I need to go."

"Where you need to go?" Wagner asked. "Where in the hell do you need to go?"

Dr. Glouster tapped some more at his tablet. "I have sent the coordinates to the bridge," he said. "Please get on your com and instruct the captain to set the ship's course for those coordinates, if you will be so kind."

"None of this makes sense, Doc," Wagner said. "You obviously have some plan in mind, but there is no way in hell you could have known I was working for NCDC and was going to move the creature. How the hell is your plan still viable?"

"Because my plan involves me, my creature, and a ship," Dr. Glouster said and shrugged. "The ship need not be an OAS ship, specifically. A NCDC ship will work just as well. In fact, it works even better since if anything is to go wrong, I can blame NCDC and come away looking like an unwilling captive. You, Mr. Wagner, have given me a cover, if I end up in need of one."

"Doc, listen to me," Wagner said. "I don't know who you are working with, and before you try to deny it, I know you are working with someone, okay? It's obvious. Like you said, you're a scientist. You're not a sailor and you are certainly not a weapons dealer. I'm guessing that whoever you are meeting at these coordinates, they are the weapons dealer. How much have you been offered, Doc?"

"I already said I am not selling my work to the highest bidder. But, you are close. Yet not quite there, Mr. Wagner," Dr. Glouster said. "And that is all I am going to say on the subject. I've said what I want and do not intend to be the man that shares his plans in a revealing monologue. Please instruct the captain to turn this ship towards the coordinates I have sent him."

"And if I don't?" Wagner asked.

Two taps on the tablet and a tentacle gripped Wagner around the throat. The pressure was surprisingly light and Wagner was able to breathe easily without any restrictions. As he felt the wet skin of the creature pulse against his neck, he knew that all it would take was one squeeze and he'd find the light pressure gone and possibly his head as well.

"Do I need to ask again?" Dr. Glouster said.

Wagner pressed a finger to his ear. "Captain? This is Wagner. Did you just receive a set of coordinates?"

"Yes, Mr. Wagner," a voice replied.

"Plug them in and head that way," Wagner said. "We're taking a detour."

"Mr. Wagner, I am under strict instructions not to deviate from our rendezvous with the NCDC facility," the captain replied.

"You have new instructions," Wagner said. "We're giving the doctor and his creature a ride, it looks like. Our rendezvous will have to wait until another time, are we clear as a bell, Captain?"

"I understand the code you just gave me, Mr. Wagner, and I'm sorry to say our long range and satellite communications systems have been disabled," the captain said. "NCDC has no idea what has happened on this ship. They won't come looking for us until we miss our arrival window. By then we'll have reached the new coordinates and whatever waits for us there will already have happened."

Wagner glared at Dr. Glouster.

"Is he informing you that the cavalry is not coming, Mr. Wagner?" Dr. Glouster asked. "By the look on your face, I would say that he is."

Wagner glanced around the vault. He calculated the lives lost, the men murdered, and realized that his life was going to be added to the list of casualties the moment Dr. Glouster got what he wanted.

"You win, Doc," Wagner said. "I can't fight you. Not with that thing in your corner. So, how about we make a deal?"

"I have no desire to make a deal, Mr. Wagner," Dr. Glouster said. "I'm sorry, but I don't."

"You sure?" Wagner asked. "This other player, or is it players? Doesn't matter. This other player on the board. Do you trust him or her?"

"Of course not," Dr. Glouster said. "I'd be a fool if I did."

"Then what is to stop this person from just killing you and taking your creature?" Wagner asked.

"Are you really so dense?" Dr. Glouster laughed and swept out a hand. "Look around you. I made this happen. These men were highly trained professionals. I have more than proven that I can handle myself."

"No, you have proven you understand the element of surprise," Wagner said. "Which you will not have when you arrive at your destination. They know you are coming, they know you have the creature, they know you can control the creature. They are counting on it. That makes you a serious liability and risk. The sooner they dispose of you, the better. You are a dangerous variable, Doc. You aren't getting out of this alive."

"I beg to differ," Dr. Glouster replied, but the tone in his voice revealed a different feeling.

Wagner heard that tone and locked onto it.

"You need someone that can navigate the world you are about to step into," Wagner said. "Trust me, Doc. What you've done here is pretty cold blooded, but I can guarantee that whoever you are working with is a million times more cold blooded. You're already dead and you don't know it." Wagner smiled. "Unless you have me watching your back and making sure the trap they have set isn't sprung."

"There is no trap," Dr. Glouster said, but his voice sounded even less convinced than before.

"Oh, there is, Doc. Probably more than one," Wagner said. "How much will you get paid to be whatever it is you think you're going to be?"

"A good amount," Dr. Glouster said. "High eight figures. But, that money will allow me to work more, create more. I do not care about riches, I care about greatness."

"That's what I'm afraid of, Doc," Wagner said. "Because for this other player of yours, it is about the money. It's always about the money." Wagner pointed at the tablet in Dr. Glouster's hand. The tentacle tightened just a hair and Wagner froze. He waited, but when his head wasn't popped off, he continued. "All they need is that tablet and some smart techs and they have your project. And those techs cost a lot less than high eight figures."

"This tablet is not the only reason my creature obeys my commands," Dr. Glouster said. "I raised it from birth. I have been there every single day of its life. It knows me, Mr. Wagner. And I know it. Techs may be able to work out the software from the tablet, but they will not be able to work my creature."

"All the more reason to stay alive, Doc," Wagner said. "Because if they can't control the creature then they'll just kill it."

"Easier said than done, wouldn't you say, Mr. Wagner?" Dr. Glouster chuckled.

"Yes, I would," Wagner agreed. "But once again, you had surprise on your side. All it would take is a couple torpedoes, or some well-placed explosives, to blow this ship to fragments. End of your creature, Doc. Your mystery friend has wasted some time, and maybe some resources, but in the end it's just another deal that didn't pan out. Trust me when I say that if this person is a true professional, they are used to deals not panning out. They are also used to forgetting about them and moving on to the next thing."

"The next thing?" Dr. Glouster snapped. "There will be no next thing like this without me!"

Wagner's hand slowly, carefully moved to his side.

"Do you think that NCDC or OAS will ever be able to replicate what I have done?" Dr. Glouster asked, his face red with anger. "No, they will not! My partner knows this and will not miss the opportunity I am presenting."

"Still doesn't mean you'll get out of this alive, Doc," Wagner said. His fingers found the hilt of the combat knife strapped to his thigh. "Yes or no? Do you want my help or not?"

"I think not," Dr. Glouster said, his finger moving towards the tablet.

Wagner pulled his knife and slashed at the tentacle around his neck. Part of it fell away, landing at Wagner's feet. It flopped about, spurting blue blood, slapping at the blood coated floor on its own. Wagner kicked it away as he rushed at Dr. Wagner before the injured tentacle, or one of the other seven the creature had, came for him.

Dr. Glouster's eyes went wide just as Wagner reached him. The tablet flew out of the doctor's hands and tumbled through the air, spinning end over end until it landed on a broken ribcage. Dr.

Glouster turned to reach for the tablet, completely ignoring the attacking Wagner, his focus only on the device that helped control the creature. With his attention on the tablet, he missed seeing the combat knife coming at him.

Wagner jammed the knife up under Dr. Glouster's ribs, pushing the blade at an upward angle until it pierced the man's lung. Dr. Glouster gasped then began to choke and cough as he fell to his knees. Wagner pulled the knife free, stepped behind the doctor, grabbed him by the forehead, then reached around and slashed his throat, sending a geyser of blood spurting out to create yet another pool on the floor.

As the man gurgled and died, Wagner shoved him aside and rushed over to retrieve the tablet. He made it halfway when the tank behind him shuddered so violently that it moved an inch across the floor, digging a deep gouge in the metal.

Wagner slid to a stop, looked at the tablet on the ribcage, then looked at the tank.

A massive eye was pressed against the glass, staring at him. Wagner met the stare, his blood going as cold as the creature's inside the tank.

Time stretched, but neither Wagner nor the creature made a move.

Then everything broke at once.

Tentacles grabbed the edge of the tank at the same time that Wagner decided to hell with the tablet and started sprinting towards the vault room exit. The creature pulled itself up out of the water and Wagner caught a quick glimpse of the massive thing, all bulbous mantle and pink red skin, before he reached the vault door. Spinning about as the thing landed on the floor, Wagner picked up a stray rifle and opened fire, making sure every shot hit the creature's soft mantle.

But the mantle wasn't so soft.

The bullets fell away without doing any damage as the creature's rosy pink skin became gunmetal grey, hardening into an armor that sent the slugs ricocheting around the vault. Wagner caught a bullet in his shoulder and nearly fell to the ground, but the adrenaline that surged through him, and his years of honing a survival instinct that refused to let him fall, kicked in and he tossed the rifle aside as he sprinted out of the vault.

Wagner put every last ounce of strength he had into shoving the vault door closed. Two tentacles made it through the gap and wrapped themselves around Wagner's legs, pulling him off his feet. But before they could yank him into the vault, the huge door's momentum slammed itself shut and the tentacles were severed, cut off from their body.

Unfortunately for Wagner, the tentacles came from a creature that did not have a central brain like other animals. The tentacles themselves had enough neurons to act independently and they proceeded to finish the task they had been sent to do.

Wagner tried to pry them from his body, but he did not have the strength to do so. His screams filled the passageway as his legs were squeezed apart below the knees. Another noise quickly joined his wailing. A noise from inside the vault. It was the noise of metal tearing and the ship being ripped apart.

With his last bit of strength, Wagner put his finger to his ear.

"Captain?" he whispered. "Captain… Correct…course…now."

"What was that?" the captain responded. "Wagner? I can barely hear you. What did you say?"

Wagner tried to speak, but he couldn't find the words. His mouth opened a few times then stayed open as his hand fell away from his ear and his eyes closed.

"Wagner? Come in," the captain called over the com in Wagner's ear. "Wagner! Are you there? I need you to repeat that order! Wagner!"

The sound of glass breaking, metal shearing, and men screaming, filled the com next.

"Oh dear God!" the captain shouted "What is that—?"

A choked gurgle and then a wet splat was heard.

Then silence.

Wagner heard none of it.

18.

One of the hulking guards stepped to Tony's side and whispered in his ear. He smiled then nodded at the guard. The large man left the game room quickly as everyone took their seats around the poker table.

"Everything cool, Tony?" Nick asked. "Your men comfortable? Finding what they need? I told them they could hang out in the upper lounge, watch some satellite TV, drink and eat whatever they want. Ashley is a great hostess, believe me."

"My men are fine," Tony said. "Just received a text I'd been waiting on."

"Text, right, about that," Nick said. He stood at the head of the poker table as everyone settled in and Manny walked over with a tray of drinks. "As much as I know this will annoy you, I'm going to have to ask that all cell phones be handed over to Manny. He'll keep them safe behind the bar while we play. Once you are done completely for the night, you can have them back."

"What's the deal, Nick?" Lane asked. "You think we're going to cheat?"

"What? Cheat? Never," Nick chuckled. "You folks are such honest, fine, upstanding people. Your moral character is beyond reproach." He pulled out his cell phone and set it on the table. "But I wouldn't trust any of you further than I could throw you overboard."

Lane smiled and fished his cell phone from his pocket. He placed it on the tray in Manny's hands, trading it for a gin martini. Each player did the same until Manny reached Ben.

"Can I keep mine?" Ben asked. "Just in case my daughters need to get a hold of me. They're at their mother's house for the weekend and—"

"Maggie can watch your phone," Nick said, nodding to Manny. Manny took the phone and handed Ben his drink. "Thanks, Benny Boy. Can't play favorites, now can I?"

The last person Manny stepped up to was Tony. The man looked Manny up and down and smiled. He turned his attention to Nick and shook his head, that smile still in place.

"I need my phone," Tony said. "Business."

"Not tonight," Nick said. "Didn't you hear me just tell my oldest friend I can't play favorites? Sorry, Tony, but house makes the rules and I have a strict rule against cell phones while a player is still in the game. Technology has really made cheating just too damn easy these days."

"I'll keep my phone," Tony said and started to reach for his drink on the tray. Manny stepped back out of reach. "You're going to regret that in thirty seconds if you don't give me my drink."

"I am sorry, Mr. Giraldi, but house rules are no cell phones," Manny said.

"Don't you fucking talk to me, you piece of shit bartender!" Tony roared as he stood up, knocking his chair backwards. "You hand me my drink or I rip your fucking throat out!"

Everyone else shot to their feet. Lane and Carlos started to move towards Tony. Before they could get there, one of Tony's men came into the game room, his pistol in hand and pointed down at the floor. Lane and Carlos backed off.

"Come on, Tony," Nick said, walking over to the man. "I've let you bring your goons and I let them keep their guns. Are you really going to push things to the edge over a cell phone?"

"I don't push things," Tony said. "I shove them." Which is what he immediately did to Nick.

Nick fell back, but reached out and caught himself on the table.

"Tony, Tony, Tony," Nick said.

"I hated that band," Ben said and received a sharp glare from Nick. "Sorry."

"Tony, if you don't want to be here then just say so," Nick said. "I'll have Captain Staggs call for a helicopter and you can leave as soon as it gets here."

"I never said I didn't want to be here, Sheeran," Tony said. "I just ain't gonna play by your rules. You think I've lived this long by doing as I'm told by Irish punkasses? The day I bow to a mick like you is the day I blow my own brains out."

"He's hardly Irish," Ben said.

"Not helping," Nick snapped.

"Let him keep it, Nicky," Ben said. "Who cares? I'm still going to take every last cent of his. He can cheat all he wants, won't make a bit of difference."

"I don't cheat," Tony said.

"Of course not," Ben said. "You only need your phone to check Facebook, right? Don't want to miss out on any new memes that might pop up."

"I don't cheat," Tony said.

"I know," Ben replied, his smile making it obvious to everyone in the room that he thought Tony was the biggest cheat in the world. "You're a man of great moral fiber."

Ben held up a hand as Tony was about to respond then pointed at the guard standing by the door.

"Give it to him," Ben suggested. "That's fair. My girlfriend has my phone, so your girlfriend should have yours."

The room went still. No one breathed as Tony's guard took a couple of steps forward, his gun hand lifting slowly.

"No," Tony said without looking back at the man. "Blogger Boy here is right. I'll give you my phone. If there is anything important I need to know then you'll come tell me."

"And you'll drop out of the game," Ben said.

"Excuse me?" Tony asked.

"Really? Are we having the Medici moment again?" Ben chuckled. "I said you'll drop out of the game. Can't have you accessing the hidden cameras your men put in here while we were eating dinner, right? Wouldn't want you to know if I was bluffing or not when I take you down for a big pot. You get up to check your phone and you are out of the game. Same goes for me. If Maggie can't handle whatever texts my girls send then I'll drop out as well."

"You have some balls, Blogger Boy," Tony laughed.

"It's Ben," Ben replied. "Blogger Boy is a guy that lives in Cincinnati and I'm pretty sure he's trademarked the name. Call me Ben or Mr. Clow."

"Fine," Tony replied. "*Ben.* Since you are the pro at this, I'll defer to you. I need to use my phone and I'm out of the game. That I can live with."

"You don't need to be out of the game," Nick said. "I'm sure we can make that call when the time comes. Put it to a vote."

"The house is now a democracy?" Tony sneered. "You break too easy, Sheeran."

"I've had an ex-girlfriend tell me that once," Nick said. "But she was wearing a strap-on at the time, so I think she had a different meaning in mind. Couldn't sit comfortably for two weeks, man."

The room was quiet then filled with laughter as everyone let Nick's self-deprecation cut the tension. Tony handed his cell phone to his man and nodded at Ben. Ben raised his glass of faux bourbon and nodded back.

"Can we play cards now, please?" Niya asked. "As much as I love this ship of Mr. Sheeran's, I did come here to put my skills up against the world famous Benjamin Clow."

"I thought you were here to flirt with me," Lane said.

"I don't flirt," Niya said. "I am flirted with."

"Consider my strategy changed, love," Lane said.

"Change it all you want," Niya said and grinned. "It will have the same result. You losing."

"Gotcha loud and clear," Lane said.

Nick took a seat and showed everyone an unopened deck of cards.

"I have decided to join the game, after all," Nick said. "Might be the last time I get to use this table since one of you will be buying this incredible yacht off me by morning."

He pulled a flip blade knife from his pocket, cut the plastic, tore it off, and tossed it aside. A quick squeeze of his thumb and he folded the blade up then stuffed it in his pocket.

"We take turns dealing," Nick said. "You've each bought in for two hundred grand. Feel free to count the chips in front of you."

Maggie snorted and coughed from the bar, reminding everyone that she was still in the game room. Her eyes looked blurry and her focus was delayed as she swiveled about to look at them all.

"Did you say two hundred grand?" she asked. "As in two-hundred thousand? Dollars? To play poker?"

All eyes shifted to her, even Ben's, and she blushed quickly. But whether the blush was from the attention or the fact she had eight empty glasses in front of her was debatable.

"Sorry," she said. "I just haven't ever seen that much money. I mean, two-hundred thousand is…a…lot…" She frowned then burped. "Yeah… I'll be quiet now."

She took a sip of her latest drink and spun about on her bar stool to face Manny. He gave her a sympathetic smile and placed a gentle hand on her forearm to keep her from slipping off her seat.

"High card deals," Nick said as he shuffled quickly then splayed the deck out in a chaotic mess across the table.

Each player took a card and flipped it over. Tony had the ace of spades and nodded as the cards were shoved towards him. He pushed them around with his hands for a couple of seconds then gathered them up in a pile, set the deck to his right, and waited as Lane cut the cards. Tony completed the cut, squared the deck then began to deal.

He tossed out two cards to each player, set the deck to his right and looked to his left at Jessica and the two white chips in front of her.

"Big blind," Tony said as he looked past her to Carlos and his single white chip. "Small blind bets."

"Give a man a chance to look at his cards," Carlos replied as he set his drink down and picked up the two cards in front of him. He grabbed a second white chip from his tray and set it on the first. "Call."

Nick was to Carlos's left and he set two whites in front of him. "Call."

"Raise," Niya announced, next up to bet. "Four thousand." She tossed in six white chips, calling the initial two thousand bet and adding her four thousand raise.

"Okay," Ben said as he looked down at his two cards. He held a six of clubs and an eight of hearts. Crap cards even if Niya's bet wasn't very big. But that was probably a trap she was setting. A small bet like that usually meant she wanted players to stay in the hand. He threw his cards face down in front of him. "Fold."

Lane looked at his cards, looked up at Niya, looked back at his cards, fingered his chips for a second, then tossed his cards on top of Ben's. "Fold."

The bet was to Tony and he quickly grabbed up three red chips. "I raise it nine grand."

"Nope," Jessica said, throwing in her cards with Ben and Lane's as well as pushing her blind bet into the center of the table. "Not on the first hand."

Carlos rubbed at his chin then followed Jessica's lead and folded, adding cards and chips to the growing piles of both on the table. Nick was right behind him, mucking his hand almost before Carlos was done moving.

That left Niya. She stared at Tony for a second, but the man wasn't giving her anything. Ben studied him, watching his every move, breath, tick, twitch, shake, shudder. But the man was like a statue, his eyes locked onto Niya's.

"Raise," Niya said. "Ten thousand."

She threw in enough chips to call Tony's raise and increase her own. Tony smiled and called immediately. He burned three cards, tucking them face down in with the folded pile, then flipped three cards over in the center of the table, one after the other.

"Ace of diamonds, queen of hearts, and seven of hearts," Tony announced. "Your bet, madame."

Niya bristled at the term, but kept her mouth shut as she picked up three reds and threw them in the pot.

"Fifteen?" Tony asked. "I raise twenty."

"Jesus, kids," Nick said. "Save some for the rest of the night."

Tony gave him a look that could kill and Nick shrugged his shoulders.

"Call," Niya said, tossing in four reds.

Tony burned one card then flipped over another, making it four cards in the center of the table. Ace of spades.

"Check," Niya said.

"Fifty thousand," Tony responded, tossing in five blue chips.

"All in," Niya said, her hands resting on her entire set of chips.

Tony's eyes narrowed and his upper lip curled at the corner.

Ben watched him closely, studying the way the man stared Niya down. He knew instantly that the man didn't have an ace in his hand. He would have called and burned and flipped the last card immediately. That meant he was either full on bluffing, had a low-to-mid pair, or had matched up something on the board.

Tony's hand hovered over his chips. He tapped at the row of blues then sighed and tossed his cards on the table. "It's yours."

Niya gave him a short nod and reached out to scoop her chips in. She quickly separated them by color and placed them in their respective rows.

While she did that, Jessica took the cards, shuffled them, and dealt out two to each player.

Ben watched everyone lift their cards and look at them. Except for Tony, who was busy looking at him. Ben smiled. Tony did not.

"At the same time?" Ben joked.

"Be my guest," Tony said.

Ben nodded and lifted his cards, careful to shield them from the other players' view. Jack of diamonds, queen of diamonds. That was a playable hand.

Nick tossed his cards in and pushed his small blind into the center of the table without saying a word. Niya threw her cards in as well and then it was up to Ben. He looked at his cards once more then grabbed four reds and two whites.

"Call and raise," Ben said. "Twenty thousand."

He threw in the chips and looked at Lane. Lane shook his head and threw his cards away. Tony did as well and Ben was actually surprised. Jessica watched Ben for a second then shook her head and added her cards to the muck. Carlos did as well, pushing his big blind in with his cards.

"Hope you didn't waste a high pair on that move," Jessica said.

"I don't know," Ben said. "Are aces high or low?"

"Cute," Jessica said.

Carlos shuffled and dealt as Ben took his meager winnings of the big and small blinds. He looked down as the cards landed in front of him, picked them up, and did everything in his power not to smile. Not that it was hard since he'd been playing poker for most of his life. A pair of aces weren't going to make him whoop and holler like a rookie.

Spades and clubs. That was what he had. Two aces. A pair of bullets.

Niya called, Ben called, Lane folded, Tony raised it ten thousand, Jessica called, Carlos folded, and Nick raised it another ten thousand. Niya folded, Ben called, Tony called, Jessica folded, and Carlos burned three cards then showed everyone the flop.

King of spades, queen of spades, king of diamonds.

Not a good flop for Ben. He kicked himself for not pushing hard with a pair of aces in his pocket. Having two kings show up on the flop meant that anyone that stayed in with a king was doing better than he was. He only had three to a royal flush, so it wasn't like he had great options.

Niya checked and Ben threw in thirty thousand before her cards settled on the felt. Tony called immediately and Ben's gut twisted. Tony had a king. No one would look at that flop and call a twenty thousand bet without having the king. Either you fold or you raise. Calling meant Tony wanted Ben in the game.

Everyone else was out. Cards were shoved into the muck and Carlos burned a card then dealt another. Jack of spades.

Ben had four to a royal flush with two aces in the hole. Or a rock and a hard place since he couldn't beat three kings, if Tony had a third, and he didn't actually have a flush, royal or not. With only one card left to see, the odds were not favoring Ben and he knew it.

He almost checked to see what Tony would do, but then Tony sniffled. It wasn't anything special, just a normal sniffle if you had a slightly runny nose. Except Ben knew for a fact Tony hadn't been sniffling at all the whole evening. He would have caught something like that.

"Fifty thousand," Ben said, tossing his chips in.

"Raise fifty," Tony said right off the bat.

"Call," Ben said just as quickly.

Tony gave him a sharp look and Ben knew what Tony's tell was. A sniffle. He wasn't sure what the man had in his hand, but it wasn't another king. Every instinct in his body told him Tony didn't have the third king.

Carlos turned over the last card, the river, and it was the king of hearts. The odds of Tony having a king hidden in his hand dropped exponentially with that reveal.

"Check," Ben said.

"Fifty," Tony said.

It was a small enough bet to instantly make Ben think it was a trap, which he knew was exactly what Tony wanted him to think. It would draw Ben in or make him fold. But why? Ben thought about it, actually putting some effort into figuring out the bet instead of just pretending to. Then it hit him.

"I raise fifty," Ben said.

"Call," Tony said and tossed in his chips. "Let's see what you got."

"Aces," Ben said. "For a full house, kings over."

Tony looked at Ben's cards and his face flushed, but not in a way that would allow him to beat the hand before him. He started to turn his cards over then stopped himself and tucked the unseen cards into the muck.

The look on Tony's face was close to pure rage. Ben knew that the man had something good. He replayed the hand over in his head and grinned as Nick started to shuffle and deal.

"What the hell are you grinning at?" Tony snapped. "You got my money, no need to gloat."

"Sorry," Ben said. "I wasn't gloating. Honestly."

"Then answer my question," Tony said. "What the hell are you smiling at?"

"Your two queens," Ben said.

"My what?" Tony growled and started to stand up.

"Need to pee, Tony?" Nick asked, his hand in mid-deal, hovering over the table with a card about to be tossed. "If not then sit your butt down. This is a friendly game. Sometimes you win, sometimes you lose. That time you lost. Let it go."

"Was I right?" Ben asked as Tony settled back into his chair.

"Benny Boy, leave it be," Nick said.

"Why?" Ben replied. "Everyone came to see me play, to meet the poker blogger and legendary screw up. It'd be false advertising if I didn't flex my muscles a little."

He looked Tony square in the eyes.

"Am I right?"

Tony only smiled in response, his lips pulling back to show a couple of gold caps spaced between blindingly white chompers. It was like a shark raised in Jersey had decided to sit down and play some cards.

"How many rebuys?" Tony asked.

"Really?" Nick laughed. "Third hand and you're already thinking of rebuying?"

"My money," Tony said. "Gives you suckers more chances to win."

"You do know we're here to have fun, right?" Nick asked. "This game is so you all can have a look at the yacht, have some drinks, eat some good food, and play the night away until you're so in love with the Lucky Sucker that you want to take it off my hands by morning."

"It's a nice boat," Tony said. "But that's not why I'm here. I'm here to win."

"Not why you're here?" Nick asked. He started to say something else then shook his head. "Buy in as many times as you want. I know you're good for it, Tony."

"Yeah, I am," Tony said and glared at Ben. "Your bet, Blogger Boy."

"I know," Ben said. "Just didn't want to interrupt you two while you worked things out."

"Nothing to work out," Tony said. "Bet or fold. Pick one."

Ben lifted up his cards and looked at a pair of twos. It was a crappy hand, barely better than a high card, but sometimes those twos paid off. He looked up to see Tony still watching him and he knew his play instantly.

"Fold," he said as he tossed the cards away.

"That's what I thought," Tony said. "I raise one hundred thousand."

Everyone folded.

The play went around and around a couple times, giving everyone a chance to deal, to lose, to win, to start to hate Ben. It was obvious from the rows of chips who the cards favored.

"Can I get another?" Ben asked after draining his glass and holding it up for Manny to see.

"What ya drinking?" Tony asked.

"Bourbon," Ben replied.

"That so?" Tony asked, sniffing the air. "Smells fruity."

"Does it? It has very heavy vanilla notes," Ben replied. "Maybe that's what you're picking up on."

"You saying I don't know the difference between fruit and vanilla?" Tony asked.

"What would you like to drink?" Nick asked Tony. "Is that a gin and tonic? Need a refill."

Manny set a glass down next to Ben and picked up the empty. He smiled at Tony.

"Would you care for another one?" Manny asked.

"I think I'll switch it up," Tony said, nodding to Ben's glass. "Gimme a sip of that so I can see if it's what I want."

"A sip of my drink?" Ben laughed. "No offense, but we're not that close. And I've been fighting off some bug this past week. You don't want to drink after me."

"You haven't taken a sip yet and that's a fresh glass," Tony said.

Ben couldn't think of an excuse. So he picked up his glass, looked at it for a second, then handed it over to Tony. He gripped the arms of his chairs, ready to jump up and get the hell out of the room the second Tony took a sip. He wanted to look at Nick, but he knew that would be a dead giveaway.

Tony took the glass, swirled the liquid around, then looked at Ben's hands.

"You going somewhere?" he asked as he sniffed the glass.

"Just need to piss," Ben said and stood up.

"Hold on," Tony said. "Let me have a taste before you go. Don't be rude."

Tony took his sip and his eyes narrowed.

Ben honestly thought his fake excuse to piss was actually about to happen for real, right then, right there.

"Vanilla, eh?" Tony asked. "You either have crap for taste buds or Manny over there is dumber than I thought and poured the wrong drink."

"Oh, uh, why's that?" Ben asked.

"This tastes like caramel, like a real bourbon should, not like vanilla," Tony said. "Kinda smokey too. Not peat smokey like a scotch, but burnt smokey."

"That's the barrels," Manny said. "They burn the insides of the barrels to—"

"I know how bourbon is made, asswipe," Tony said. "Do not interrupt the adults when they are talking."

He handed the glass back to Ben. Ben took it and stood there.

"I think a pee break is a great idea," Nick said to fill the silence. "I know I need to. Also, if anyone wants to join me, I'm going to smoke a fat joint up on deck and get some fresh air. How about we sit back down in thirty minutes? Everyone cool with that?"

There were plenty of agreements, but none too enthusiastic as Tony continued to glare at Ben.

"You going?" Tony asked.

"To smoke?" Ben asked.

"No, to piss," Tony said. "You said you needed to piss, so are you?"

"He is," Maggie said, taking Ben by the arm. "In our cabin. I have to go too and need to talk to him about a text from his daughters."

"A text?" Ben asked. "It's late for them to be texting."

Maggie smiled and her fingers dug into his arm.

"Must have been before they went to bed," Ben said.

"Must have been," Tony echoed. "Get along now. I'm sure you're dying to know what Tanni and Norma have to say."

19.

Ben's veins turned to ice and the only way he was able to walk away from the table was because Maggie was pulling him along. By the time they reached their cabin, Ben was close to hyperventilating.

"This is why I got out," Ben said as he collapsed on the bed. "I can't do this, Mags! People like that! Crazy mobsters and thugs that do their homework before they sit down. Did you hear what he said? He knows my girls' names!"

"I heard," Maggie said, her voice solid and sober. Ben frowned. "But that's not the real problem. Scary as shit, but not what we need to talk about."

"Huh? What's wrong?" Ben asked.

"You did get a text, but not from Tanni or Norma," Maggie said. "It was from Bobbi. I've been texting back and forth with her all night."

"Bobbi? What's wrong?" Ben asked. "And while you're drunk?"

"Tanni snuck out and has been missing all night," Maggie said, "and I'm not drunk. Well, not too bad."

"Tanni and I talked about her going out," Ben said. "She probably didn't tell Bobbi because she didn't want to deal with the grilling."

"She told Norma that she wasn't coming back," Maggie said. "But I think she said that because of what we said earlier about taking Norma with her."

"Maybe," Ben replied and got to his feet. "Probably. Is she still gone?"

"Yes," Maggie said. "That's why we're talking."

"Does Bobbi have any idea who she's with?" Ben asked. "Did you try texting her from your phone? She listens to you, Mags. She'll respond because she knows you won't bust her ass."

"Bobbi doesn't know who she's with," Maggie replied. "But I do. And, yes, I have been texting with Tanni on my phone. She's at a party, but doesn't want to be there anymore. Everyone is too drunk to drive and she's afraid if she tells her mom then Bobbi will try to go pick her up, make a huge scene, and embarrass her in front of Alex."

"Alex? Is that who's she with?" Ben snapped. "Well, tough shit if she gets embarrassed! Maybe that boy of hers needs to see what happens when he takes my daughter to a party with alcohol and gets her drunk! Bobbi'll rip him apart, trust me."

"I know she will, but that's not the real issue," Maggie said. She fidgeted and Ben saw it right off, his observation skills at their full power due to hours of poker.

"What aren't you telling me?" Ben asked and sat down without being told to.

"Alex isn't a boy," Maggie said. "Alex is short for Alexandria and she's your daughter's girlfriend, not boyfriend."

"Oh," Ben said. "Oh. Oh…"

He looked up and Maggie shook her head.

"No, it's not just an adolescent phase," Maggie said. "This is Tanni's third girlfriend, Benjamin. She's gay. Your daughter is gay and is terrified to tell you or Bobbi."

"That explains the sulky attitude," Ben said. "More than just usual teenage BS."

"Yeah," Maggie said, sitting next to Ben on the bed. "You okay?"

"I have no idea," Ben said. "Not a clue. I've been faking this parenting thing since I was nineteen and Tanni was born. God, we were so young and stupid, but Bobbi was rich and I was playing poker, so we learned to handle it. I haven't done the greatest job as Dad, but at least my girls wanted to live with me after the split, so I always thought I'd done okay since they chose me over money. But now this?"

"How does this reflect on your job as a parent?" Maggie asked.

Ben sensed her anger and shook his head, placing a hand on her leg.

"No, I don't mean that my parenting could have changed this at all, just that I should have known," Ben said. "I should have seen the signs or something and been there to support her. It breaks my heart she is scared to tell me. Bobbi, I get. That woman would embrace it to the extreme and try to sign Tanni up on gay dating sites and crap."

He looked at Maggie.

"Are there gay dating sites?" he asked.

"Yes, babe, there are," Maggie laughed. "It's the 21st century."

"Right, yeah, of course," Ben said. "Wow. Gay. My little girl is gay." His brow furrowed. "Is Alex cute or kinda dykey?"

"Should I pretend I didn't hear that question?" Maggie asked as she got up and walked away.

"Where are you going?" Ben called after her.

"I really do need to pee," Maggie called back from the bathroom. "You should go back and find Nick. Have a toke to calm down so you can get back to playing."

"Good call," Ben said and stood up.

He was out of the cabin, down the passageway, up a set of stairs, and through most of the ship before it all hit him again.

"My daughter is gay," he muttered.

"That so?" a woman asked from a chair in the corner of the lounge Ben was walking through. Ben jumped and steadied himself against the wall. "Sorry. I apologize." The woman stood up and offered a hand. "Ashley Mulgrew. Can we talk?"

"Ashley? The hostess?" Ben asked. "Uh, you haven't exactly been hostessing much."

"No, not so much," Ashley responded. "Listen, before you go back to the game, I think you should be filled in on something. Nicholas didn't want you to know, neither did Manny, but this is my op and I get the last say."

"Oh, okay, what is it?" Ben asked then shook his head. "I'm sorry, did you say op?"

Ashley smiled and nodded then gestured towards a chair.

"Have a seat, Mr. Clow, we have a lot to cover in only a very short time."

20.

The ship rose with the swells and crested the tops of the good-sized waves then dove down into the trenches. Over and over it did that as it moved across the open ocean. Nothing unusual, as it would have been the strategy of any good captain to aim into the waves and keep the ship from capsizing.

Except the NCDC ship no longer had a captain. Not in one piece, at least.

The navigation system was running on autopilot, and being a ship in the fleet of a major defense and tech contractor, that autopilot was an exceptional piece of programming. It could sense the changes in weather patterns and adjust to the expected changes in the sea. It knew when to adjust the rudder and when to increase or slow the engines.

The ship could handle navigating the waters all on its own. Which was a good thing since every human being onboard was ripped to shreds and being fed upon by the massive creature that had returned to the safety of its tank. Despite the thing's incredible strength and ferocity, it was still a member of the octopodidae family and shy by nature.

It preferred to be safe and comfortable. At least until it sensed prey. Then nothing was safe and or comfortable.

It supped on the femurs of half a dozen men, sucking the marrow straight from the bones, savoring the flavor as it passed through its incredible beak. Not that it needed the beak to taste. Its tentacles and suckers had the ability to taste food as well as any human's taste buds. It knew what it liked and what it didn't before the food even got close to the sharp, parrot-like beak.

Having finished off the femurs, the creature slid from its tank and hunted around for something new to eat. Its hunger was never sated; the creature lived in a perpetually ravenous state. Something in it, a part of that uncanny octopus intelligence, knew that its hunger was not natural. It knew that it didn't need to eat anywhere near as much as it was. But it couldn't stop. Once it had tasted blood, tasted the flesh of humanity, it couldn't stop the urges. Or, more accurately, the urges that had been built inside it.

As the thought sped through its complex and fairly alien mind, the creature came upon the corpse of Dr. Glouster. It hesitated, its tentacles waving slowly, lightly, over the man's body. Its hunger told it to grab the corpse up and eat, eat, devour, but it couldn't do it. The man raised it, the man cared for it, the man taught it many things and showed only kindness. The hardest part of the creature's impossible life had been watching Dr. Glouster bleed out on the vault's floor.

The creature couldn't quite come to terms with the event and one of its tentacles settled on the man's body, nudging it carefully, gently. When there was no response, it started to withdraw the tentacle then thought better of it. It grabbed up the corpse and walked it back to its tank. There was a rattling in the man's pocket and the creature hesitated. Before dumping Dr. Glouster's body into the saltwater, it plucked something from the dead man's pocket, looked it over, then threw it aside. The corpse bobbed up and down in the tank and the creature stared at it for a minute before it went back to gathering more food.

Arms loaded to capacity, the creature entered its watery sanctuary once again and began to feed some more. It pressed itself up against Dr. Glouster's corpse, feeling a slight comfort in having the man near even if the doctor was no longer part of the living. It paused only briefly in its feast to observe the corpse, a hope that the man would suddenly come to life.

The creature instantly began to grow from all the feeding, its enhanced genes kicking into over drive. The accelerated growth made the tank uncomfortable and the creature grew irritated. The irritation became frustration with the frustration quickly turning to anger, anger against humanity at allowing Dr. Glouster to be killed, to be murdered, to die.

The anger became rage and the creature took up Dr. Glouster's corpse with four of its tentacles ready to tear it apart. But it couldn't do it and instead it slowly, carefully, kneaded the body until the bones were nothing but dust and the corpse was soft and pliable. Just like the creature. It had changed Dr. Glouster just like the doctor had changed it.

But with that act it struggled with a feeling that grew alongside the rage. It didn't know grief, but it knew it had lost something when Dr. Glouster had died. It also knew it had lost something when it was changed from what nature had meant it to be. It looked outside the tank and its eyes fell on the human remains scattered about the vault, falling on a body that it was surprised was still a part of the living.

Its grief could not be vented, but its rage could be.

The creature crawled back out of the tank and rushed over to the body of Wagner. It lifted two tentacles, ready to bring them down onto the unconscious man's chest, but it stopped. Next to Wagner was the item the creature had thrown from Dr. Glouster's pocket. A USB drive.

Instead of ending Wagner's life right then, the creature undid two belts from the dead men on either side of Wagner and tightened them around his bleeding stumps for legs. The man moaned and the creature jammed an eye right in Wagner's face, but Wagner did not wake up.

Once it knew the man wouldn't die right away, the creature set the USB drive in the man's hand. It did not know why, but the act felt like what it should do. It knew the drive had been important to Dr. Glouster. The drive needed to be saved.

The creature turned to face the vault and its rage still boiled. It crawled from the no longer secure space and began to collect body parts. It wanted to feed, but the hunger of its body could not override the hunger of its rage. A rage that began to create a new need with every body part it lifted into its tentacles.

A need for vengeance.

21.

The woman had asked Ben to take a seat while she explained the situation he was in, but he'd declined and said he'd prefer to stand, as most people do when presented with a suspicious scenario. As soon as she had finished talking, the idea of sitting down seemed like a very good one as Ben's knees became weak and his legs started to tremble.

"This is a sting?" Ben asked then looked around quickly, alarmed that he had been overheard.

"Don't worry, Mr. Clow," Ashley said as she tapped the screen of her phone. "I have access to the ship's entire surveillance system. I know where everyone is at all times." She showed him her phone and the image of Tony Giraldi talking to a couple of his men at the bow of the ship. "His men are keeping watch over him. They've established a perimeter so that the bow is all Tony's."

"He's the king of the world, eh?" Ben laughed then coughed then went silent as Ashley stared at him, her lips not even coming close to cracking a smile. "Sorry."

"I need you to take this very seriously, Mr. Clow," Ashley said. "We have been tracking Mr. Giraldi for months and know he has something planned. What we believe is that he's going to intercept a ship that is en route now. I have satellites hunting the sea for miles around us, but so far, other than legitimate commercial vessels and a couple of cruise ships, there is nothing out of the ordinary."

"Yes, okay, great," Ben said. "So what does this have to do with me? You could have kept me in the dark. Nick has and he's as close to a best friend as I have in this world. You sure didn't need to spill the beans."

"Actually, I did need to spill the beans because you are close to ruining this entire operation," Ashley said. "That is why I have told you everything and why we are talking right now." She leaned forward and the button-down white shirt she wore went tight across her chest. She adjusted her position and pulled at her shirt.

"Stupid uniform. I guess being a hostess on a yacht like this means showing as much cleavage as possible. Degrading."

"I have two daughters," Ben said. "I agree one hundred percent on that."

"The problem is, Mr. Clow," Ashley continued, "is that you are pissing Mr. Giraldi off so much that I'm afraid you are going to blow this entire operation. He's either going to abort what he has come to do or he's going to shoot you between the eyes which means I am forced to get involved. As much as I want to arrest him for what he has planned, I will have to arrest him for homicide if he kills you. That's just how the law works."

"International law," Ben said. "Because you are INTERPOL? Why should I believe you? A laser printer and a laminator can make the ID you showed me. Easy enough to buy fake badges on the internet."

"Feel free to talk to Nicholas about this," Ashley said. "Discreetly, of course." She leaned back and relaxed into the chair. "You will quickly find that my partner and I are legitimate."

"Your partner?" Ben frowned then nodded. "Manny."

Ashley smiled. "What I need from you, Mr. Clow, is to pull back on the irritation level. I need you to stop pushing Mr. Giraldi's buttons and start making him feel confident. I want him relaxed, at ease, thinking he is in total control at the table. If he thinks he's in control at the table then he will assume he is in control of everything else. Pissing off a man like Giraldi is never a good idea, Mr. Clow, regardless of whether there is an INTERPOL operation in place or not."

"You know who I am, so I assume you know my background," Ben said. "Then you also know I've been at tables with way scarier men than Giraldi."

"No, you have not," Ashley stated.

"Actually—"

"No, you have not," Ashley repeated. "Do not kid yourself, Mr. Clow. Yes, you have played against some very, very bad men and women while you were a rounder with Nicholas, but at no point have you been in the presence of a monster like Giraldi. This is a man that blinds children in front of their parents with a cocktail fork just to make a point. Giraldi is not, and let me be very clear as

I repeat this, Giraldi is not a man you piss off. Not unless you want your daughter and her girlfriend to be raped and dismembered, left on the wet Olympia streets to be found by some yuppie walking her labrodoodle tomorrow morning."

Ashley showed him her phone again and it was an image of Tanni and some girl laughing at a party. Ben's eyes took in the entire scene and he gasped when he realized there was a young man passing as a teen standing only a few feet behind the two teenage girls, his eyes locked on to them. And those eyes were deep, dead pools of violence. Ben kept the gorge from rising in his throat, but only barely.

"The good news is that I am seeing this video because one of my people is at that party," Ashley said. "I also have people watching your ex-wife's house while she and your youngest daughter sleep."

"The bad news?" Ben asked. "Because I know there has to be some of that."

"There is," Ashley said. "The bad news is that the guy Giraldi has sent to watch your daughter Tanni is known as the Guillotine. He is very good at his job and very fast. No guns, just one deadly sharp blade. Even with my agent in place, there is the risk that the Guillotine will be too fast and kill either Tanni or her girlfriend before he can be stopped."

"Then stop him now!" Ben shouted. "Put a bullet between his eyes and keep my girl safe!"

"The second we make a move on him then we risk Giraldi being contacted," Ashley said. "I'm sorry, but as much as I want to make sure your daughter stays alive, I have to take Giraldi down. Whatever he has planned probably has to do with illegal arms, since he rarely involves himself with the other parts of his business. If it is arms then it has to be missiles or worse in order for him to go to all the trouble of using Nicholas as a front. Mr. Giraldi has put a lot of work into this deal and so have I. I can't jeopardize it all to save your daughter."

"You have got to be kidding me," Ben said and stood up. "Then I'm getting her out of there. I'm going to text her right now and tell her she needs to get her ass home."

"How?" Ashley asked. "No one there is sober enough to drive and she's too young to call a cab. Even Uber would probably balk at giving an intoxicated teen and her girlfriend a ride. Liability insurance is a bitch."

"Have you been listening to me and Maggie talk?" Ben asked.

"Of course we have," Ashley said, wiggling her phone. "I have access to this entire ship."

"You suck," Ben said. He was about to say more, but Nick came hurrying into the lounge.

"There you are," Nick said. Then he saw Ashley. "Oh, uh, hello, Ashley. The game is starting back up. Could you maybe have the chef set up a buffet of snacks? That would be great."

"I know," Ben said.

"You know what?" Nick asked. "That snacks are a good idea when poker players get hungry?"

"I know who Ashley is," Ben said.

"Oh, that," Nick said. He grinned then frowned then settled on an expression half way between the two which made him look constipated and confused. "I was going to tell you about that."

"No, you weren't," Ben responded.

"No, I wasn't," Nick admitted. "But, how exciting, right?"

"Giraldi has a killer watching Tanni and her girlfriend right now," Ben stated. "How excited about that do you think I am, Nicky? On a scale of one to ten, tell me how excited I am that my baby girl could have her throat slit open because you got your ass busted and now have to be INTERPOL's bitch."

"I never said he got busted," Ashley said.

"You didn't have to," Ben replied. "I've known this man my whole life. No way he'd get involved and risk his rep as a playboy that can weave in and out of legitimate and illegitimate circles just to do the right thing. What was it, Nicky? What crime are they wiping away so you could get Giraldi onto this boat?"

"Yacht," Nick said. "And it was heroin."

"What?" Ben nearly shouted. "Smack? Since when did you start dealing smack?"

"I don't!" Nick exclaimed. "I hate that shit, you know that."

"Not sure what I know," Ben scowled.

"It was a girlfriend of mine," Nick said. "I had no idea she was a junkie. I just thought she liked to take naps in public at strange times."

"Seriously?" Ben grumbled.

"Dude, if you saw how hot she was you'd have been happy to let her nap wherever and whenever she wanted," Nick said. "Plus, she didn't have tracks in her arms or anything. She shot up in that vein in her upper thigh. I'd noticed the marks when I went down on her, but it's not like my mind was exactly putting two and two together at those moments, man."

"So she got busted?" Ben asked.

"She died," Ashley said. "She was a mule for her dealer and had seventeen balloons inserted in her rectum. Five burst at once and she overdosed just as Mr. Sheeran and her were crossing the border from Germany to Austria last year."

"So you nabbed him and turned him for good," Ben said. He waved his hands around. "So this yacht isn't even yours, is it? It's all a front."

"Uh, no, the yacht is mine," Nick said. "That's all true. It's why INTERPOL decided I was worth making a deal with. They knew I had been trying to unload it for a while and they knew Giraldi was in the market for a yacht as a front to conduct some business. One thing led to another and now we are all here. Yay…"

Things clicked into place for Ben at that moment and he looked at Ashley.

"Giraldi suggested the route we're taking tonight, right?" Ben asked. "It was part of his security terms to agree to play cards. He decided where the yacht would be and where it would go while we're at the table. Use someone else for transportation and if his deal goes bad he can walk away like he had nothing to do with it. Am I right?"

"You are right," Ashley said. "We have let him run things from the very beginning. All we had to do was be ready for tonight."

"And along comes the ex-poker pro with the mid-list blog to ruin it all," Ben said.

"Almost ruin it all," Ashley said. "Now that you know what's going on, you can switch your strategy from pushing him off his game by getting him riled up to making him feel like he's a winner and kicking your butt. Can you handle that, Mr. Clow?"

"Yeah, I can handle that," Ben said. "I've run harder cons with Nicky. At least this one is for the good guys."

"And maybe I can still sell this yacht," Nick said. "Yeah? You're busting Giraldi, not the others, right? Leaving me out of it so no one suspects?"

"Yes, Nicholas," Ashley sighed. "You get to sell your boat."

"Yacht," Nick corrected. He clapped his hands and grinned. "Alright. Let's get back to the cards, shall we?"

Ben studied his friend for a brief second. Alarm bells went off in his head. Nick was too agreeable. He was rolling over and letting Ashley push him around like he didn't have a care in the world. That wasn't how Nick had acted around authority when they'd worked together. Ben had always had to shut the man up and keep him from making things worse.

"Yeah, let's get back to the cards," Ben said as he saw a brief flicker in Nick's eye. A dangerous, secret flicker that no one but him would have ever seen.

There was more going on, but Ben didn't know what. He shoved the suspicion aside as Nick gestured for him to follow. The two head back to the game room and Ben had to restrain himself from grabbing Nick and pounding him in the face until he told the truth. Because Ben believed at that moment that the real truth Nick was hiding was key to getting Tanni to safety, not relying on the INTERPOL agents.

It may have been a hunch, but Ben had been at the game long enough to know when a hunch should be relied on.

22.

Ben checked his two cards again then mucked them, sighing heavily as he turned a harsh glare on Tony.

"I know you're bluffing," Ben grumbled.

"But you didn't call," Tony said as he raked in the chips. "If you were so sure, you should have called."

Ben mumbled something and Tony stopped what he was doing. He turned his full attention on Ben and the temperature in the room dropped a few degrees.

"What was that?" Tony asked. "Did you just call me a cheater?"

"No," Ben replied. "All I said was the last time someone took me like that, they'd been cheating off the deal."

"I dealt," Niya said, her eyes watching the two men carefully. "Are you saying I am in league with this man?"

"I have to say, Nicky," Lane said as he held up his empty glass. "Your poker blogger isn't exactly living up to his reputation."

"You promised a top notch game, Nick," Carlos added. "This is just another boring game on some spoiled brat's boat."

"Yacht," Nick said, his face red. "And you guys know how cards can be. They turn on ya in a heartbeat."

"So do I," Tony said. "How about we talk less and play more?"

"You got somewhere to be, Tony?" Carlos asked.

"Yes, Mr. Giraldi, do you?" Niya asked. "You keep whispering to your men and checking your watch. Do you have a big date?"

"I'm a very important business man," Tony said. "The world doesn't stop because I'm playing cards. If the world don't stop then neither do I. Gotta keep the wheels greased and motor running."

"We fixing an old Mustang or playing poker?" Ben snapped. "Who's deal is it?"

"Yours, smart ass," Tony said, grinning. "But maybe you should pass the deal until you calm down. I know how emotional this game can get when things aren't going your way."

"I'm cool," Ben said as he shuffled and dealt. "You'll see."

It was Tony's turn to bet. He looked at his two cards, fingered the small blind in front of him, then went back to his rows of chips and fished out a single black chip in addition to the two white chips needed to call the big blind.

"I raise twenty-five," he said as he threw out the black chip. "Twenty-seven to you, sweetheart?"

"What was that?" Jessica growled. "Call me sweetheart again and you'll be finding out what those cards taste like as I jam them down your throat."

"Hey, hey, hey!" Nick exclaimed. "Everyone calm down! No one needs to get offended at a little trash talk."

"Only talk he knows," Jessica said as she grabbed two white chips and a black. She started to throw them in the pot then held back, looked at her cards, and instead threw her hand away, tucking the chips back into their rows. "Fold."

"Fold," Carlos said.

"Fold," Nick said and held up his glass as Manny brought Lane his fresh cocktail. Manny took the glass from Nick and moved quickly to the bar. "Anyone else need a fresh drink?"

No one replied as they focused on the game.

Niya folded and stood up. "I need to use the restroom. Deal me out if I'm not back in time for the next hand."

Ben watched her go then looked down at his cards. Eight and nine of clubs. Decent cards to make a play if the bet wasn't twenty-seven thousand. A ten thousand raise would be worth chasing a straight flush for. Maybe even a straight. But twenty-seven? Stupid move with the dwindling rows of chips in front of him.

"Call," he said as he threw his chips in the pot.

"You sure?" Tony grinned. "You hesitated there, Blogger Boy."

"I'm sure," Ben said. "I tossed in my chips, didn't I?"

"Raise," Lane announced. "Another twenty-five."

Tony bristled at the raise. He started to look at his hand, but held back, his thumb flicking at the corners of the cards. His entire body turned to regard Lane, not just his eyes.

"You trying to play me?" Tony asked. "Catch me off guard because I've been focusing on the weak one to your right?"

"Hey," Ben said. "Not cool, man."

"If you've got a strong hand then I can't catch you off guard, can I, mate?" Lane asked. "Unless you're full of shit and just trying to bully the table."

"Guess we'll find out," Tony said. "Call."

He threw in another black chip and all eyes turned to Ben.

"Might as well," Ben said and added his second black chip to the pile.

"Good strategy," Carlos laughed. "Might as well."

Ben burned three cards then dealt out the flop in the middle of the table. Seven of clubs, ten of clubs, ace of hearts.

Ben kept himself calm. His hopes of a straight flush increased exponentially with the arrival of the two clubs. If he wasn't forced out of the hand by huge bets then he had two chances to draw to an outside straight flush. He'd even take a regular flush, but the odds of someone having a higher club than him were pretty good, so that would be a risky hand to play.

Unless he didn't play the hand at all and let the cards decide the risk for him...

"All in," he said and counted out his remaining chips. "Eighty-four thousand."

"Only eighty-four?" Tony asked. "Kinda sad. I guess I'll have to—"

"My bet, Guido," Lane said.

Tony's chair hit the ground hard as the man leapt to his feet, his right fist connecting with Lane's jaw before the man knew what was happening.

"Whoa! Hold on!" Nick yelled as he got up.

Everyone was up on their feet and yelling as Ben got between Tony and Lane.

"Chill, man!" Ben shouted in Tony's face. "He's just messing with you to see if you're gonna break! Pushing buttons just like you do, okay? No need to get all gangster on him!"

"Gangster? Guido? That what all of you think?" Tony asked, his fists shaking with rage as he held them to his sides. "The Italian guy is here so he must be some pasta eating, Chianti drinking, tracksuit wearing stereotype, right? You think I'm some stupid wap right out of The Godfather?"

"Are we back on The Godfather again?" Jessica sighed.

"Love that movie!" Maggie announced from the bar. She raised her drink over her head and Manny took it from her before she could spill it. She gave him a wet raspberry then laughed.

"Nice right hook," Lane said to Tony, picking himself up off the floor. "And I was just fucking with you, mate. All good." He took his seat and counted out eighty-four thousand in chips. "Call."

Tony looked around the room as the others turned their attention from him to Lane, back and forth, until they all sat down. Ben was the last to sit and he glanced over at Nick, but the man wouldn't meet his gaze.

"I call," Tony said before he was fully back in his seat. "Never say this guido hesitates."

"Alright," Ben said as he burned a card and turned the next one over.

Jack of clubs.

Ben barely glanced at the card before turning to Lane.

"Your bet," he said.

"Check," Lane said.

"Check," Tony echoed.

"Last card," Ben responded.

He burned and flipped. Ace of spades.

"Check," Lane said automatically.

"All in," Tony said, his eyes locked onto Lane.

"Yeah," Lane nodded. "I had a feeling." He threw his two cards into the muck and leaned back. "You two have fun."

Ben turned over his hand to show the straight flush he'd drawn to. Tony stared at the eight and nine of clubs for a while before he threw his own hand into the muck.

"Let's see them," Jessica said.

"I lost," Tony replied. "That's all you need to know."

"Actually, we need to see your cards," Jessica insisted. "As soon as Lane folded both of you should have shown your hands, not just Ben. You flip 'em over in a showdown."

"That so?" Tony asked. He turned his attention to Nick. "What's the ruling on that, Sheeran? What does the house have to say?"

"Uh, well, you know how it is, Tony," Nick sputtered. "That's the way the game is played."

"Not much of an answer," Tony said.

"Show them," Ben said as he raked in his chips. "That's how the game is played."

"Fine," Tony said without any more of a fight. "You want to see what I had? Here ya go."

He fished his cards out of the muck and flipped them over. Pair of aces.

"Damn," Nick said. "Ouch."

"Lucky bastard caught his straight flush," Tony said. "Ain't a damn thing I can do about that."

"No, there isn't," Ben said. "Good hand. You played that perfectly. Good show of strength and nice effort trying to push everyone out. If I hadn't been short stacked, you would have taken that one."

Tony watched Ben for a few seconds then laughed. "I think that was a real compliment," Tony said. "No BS, right?"

"Right," Ben said. "No BS. Pretty sure you can find me talking about a hand just like that on my blog. You checked when you only had three aces then went in hard when you caught your fourth. At that point, I was irrelevant and you were playing Lane. Which was the only mistake you made in the hand. If he'd called you then you'd have made a nice chunk, but he folded and it all came down to the two of us."

"You think I should have bet less?" Tony asked. "Kept Lane in?"

"Maybe," Ben said. "You had four bullets, so it would have been near impossible for him to beat you. If he had his own straight flush then you were dead whether you bet big or bet small. But, at least by betting small you may have squeezed some chips out of the loss to me with the side bet."

"Good to know," Tony said and started laughing. "Very good to know!" He pointed at Nick. "This guy of yours ain't half bad. I think I'll let him live a while longer as long as he keeps giving advice like that."

Ben bristled and almost lost the cool he had been working so hard to build up. All he wanted to do was grab the man's drink glass, crack it on the side of the table, and stab the shards into the son of a bitch's throat. But, instead, he sat back and pushed the image of the Guillotine staring at Tanni out of his mind and gave Tony a huge grin.

"You're a giver," Ben laughed. "I appreciate the gift of life."

"Never say I ain't got a soft side," Tony said, laughing as well.

Tony's guard cocked his head and nodded, moving quickly to the table. A quick whisper in Tony's ear and the man was up on his feet.

"Ladies and gentlemen, I'm afraid my time at the table is over," Tony said. He hooked a thumb over his shoulder at his guard. "Feel free to keep playing. In fact, I insist on it. My man here will make sure you remain in the game room while I conduct some business."

"What?" Carlos exclaimed.

"Hold the hell on!" Lane snapped.

Jessica slid away from the table, her hand halfway up her dress. Ben caught her eye and shook his head. Jessica frowned then glared at him. Ben shook his head harder. Jessica pulled her hand out of her dress and turned her glare onto Tony.

"What you got tucked up there?" Tony laughed. He motioned with his head to his guard. "Have a look."

The guard took one step and Jessica stood up.

"I don't need my .32 to put you down," Jessica said to the huge man with the big gun pointed at her. "I'll cram your own gun up your ass and empty it before you know what's happening if you take one more step towards me."

"Let her be," Tony said to his guard. "But you keep an eye on her. She goes to scratch her snatch and you put two between her eyes."

"Tony, man, this is so not cool," Nick said. "What the hell are you doing? This is not the time for business. I made that clear when you were invited. Friendly game of poker so everyone can see the yacht and—"

"I'll take the yacht," Tony said. "Full asking price. How does that work for you, Sheeran? You think I'm being cool now?"

"You'll take it," Nick said. "Uh, well, awesome."

"Is it? Because you don't sound too thrilled," Tony said. "Why is that?"

"What? No, I'm stoked, man," Nick replied, clapping his hands together. "It's just that you're kind of threatening everyone and it puts a damper on my excitement. Hard to celebrate the sale of my yacht when someone could be getting shot on it any second now. You know what I mean?"

"I've had the money wired to you already," Tony said. "I assume you have the ownership paperwork ready to go?"

"Yeah, yeah, of course," Nick said.

"Good," Tony said. "Let me handle my business while you get that together. I'll sign it all once I know my other endeavor is handled. Then we can sit down and finish our game. On my new yacht."

"Nope," Lane said. "Nicky may be cool with this, but I am not."

"Me neither," Carlos said.

"Want to guess my answer?" Jessica asked as she held up two middle fingers. "Can you read between the lines?"

"Let the guy do his thing," Maggie said from the bar and all eyes turned on her. Everyone looked completely surprised since most of them had assumed she'd passed out. "The sooner he does whatever he's going to do then the sooner this game can be over and we all go back home and forget any of this crap happened."

"That's the booze talking," Ben said.

"Smart booze," Tony said. "Your lady is right. Let me do my thing, as she put it, and we will all be good. Try to stop me and my thing will turn ugly pretty fast."

"I'm guessing your thing is pretty ugly already," Jessica said. "If your dick matches your face."

"Jessie," Nick said. "Tony's a guest of mine. Let's be civil and not piss off the guy with the henchmen, okay?"

"I blame you for this, Nicky," Jessica said as she walked over to the bar and sat down next to Maggie. She tapped at the bar then snapped her fingers at Manny. "I have people waiting back on shore for me to turn up safe and sound. If I have even a scratch on this bod when I get back there, they will take it out on you."

"Maybe next time you want to sell a boat, you put it in the classifieds, mate," Lane said.

"It's a yacht," Nick replied. "And you don't put a sixty-five million dollar yacht in the classifieds."

Tony's guard cleared his throat.

"This discussion is over," Tony said. "I will return as soon as possible. Nobody go anywhere."

He turned and walked out. Two of his guards were waiting for him outside the doors. A third one closed the doors and everyone could see he was taking a position right outside before the doors closed.

"Niya is out there," Carlos said, glancing at Tony's guard. "Let's hope that is not a problem."

"I will have someone detain her," the guard said. "For her safety."

"Downright kind of you," Lane said and slapped his hands on the table as he stood up. "Manny? Set me up with a row of martinis. Since the night isn't about poker anymore then I might as well get really drunk."

"It'll dull your senses," Jessica said. "May want to stay sharp if things get dicey."

"Thanks, Mum, but things have already gotten dicey," Lane said. "I think some bar therapy is the way to take the edge off the testosterone dump that Tony just took on us."

"Nice," Carlos said. "Now I can't get that image out of my head."

Ben hurried to Maggie's side and put his arm around her shoulders.

"Are you okay?" he asked her.

Maggie held up a full glass fast enough that some of the cocktail sloshed out onto the bar.

"I've been working on getting to okay as soon as the Italian gorilla arrived and started pushing people around," Maggie said. Sipping from her drink. "Comfortably numb has been achieved."

"Sorry about this, guys," Nick said. "Really, I am."

No one responded and he shrugged.

"At least I get to sell my boat," he said then smacked himself on the forehead. "Yacht, I mean. Dammit."

23.

Ashley kept to the shadows, making sure she was well hidden by corners and blind spots as Tony and his armed entourage made their way from the game room to the sun deck above. She typed a quick message into her phone and sent it to Manny then slid the phone in her pocket, opened her blazer, and pulled out her 9mm pistol.

"Now, what would a hostess need with a Glock?" Niya asked as she came out of the restroom and blocked Ashley's way. "Or is that a Beretta? Yes, on second examination, I can see the difference. Still…"

"Nothing you need to worry about," Ashley said, as she held the gun down at her side. "You should go back to the game and join the others."

"Ms. Romanski?" a man called from the end of the passageway. "I have been asked to escort you back to the others."

"Have you now?" Niya replied over her shoulder, her body and attention still facing and focused on Ashley. "And who asked you to do this? Our host?"

"Mr. Giraldi has requested it while he attends to some business," the man said. "He will return to the game as soon as he can, but in the meantime he would prefer no interruptions or possible distractions. It is for your own safety."

"My own safety?" Niya asked. She glanced down at Ashley's pistol then turned her back on the woman and faced the guard at the end of the passageway. "And if I do not comply with Mr. Giraldi's request?"

"Then your safety would be in jeopardy," the guard said, "and Mr. Giraldi could not be held to blame for anything that might accidentally happen to you."

"I see," Niya said.

She started to walk towards the guard, her hips swaying back and forth, making good use of the tight dress she wore. She slowly, almost playfully, unclasped her heels and slid one off then the other. She twirled the shoes by their straps on her index finger as she continued walking towards the guard.

"This accident, you speak of," Niya said. "Would it involve you? Because I'd hate for a handsome, obviously kind-looking gentleman to get involved in something as nasty as harming a woman."

"Ma'am, all you are being asked to do is return to the game room," the guard said. "There is no need to make this difficult."

"It won't be difficult at all," Niya said as she casually tossed her shoes at the man.

He hesitated for a second, unsure of whether to catch the shoes or bring up his semi-automatic. That hesitation was all Niya needed. She leapt to the side, her stockinged feet pushing off the wall and sending her flying at the guard, her left arm raised, fist closed. She came down fast and hard and the man's head snapped to the side. He wobbled for a moment then fell to his knees.

Niya grabbed him by his lapels before he could fully collapse. His eyes swam in his head and struggled to focus on her. She brought his face down and her knee up at the same moment. The crunch of bone echoed in the passageway and Ashley flinched at the noise as she came hurrying up behind Niya.

"Giraldi will wonder where this guy went," Ashley said.

"Yes, he probably will," Niya said, relieving the unconscious man of his weapon. She bounced the pistol in her hand, feeling its heft. "Heckler & Koch .45 auto. I would have expected him to have an Italian pistol like your Berretta, Agent Mulgrew. Surprising he went German."

Ashley began to raise her 9mm, but Niya beat her to the punch and had the .45 up and aimed at the woman first.

"Tut, tut, Agent Mulgrew," Niya said. "You can't be surprised that I know who you are. Do you think a woman would make it this far in the Ukrainian underworld without having friends in high places? I like to keep tabs on those that are keeping tabs on me."

"I don't know what you're talking about," Ashley said. "I'm just a hostess."

"A hostess that grips her pistol like she knows how to use it," Niya laughed.

"I've had training," Ashley said. "Every member of the crew has. International waters can be dangerous."

"Did you really think I would accept an invitation to join a poker party from someone like Nicholas Sheeran?" Niya laughed again. "The man is small time and has a reputation as a flake. Mr. Garfield, Mr. Whittier, and Ms. Holstein have had dealings with Mr. Sheeran in the past. I have not. He is not on my level."

"Then why accept?" Ashley asked.

"Because my friends in high places let me know that Mr. Giraldi had something in store and maybe it was worth me checking out," Niya said. "The fact that there's at least one INTERPOL agent on board tells me that my friends were correct. Of course, they told me to expect you, and that maybe this mission isn't precisely sanctioned. So many players."

Ashley didn't reply, she just stared at the muzzle of the .45.

"Still don't want to play along?" Niya said. "Then I think we will have a problem here. I certainly know Mr. Sheeran is going to have a problem. Snitches don't last long in my world. I doubt the man will ever see solid ground again in his soon to be very short life."

"You have this all wrong," Ashley said. "I'm not what you—"

The gunshot was exceptionally loud as Niya squeezed the trigger. The .45 bucked, but not much, and Niya turned the pistol back and forth in her hand, admiring the gun.

"Ah, I see why they went for the H&K," Niya said as she stood over Ashley's corpse, blood pooling into the carpet from the good sized hole in the woman's head. "I may have to keep this one."

She turned and put two rounds in the back of the unconscious guard's head. The man's body shook from the impact then went permanently still.

Niya reached up under her dress with the hand not holding the pistol and pulled down the legs of the tights she was wearing underneath. She then grabbed the hem of her dress from behind and yanked it up and over her head, shimmying out of it in record time, all without letting go of the pistol or taking her eyes off the end of the passageway.

She tossed the dress aside and stood there in an athletic top and black tights, her head cocked and listening. When she didn't hear footsteps coming her way, she knelt by the dead guard and patted him down, removing the two extra magazines from his belt and tucking them into the waistband of her tights before standing up and giving Ashley's corpse one last look.

"I believe I may have burned a bridge with my friends in high places," Niya said. "But sometimes you must burn things down before you build them back up."

She strolled down the passageway, her feet bare, back straight, and pistol out in front.

"Now, let's see what Mr. Giraldi is up to, shall we?"

24.

The guard by the game room door didn't even flinch at the far-off sounds of the gunshots. But he did tighten his grip on his pistol and made sure everyone knew he wouldn't be distracted and that they'd have to get through him if they wanted to try to leave.

"Giraldi's men are the only ones with firearms, right?" Lane asked. "Sounds as if one of them is having a bad day."

"More like the person on the receiving end of those shots is having a bad day," Carlos said.

"You may want to contact your crew and see what's happening," Jessica suggested to Nick as the man just stood by the poker table and stared across the room at the guarded doors. "Sheeran? Nicky? Are you listening?"

"He's still going to buy the yacht even if it has a few bullet holes in it, yeah?" Nick asked no one in particular.

"Nicky," Ben snapped as he walked over and grabbed the man by the shoulders. "Dude. We are way past you selling this boat."

"Yacht," Nick said then cried out as his head rocked back from the slap Ben gave him. "Jesus, Benny! What the hell?"

"You need to get your head in the game!" Ben shouted. "Yacht selling is not our priority! Everything is going down and I need to know you aren't going to fall apart like that time in Omaha!"

The mention of the Nebraska city got Nick's attention and he shoved Ben away.

"You don't get to bring up Omaha," Nick growled. "That is below the belt, man, and you know it. There was no way any of us could have known what that place was. No way."

"What happened in Omaha?" Maggie asked, her speech slurred considerably from alcohol and fear.

"Not the time, baby," Ben said.

"Hold on, now," Lane said. "You've piqued my interest, mate. I kinda want to know what happened in Omaha too."

"Not the time!" Ben snapped and looked back towards Manny. "We need to get out of this room then get off this ship!"

"None of you are going anywhere," the guard said then focused on Ben. "Why'd you look at the bartender?"

"What?" Ben replied, his head whipping back around to focus on the man that held the gun on them all. "I didn't look at him specifically. I was just looking behind me at everyone at the bar."

"Didn't seem like that to me," the guard said. "You had a reason you were looking at the bartender. Why?" The guard nodded in Manny's direction. "How about you come out from behind there? Nice and slow. Hands where I can see them."

"I'm just washing glasses back here, sir," Manny said. "I'd prefer to stay out of all of this. I'm not getting paid to be involved in whatever is going on. I'm getting paid to look the other way and keep my mouth shut. That's all I want to do."

"You think I'm asking?" the guard snarled. "Get your ass out from behind that—"

His brains exploded out the back of his head and splattered against the game room doors. There were more than a couple of startled screams from the guests and all eyes whipped about to focus on Manny and the smoking pistol in his hand.

"Mr. Sheeran? Would you please relieve the corpse of its weapon?" Manny asked. "Then bring it to me, if you will."

"Nicky, Nicky, Nicky," Lane sighed. "What the bloody hell have you gotten us all mixed up in?"

"I just want to say for the record," Carlos announced, his voice raised and eyes looking about the room. "To anyone listening right now, that I was only here to play a friendly game of cards and get some free drinks and food. If this yacht is stolen, I had no prior knowledge and would never consider buying anything in an illegal manner."

"Pussy," Jessica said, spinning on her barstool to face Manny. "Who are you with, Wyatt Earp?"

"Wyatt Earp?" Manny asked. "Funny. I'm not a US Marshall, I can say that for sure."

"We're in international waters," Lane said. "He's either INTERPOL or secret intelligence. That it? You NSA, CIA, MI6 or something else?"

"He's INTERPOL," Ben said. "They're after Giraldi, not you guys."

"Jesus, Benny," Nick said. "You really weren't supposed to announce that."

"Time to put all of our cards on the table," Ben said. "Manny's cover is blown."

"Because you told them," Manny said.

"Pretty sure you putting a bullet in that guy's head was the give away," Ben said. "But that doesn't matter. What does matter is that Giraldi has zero intention of letting any of us live through tonight. I could see it in his eyes after that last hand. He had the look of a man that can't lose. Same look some guys get when they are planning on jacking the winnings anyway, no matter how the game turns out. You learn the look on the circuit and you leave the game as early as possible."

"That what happened in Omaha?" Lane asked. "You didn't leave the game early enough?"

"We can't really leave this game," Jessica said, nodding at Manny. "Not with secret agent man there keeping us covered."

Ben held up his hands and faced Manny.

"I know you have a job to do and most of these people aren't exactly the type you fight to protect," Ben said.

"Oy!" Lane snapped.

"Hey!" Carlos said.

Jessica shrugged. Maggie burped.

"But this has all gone sideways," Ben continued. "You have to admit that. What you need to do now is get in contact with Ashley and find out what's going on outside this room. Then you need to tell her to have your guy get my daughter and her girlfriend out of that party and somewhere safe so the Guillotine doesn't hurt her."

"Guillotine?" Nick asked. "Party? What's that about? Why is the Guillotine after Tanni?"

"Because INTERPOL had you invite Giraldi onto this boat," Ben said and held up his hand. "*Yacht*. He sent the killer to watch my daughter in case things went bad and he needed a bargaining chip. I'd like to remove that chip from the table right now."

"Yeah, and I'd like my cell phone back, mate," Lane said. "I need to check in with my people and make sure Giraldi hasn't made any moves against them."

"Going to have to agree with Lane there," Jessica said.

"Back away from the body!" Manny shouted as he brought his pistol to bear on Carlos.

But it was too late. Carlos already had the dead man's gun and was aiming it at Manny.

"Shit," Nick said. "I was supposed to get that, wasn't I?"

"Hold on!" Ben yelled. "How about we just set the guns down? Giraldi is the problem, not the people in this room."

"I have an INTERPOL agent aiming his pistol at me," Carlos said. "That makes him a problem in this room."

"I am not setting my weapon down for any reason," Manny said. "But he will be setting his down or I will fire."

"No!" Ben shouted. "No firing! We can figure this all out! No firing!"

"Set the gun down!" Manny yelled at Carlos.

"Not happening!" Carlos yelled back.

"Everyone is so loud!" Maggie cried. "Shhhhh!"

The tension in the room was about to break. Ben could feel it building to a crescendo. As soon as that happened then there would be bullets flying and he'd be lucky not to catch one. So he did the dumbest thing he could think of.

"Knock it off," he snarled as he stepped directly between the two men's lines of fire.

"Benny Boy, that is not a good move," Nick hissed.

"Cram it," Ben responded. "You no longer get a say in any of this."

"Mr. Clow, please get out of the way," Manny ordered.

"Yeah, Clow, you best move," Carlos said. "You are in way over your head right now."

"No, I'm not," Ben said. "Just listen. Manny, there are armed men on this ship that will kill you when they find out you are INTERPOL. I don't know how many agents you have on board, but my guess is that's it's just you and Ashley. You need these people to help if we are going to live through this." He looked at Carlos. "You. Where are you going to go after you kill an INTERPOL agent? You'll still be on this ship. That helicopter that brought you here? Gone. Not like you can call a water taxi and slip away. You need INTERPOL's help to get off this ship alive."

Neither of the men lowered their weapons even a hair.

"What if Manny swears you won't be prosecuted for anything that happens tonight as long as you promise to help against Giraldi?" Ben asked Carlos.

"I can't make that deal," Manny said.

"Dude," Ben sighed. "Work with me here."

"I can make a request, but it's not up to me," Manny insisted. "But he lowers that gun before I even think of making that call."

"Carlos? Please?" Ben asked. "I really have to make sure my daughter is safe."

"Guns down at the same time," Carlos said. "Only way this will work."

"Manny? You're the good guy here," Ben said. "Guns down at the same time. I'll stay right where I'm at in case one of you tries to make a move. You'll risk hitting me."

"Benny, that's not a risk you want to wager on," Nick said.

"I'm not," Ben said. "The odds are we all die if we don't band together. Everyone do a quick calculation in their head and you'll see I'm right. The only way we live is if you two set your guns down and we come to an understanding."

Neither man lowered their weapon.

"Son of a bitch," Ben muttered.

25.

"Just ease it along side, Captain," Tony said as he stood on the bridge, a very large revolver pressed to the back of Captain Staggs head. "Get us as close as possible and my guys will do the rest."

"That ship has no running lights," Captain Staggs responded. "It's going to be hard to maneuver close to it. I can barely see the hull with the way it's painted."

"Yeah, ain't that paint something?" Tony chuckled. "I'm going to have my guys look at it closely. Supposed to help keep the ship off radar. Imagine that. A paint that blocks radar."

"I've come across it before," Captain Staggs said.

"Have you? First I've heard of it," Tony said. "But you can see the ship now. It's right there. Just ease up alongside it and then cut the engine."

"These waters are too choppy to tie up to that ship," Captain Staggs said. "It would make more sense to settle away from it and take one of the speedboats over there."

"But I don't want to take a speedboat over there, Captain," Tony said. "What I want to do is get right up next to it so my men can hop aboard and make sure what I'm looking for is actually on the ship."

"Mr. Giraldi, sir, you have to understand that I know more about piloting a ship than you do," Captain Staggs said. "No disrespect meant, but you should really listen to me."

"Should I? Is that what I should do?" Tony asked. He raised the gun to smack the captain on the back of the head then stopped. "Okay. Okay, I'll listen. So you want to settle how far away?"

"At least a hundred meters," Captain Staggs said. "That way if a wave hits the other ship and brings the bow around, I'll have time to move us out of the way."

"And this thing has a speedboat? Where? I didn't see one on the back when we flew over in the chopper," Tony said. "You got it up your ass, is that it? Hiding a speedboat in your butt, Captain?"

"It's below," Captain Staggs said. "In the lower deck hold. Two speedboats and two speed rafts."

"Speed raft? What's that?" Tony asked. "Like those Zodiac things you see in the movies?"

"Exactly like that," Captain Staggs replied. "Let me get this ship set and I'll have one of the crew show you down."

"Right," Tony laughed. "So you can make a distress call and ruin everything? I don't think so. Which panel is communications?"

"I'm sorry, what?" Captain Staggs asked.

"All these lights and dials," Tony said. "Which panel controls the radio and intercom and all of that?"

"That one there," Captain Staggs said as he pointed at a console a couple feet away. "But I don't see why—"

He cried out as Tony pointed his pistol at the console and pulled the trigger three times, leaving the panel a smoking, sparking mess.

"You're still coming with me," Tony said. "I just want to make sure none of your crew can call out while we're down below. Once my men are safely off in one of them speedboats then we'll walk ourselves back up here and relax until they confirm what I need confirmed."

"Yes, sir," Captain Staggs said.

"I like your manners, Captain," Tony said. "You know how to speak to your betters. Shows respect. That gets points with me."

"I am glad to hear that, sir," Captain Staggs said. "I try to treat everyone equally when I interact. It makes things more pleasant and keeps a calm atmosphere. Tension and high emotion are never a good thing on a ship at sea."

"Now you're ruining it," Tony said. "No need to pile it on."

Captain Staggs went quiet until they got closer to the other ship. He frowned and glanced back at Tony.

"No running lights and I don't see any lights on the bridge, either," Captain Staggs said. "Will you hand me those binoculars there, please?"

Tony pressed the muzzle of the gun up against Captain Staggs's head as he reached for and retrieved the binoculars. He handed them to the captain and waited.

"What do you see?" Tony asked.

"Nothing," Captain Staggs said. "Is the ship supposed to be deserted?"

"Not entirely," Tony said. "But it shouldn't exactly be bustling with crew members. Don't worry about lights."

"Well, the problem is that the ship obviously still has power," Captain Staggs said. "The engines are running and it is moving at a nice clip. It makes more sense for us to pace it than to settle in place. By the time your speedboats get over there, it will be quite a ways away, leaving them with a large part of open ocean to travel when they come back."

"What you're saying is that you need to be up on this bridge the whole time, is that it?" Tony asked. "I need someone else to show me the speedboats?"

"Yes," Captain Staggs said. "I'm not trying to play you, sir, I promise. You do not strike me as a man that likes to be played."

"You got that right," Tony said. "Fine. Get on the intercom and call your boss up here. He can show me where the speedboats are."

"You shot the intercom system, sir," Captain Staggs responded.

"No problem," Tony said and pulled a radio from his belt. "Lou? Get your butt down to the game room and tell Frank to send Sheeran up here. I want that man in front of me in five minutes tops or I get upset."

"Yes, Mr. Giraldi," a man replied.

"Sheeran knows how to handle the speedboats, right?" Tony asked.

"Yes, he does," Captain Staggs said. "He is surprisingly good with boats."

"Well, everyone has to be good at one thing," Tony said. "You probably don't want to know what I'm good at."

"Only if you feel compelled to tell me, sir," Captain Staggs replied.

"I'm never compelled to do anything," Tony said. "So count yourself lucky."

26.

"Frank? Come in," a voice called out from the radio clipped to the dead man's belt. "Frank? You copy? Come on, man, don't make me come down there. The boss needs that Sheeran guy up on the bridge in five. He was very clear about the five part."

Everyone looked at Nick. He shrugged.

"He should go up there," Ben said. "He can tell them Frank is having radio trouble. If he shows up then no one will suspect Frank is having living trouble."

"Gee, thanks, buddy old pal," Nick said. "Boot me from the frying pan and right into the fire."

"Why wouldn't Frank go with him?" Lane asked. "Sending Sheeran up there alone is just as suspicious." He looked over at Carlos and gave the man a nod. "Lower the pistol, mate. Blogger Boy is right. We need to work together to get off this boat."

Nick started to open his mouth in response, but just shook his head instead.

"INTERPOL lowers his gun first," Carlos said.

"Jesus," Ben sighed. He looked at Manny. "Other than pointing a weapon at an INTERPOL agent, has Carlos done anything for you to arrest him?"

"He has no current indictments or warrants," Manny said.

"Does anyone else in this room?" Ben asked.

Jessica raised her hand.

"I'm wanted in Greece for wire fraud," Jessica said.

"You are?" Ben asked.

"She is," Manny said.

"Wire fraud, not terrorism or murder or anything violent," Ben said, still focusing on Manny. "We need them."

"I need to go up to the bridge," Nick said.

"That would be stupid," Manny said. He glared at Carlos. "I lower this and you lower yours. Then all of you help me and Agent Mulgrew get off this boat with Giraldi in hand. The helicopter can be here in two hours once I call them. That means we have two hours to secure this boat and catch Giraldi alive."

"Does it have to be alive?" Lane asked. "I mean, it would be a lot easier if we just put two taps behind his left ear and called it good, mate."

"I'd feel better knowing he's dead," Carlos said. "If he knows we helped, then even in custody he's going to be trouble. He'll still be making the calls from a cell."

"He won't have access to any communications where he's going," Manny said.

Lane looked at Carlos. Carlos looked at Jessica. Jessica looked at Lane. They all started laughing hysterically.

"Oh, mate, that is rich," Lane exclaimed.

"Which facility will he be taken to?" Carlos asked, tears streaming down his cheeks.

"Brussels? Paris? Berlin?" Jessica asked.

"I can't disclose the location of the facility," Manny said.

"If it's Brussels then he'll have access to a cell phone within two hours of walking in the door," Lane said. "Paris and Berlin only means he has to wait an hour longer."

"It's true," Nick confirmed. "Brussels is a joke."

"How would you know that?" Ben asked.

Nick shrugged.

"The only way we make this work is if Giraldi dies," Carlos said. "Otherwise we have no incentive to do anything since we'll all be dead in a couple weeks anyway."

Manny thought it over, his internal debate plain on his face.

"I'm going to try to take him alive," Manny said. "If he's shot by one of you accidentally then that's how I'll report it."

"That's fair," Ben said, looking around at everyone in the room. "Right? That sounds fair." He frowned and looked at the closed doors. "Why isn't Niya back yet? She's been gone a long time."

27.

The guard at the end of the passageway looked at Niya and cocked his head. His resemblance to a confused golden retriever was a little too on the nose and Niya laughed as she put a little more sway into her hips, keeping her hands, and the pistol, behind her back.

"I think I got lost," she said, her voice nothing but coquettish innocence. "Is the ladies' room this way?"

"There is one down by the game room," the guard said, turning his body so he was blocking the end of the passageway. "You should go back and use that one."

Niya did the universal squirm that said she really, really had to pee.

"Is there one closer? I'm about to embarrass myself," Niya replied.

"Why are you dressed like that?" the guard asked, finally noticing that Niya wasn't wearing her dress or heels any longer.

"I like to be comfortable when I play cards," Niya said. "You try wearing a skin tight dress meant for a woman with two less ribs. Does not make for an evening of fun."

"Ma'am, you need to turn around and return to the lower deck," the guard said.

"No," Niya responded, her hands no longer behind her back.

The .45 barked and the guard was down and dead before his hand even twitched on his gun. Niya was at his side in two steps. She knelt and patted him down, finding another .45 and two more magazines. She tucked those into her waistband, but kept the second .45 out, giving both hands something to do.

She stood and looked back the way she came, listened, waited, then hurried forward, her destination only one deck up.

28.

"Lou? You want to tell me why Frank doesn't have Sheeran's ass up on the bridge?" Tony growled into the radio. "When I say five, I mean five."

"Not sure, boss," Lou replied. "I'll go do it myself."

"Yes, you will," Tony said. "And have everyone check in. Open channel. I want to hear every single voice respond. If one of you found that pretty hostess and has her in a linen closet right now, there will be hell to pay." Tony winked at Captain Staggs. "Especially since I always get first shot at a fine piece of ass like that."

Tony set the radio down and sighed. He patted Captain Staggs on the shoulder with one hand while keeping his pistol trained on the man with the other.

"How long you been doing this, Cap?" Tony asked. "You look like you know what you're doing, but you don't have the look of a salty dog."

"I've been captaining yachts for ten years," Captain Staggs replied. "I worked as crew for ten years before that."

"Always yachts?" Tony asked.

"Yes, sir," Captain Staggs said.

"You never worked on a fishing boat or charter?" Tony asked. "Never ended up stinking of halibut or cod for months?"

"I may have done some of that type of work when I was young," Captain Staggs said.

"See there, Cap," Tony said and grinned. "Never be ashamed of doing an honest day's work. You're so used to sucking up to rich assholes that were born sucking caviar out of their mommies' tits that you've forgotten where you come from. Be proud of who you were."

"Yes, sir," Captain Staggs said then whipped the wheel to the left. "The waters are getting worse. I need to put more space between us and that ship." He started to say something then paused.

"Out with it, Cap," Tony ordered. "You got something to say then say it."

"It's just that, I was wondering if what you are looking for on that ship will need to be brought over to this ship," Captain Staggs inquired. "I just need to know if it's flammable or explosive. If so then we have a secure locker it can be stored in down in the lower deck."

"Don't worry about that, Cap," Tony said. "Whatever it is, will be staying on that ship. I only need to confirm it's there and my men will do the rest."

"You have someone that can pilot that ship?" Captain Staggs asked.

"Why would I need that?" Tony responded. "When I have a perfectly good captain right here."

"Sir, no offense, but I have never captained a ship that size before," Captain Staggs said. "Or that class. I've piloted yachts slightly larger than this, but never a military cruiser."

"Who said it was military? You see any insignias or flags on that thing?" Tony asked. "I don't."

"I know a military cruiser when I see one, sir," Captain Staggs said.

"I don't think you do," Tony said. "Because I know for sure that ship isn't military."

"Then what does a pig like you want with it?" Niya asked as she stepped onto the bridge with both hands up, her two .45s aimed at Tony. "If it's not military then it must have something very valuable on it."

"Niya," Tony said, chuckling as he slowly set his gun on the dash by Captain Staggs. He held up both hands and faced the woman as she squared off with him. "Nice look. Yoga assassin?"

"I like to be comfortable when I work, Tony," Niya said. "You know that."

"Oh, I do," Tony chuckled some more. "I certainly do. You aren't still sore about Morocco, are you?"

"That and Croatia," Niya said. "And Lisbon and Dublin and Hong Kong."

"Hong Kong wasn't me," Tony said. "That one was Cooper."

"The Canadian?" Niya asked. "Do not insult me, Tony. It was not him. I put a bullet in his belly three weeks before Hong Kong. He was still learning to crap in a bag back in Toronto when you hijacked my shipment."

"Nope, not me," Tony said. "Dublin, Lisbon, and Croatia were me, but not Hong Kong. And if it wasn't Cooper then I guess we're both in the dark on that one. I'm gonna have to find some new sources if they are going to be wrong on important facts like that."

Niya glanced past Tony and frowned.

"Is that the ship?" Niya asked. "It looks abandoned. You getting into the salvage business, Tony?"

"A man should always diversify," Tony said. "And ship salvage can be very lucrative."

"What's on the ship, Tony?" Niya asked. She kicked backwards and shut the bridge door.

"Why'd you ask me if it was the ship?" Tony asked. "You specifically said 'the ship.' Kind of like you knew there would be a ship here and I was looking for it."

"We all have our sources, Tony," Niya said. "Some of mine work in circles well outside your reach. There is an advantage to being a beautiful woman in this business instead of an ugly thug like you. I look like I fit in at even the most grand of galas. You barely look like you fit in at a New York deli."

"I prefer Jersey delis," Tony said. "When I'm in the States, at least. Not a fan of the city. Too noisy."

"Tell me about the ship," Niya said.

"Why should I do that?" Tony asked. "I tell you anything and you'll put more than a few holes in my body. That don't work for me, Niya."

"You can tell me or not," Niya said. "But even with what happened in Morocco, I didn't come here to kill you."

"I find that hard to believe," Tony said.

"If I kill you then Lombardo takes over your territories," Niya said. "I hate Lombardo more than I hate you. With you, I know what I'm getting. Lombardo is a lazy psycho. He kills anything and everything he doesn't like, doesn't understand, or doesn't get a cut from. He's bad business and I'll spend more time defending my operations from him than I ever did from you."

"I don't exactly agree with you," Tony said, "since I've known Luci most of my life. But, I do understand the need to keep the devil you know. That's always a good philosophy."

Tony cocked his head in the direction of the bridge windows.

"Tell you what," he said. "You work with me and I'll cut you in on a percentage when I make delivery to the client."

"A percentage?" Niya laughed. "Do these pistols look like they want a percentage?"

"You can't have it all," Tony said.

"You got all of Morocco, Lisbon, and Croatia," Niya said. "I want all of this. Make that happen and you live."

"Dublin," Tony said.

"Excuse me?"

"Dublin. You forgot I took Dublin too," Tony said.

"I didn't forget," Niya said. "I just didn't say it because I'm saving that debt for another time."

"But if I give you this job you'll forget about the others?" Tony asked. "We'll be clean on those?"

"We'll be clean on those and the hit I put out on you last week will be lifted," Niya said.

"Hit? Damn, my sources really are not doing their jobs," Tony said. He slowly lowered his right hand and held it out. "Throw in Dublin and we have a deal."

"I keep Dublin for later," Niya said.

"No, I can't agree to that," Tony said. "What's on that ship is worth a clean slate. No debts, no grudges. We start clean and go back to being friends."

"We were never friends," Niya said.

"Then we go back to just fucking when we run into each other," Tony said. "I miss that." He moved his hand about to indicate Niya's body. "I miss that a lot. Brains, beauty, and a bod that surpasses both. You got it all, Niya. We both know that finding someone to be within our line of work ain't easy. I get the airhead bimbos that just want my money and you get the sycophants that only want to use you to get ahead in the game."

"That's what vibrators are for, Tony," Niya said. "They never stab me in the back."

"Come on, Niya," Tony said. "It'll be worth it, trust me. I give you this job and we're even. But you have to let me handle the deal. They'll never trust you."

"Because I'm a woman?" Niya asked.

"Well, yeah," Tony said and shrugged. "These guys are old school. They aren't the kind that deal with Russians, let alone Russian women."

"Ukrainian," Niya said and her grips on the pistols tightened.

"Ukrainian," Tony said. "My apologies."

"Sir? The weather is turning fast," Captain Staggs said. "I know you two are in the middle of delicate negotiations, but you are about to lose your window to board the other ship. You have maybe an hour before we need to head back to land."

"That so?" Tony said. "You aren't exaggerating, are you?"

"He's not," Niya said. "I checked before we left for this ship. Bad weather is coming this way. Mr. Sheeran's proposed route put us outside of it, but looks like you changed the route."

"Sir, I must also say that there is no way I can pilot that other ship," Captain Staggs said. "I am sorry, but in the time we have, I won't be able to orient myself with the controls."

"Did you know ships aren't ships aren't ships?" Tony asked Niya. "I thought they were. Doesn't matter. I was only testing you, Cap. Just in case things went weird. The gentlemen I'm making the deal with are coming to us. Bringing a helicopter right to the ship with their very own captain. All I need to do is make sure the cargo is on board and secure and give a call."

"A helicopter is going to have an even harder time in this weather, sir," Captain Staggs said. "They had best already be on their way."

"Let me worry about that, Cap," Tony said. "You just keep doing the fine job you are doing." He raised his eyebrows and focused on Niya. "Do we have a deal or what? You heard the captain, time is ticking."

"We have a deal," Niya said. "But I'm going over there to inspect the cargo."

"I assumed you would be," Tony said. "You've always been so hands on." He glanced at the radio. "Where the hell is Sheeran?"

29.

The tenuous alliance held for exactly ten minutes.

Everyone left the game room as allies, but it only took a couple passageways for it to all go to shit.

"That's one of Giraldi's men," Nick said as they came across the corpses in the passageway. "They must have shot each other."

"He shot Ashley while he was face down?" Manny snapped. "Then his ghost shot her point blank?"

"No?" Nick replied.

"Niya," Ben said. "She's the variable."

"Why'd she shoot Ashley?" Nick asked. "Because she was INTERPOL? That's a huge risk even with Niya's reputation."

"I need to get Maggie to our cabin," Ben said. "I'm doing that first so she is locked in and safe. You all head up to the bridge."

"I'm going with you," Jessica said.

"Why?" Ben asked.

"Because you are out of your depth, Clow," Jessica said. "You want Maggie safe?"

"Yeah," Ben replied.

"Then one of us should be with her," Jessica said. "And no offense to Lane and Carlos, but I wouldn't trust them with my eighty-year-old grandma. And that woman doesn't go anywhere without a Buck knife sharp enough to cut atoms."

"What the bloody hell, Jessie?" Lane exclaimed. "I'm not the rapey type."

"You are the hold someone hostage and use them as insurance type," Jessica said. "Or do I have you pegged wrong?"

"No, that's me," Lane said. "But you owe Carlos an apology. He's shite at holding hostages."

"Am not," Carlos said.

"San Diego," Lane smirked.

"Oh, yes, well, that was unfortunate," Carlos admitted.

"I'll take you to your cabin and then you can catch up with the others," Jessica said. "Which way is the bridge?"

"Up this passageway, two turns then the stairs all the way up," Nick said. "No, wait. Three turns, two sets of stairs. Hold on, no. Two turns is right, but three sets of stairs because of the deck we are on."

"I'll find it," Jessica said.

"I'm not splitting up until I know Manny has called in to his man to save my daughter," Ben said.

"I already did," Manny said. "She's being moved right now."

"Good," Ben replied. "Thank you."

"Move ass," Nick said to Ben. "I'm not thrilled being alone with these assholes. You I trust. Them not so much."

"Your words hurt, Nicky," Lane said. "They hurt deep."

"Whatever," Nick said, looking to Ben again. "Hurry."

"I will," Ben replied. "See you on the bridge."

He held Maggie to his side and helped her walk around the dead bodies until they came to their turn in the passageway. Jessica walked close behind him, her hand on the small of Maggie's back to help with support. Maggie showed no signs of noticing the corpses or Jessica's hand as her head lulled against Ben's shoulder.

"How much did she drink tonight?" Ben asked.

"Why are you asking me?" Jessica replied as they walked down the next passageway. "I was at the table with you."

"You two seemed to get along," Ben said. "Thought maybe you were watching."

"She's your girlfriend," Jessica said. "Yeah, I think she's a nice woman, but we're not besties or anything. She's your responsibility, Clow."

"It's Ben," Ben said.

"I prefer Clow," Jessica said. "Keeps things in perspective."

"In case you have to shoot me?" Ben asked.

"I leave all options open," Jessica said. She stopped at a door. "Hold on."

"For what?" Ben asked. "My cabin is after the next turn."

"This is mine," Jessica said. "Just wait."

Ben started to argue, but there was no point as Jessica entered her code on the keypad outside her cabin and was inside and out of sight in seconds.

Ben leaned Maggie against the wall and pushed her hair out of her face. The woman stirred some and her eyelids fluttered, but she made no show of actual consciousness. For a split second, Ben regretted inviting her along, but then he pushed that guilt away since it was Nick that held all the blame. Ben had thought it was going to be an easy weekend on a nice boat, not a set up to play poker with some serious players involved in international crime.

"What are you doing down here?" a voice asked from the far end of the passageway. "You should be in the game room."

"Uh, yeah, taking a break," Ben said, his voiced raised. "My girlfriend had a little too much to drink so I'm walking her back to our cabin."

"That so?" the man asked as he walked forward, his .45 up and aimed at Ben. "We've been trying to get a hold of Frank and he's not answering."

"Don't know a Frank," Ben said. "I know Manny the bartender."

"Frank wouldn't have let you out without instructions from Mr. Giraldi," the man said. "How about we turn around and go see what's really going on?"

"Can we drop her off first?" Ben asked, nodding at Maggie. "She's a puker and I'd rather she didn't embarrass herself in front of the others."

"Do you really think I'm that stupid?" the man asked, moving closer.

Three thwips and the man collapsed against the wall, blood trailing on the paneling as his body slid to the floor. Jessica stepped all the way out of her cabin and placed the suppressor against his temple and squeezed the trigger again, putting a fourth bullet in the man. She glanced over at Ben and smiled.

"I don't care what Nicky's instructions were," Jessica said, holding up the pistol with the long suppressor on the end. "I never go anywhere without Teddie."

"Teddie? You named your gun?" Ben asked.

"Some have stuffed animals, I have a Sig Sauer Enhanced Elite," Jessica said and grinned. "You like guns?"

"Not really," Ben said. "I know too much about them."

"I love guns," Jessica said. "Probably how I ended up in this line of work. Smoked too much pot to go into law enforcement. And I hate rules."

"But you love your gun," Ben said. "I guess Giraldi's men didn't search your bags well enough."

"No one finds Teddie unless I want them to find Teddie," Jessica said. "Not even the TSA. This baby has more frequent flyer miles than a mid-level corporate manager."

"That's a good one," Ben said.

"Let's get her to bed," Jessica said, nodding at Maggie. "Come on. I'll lead in case we meet more muscle."

They took the last few turns and then found Ben and Maggie's cabin.

Ben keyed in the code and the door clicked open. Ben and Jessica helped Maggie to the bed and she groaned.

"Too many clothes," she muttered and started to pull her dress over her head.

"Hold on, hold on," Ben said and helped her get undressed.

She swatted at him and then tried to grab for his crotch, but he gently pushed her hand away. Maggie tucked her knees up under her, her face pushed into the bed and her underwear clad butt in the air.

"Sorry," Ben said to Jessica. "She, uh, can be a handful when she drinks."

"We've all been there," Jessica said. She nodded at the cabin door. "You better get back to the others. I'll keep her safe."

"Back to the others?" Ben asked. "Do I need to?"

"It'll make them feel more at ease," Jessica said. "If you're gone too long, they'll think we're colluding and then things could go bad for both of us."

"Jesus," Ben said. "How do you live like this? Being a rounder was hard enough, but your life is beyond complicated."

"We all live the lives we're given, Sheeran," Jessica said. "Now go make sure Lane and Carlos don't get any ideas."

Ben hurried from the cabin and Jessica shut the door behind him, her pistol at the ready in case any of the rest of Tony's men came calling.

30.

Before Nick could step one foot through the door, he was grabbed and thrown halfway across the bridge, his head slamming into the very expensive brass railing bolted to the teak and mahogany wall.

"What the hell?" he cried out as he rubbed at his head. "Your guys said you wanted to... Oh..."

"Yes, Mr. Sheeran, oh," Niya said, her .45s aimed at Nick. "Who's outside the door?"

"What? No one," Nick said. "Just me. Giraldi's guy's radio was all weird so he sent me out to meet with some guy named Lou, I think and—"

"Just stop," Tony said as he moved to stand over Nick and leaned down, his hand gripping the brass railing, squeezing it, working at it like he wanted to tear it off and give Nick a good, hard whack with it. "Lou's dead. Ms. Romanski admitted as much, unfortunately. I'm guessing so is Frank. Be honest, Sheeran."

"Yeah," Nick replied in a very quiet voice. "Frank's dead."

"Who's outside the door?" Tony asked.

"The others," Nick said, still keeping his voice down

"That include the rogue INTERPOL agent slash bartender?" Niya asked.

"Rogue what?" Nick replied. "What are you talking about?"

He cried out and grabbed his nose as Tony gave him a hard shot to the face.

"Shit, man!" Nick yelled. "What was that for?"

The bridge door started to open and Niya put four bullets through it. There was a cry and several shouts then silence.

"You were right," Tony said, crouching next to Nick and looking over his shoulder at Niya. "They all caved fast and followed like little ducklings."

"I knew they would," Niya said. "Simply because they believe the INTERPOL guy is legit. But I know he's not."

"He's not?" Nick asked. "Oh, shit..."

"Your entire world just came crashing down, didn't it?" Tony asked then laughed. He patted Nick on the cheek. "Only one way you're getting out of this, Sheeran, and that is to do exactly what I say."

"Great," Nick said. "But they aren't going to. Sounds like you hit one of them, but the rest are still out there. You can ask me to do whatever you want me to, but they're going to still come for you."

"No, they aren't," Tony replied. He fished out his phone and started flicking through pictures. "See that? Whittier's niece. See this one? Garfield's sister. Here's Holstein's nephew and sister-in-law. Clow's daughter and her dyke girlfriend are in this one. I'm being sent these every five minutes."

"Bullshit," Nick said. "Ben's daughter is safe. The Guillotine won't get her."

"The Guillotine? He's not my guy," Tony said. "Last I heard he turned and is working for whatever agency needs him."

Nick's stomach lurched and he burped up rancid crab cakes and bourbon.

"Pardon you," Tony said as he stood up, waving his hand in front of his face. "Warn a person when you're going to do that."

"You have someone watching my family?" Niya asked.

"You don't have family," Tony replied. "And I didn't know you would be here. That bit of intel snuck by."

"Lucky me," Niya said. She fired through the door again and there was more shouting, but obviously from further away. "Can we get on with this?"

"You are going to take one of the speedboats over with my guys to that ship," Tony said to Nick. "You do that, they find what I want them to find, everyone gets back here alive, and I don't cut your dick off and feed it to you."

"What *will* you do to me?" Nick asked. "Because I know you aren't just gonna give me a hug and a pat on the ass and send me on my way."

"That's entirely up to you, Sheeran," Tony said. "I honestly may do nothing. I know the connections your family has. It could make my legitimate business dealings uncomfortable if I harm you significantly."

"But you might still harm me insignificantly?" Nick asked.

"Again, entirely up to you," Tony said. "You can drive one of the speedboats, right?"

"Yeah," Nick said.

"Good," Tony said. "Then Niya here will escort you down to the hold where you'll meet two of my men since I think that's all that's left alive after your little poker party decided to hunt them down."

"Manny killed one, we aren't sure what happened to the others," Nick said. "Honestly, Mr. Giraldi, I have no idea what happened to the others."

"I did," Niya said to Nick. "I happened to them. So do not mess with me, alright? You even smell like you're going to screw around and I'll put two in your head and figure out how to drive the boat myself."

Nick looked from one gangster to the other and swallowed hard. He slowly stood up and faced Captain Staggs. "You aren't going to do anything, are you?"

"There is nothing I can do, Mr. Sheeran," Captain Staggs said. "I am keeping this ship from succumbing to the growing waves. Right now that is my one and only job."

"Which he gets to keep doing," Tony said. "I got nothing against Cap here. I got nothing against you either, Sheeran, except you're a spoiled piece of shit. Despite that, if you do what you're told, you get to live. That's going to be a hard deal to pass up."

"Fine," Nick said. "I'll drive the boat. But where the hell are we going?"

"There's a special ship just off our port side right now," Tony said. "You take the speedboat over there and let my men handle the rest. You get them back here and your job is done."

"That's it?" Nick asked. "Nothing else?"

"For now," Tony said. "I do reserve the right to change my mind."

"Of course you do," Nick said. "One problem."

"What's that?" Tony asked.

"It's not going to be easy to get past the others," Nick said.

Tony tossed him the phone.

"Show them those and I think they'll fall in line," Tony responded. He looked at Niya. "You ready, beautiful?"

"I'm ready, ugly," she replied. "Come on, Mr. Sheeran. Let's get this over with."

31.

"Where the hell are the Carls?" Nick snapped as he and Ben stepped off the platform and onto the speedboat. "They hid their asses fast."

"This is crap, man," Ben said as Nick readied the speedboat. "You have no idea what you're getting in to."

"I have no idea what I'm already in," Nick replied. "None of us do."

He looked over his shoulder at the two men standing a few feet away, their hands occupied with automatic rifles, not semi-auto pistols.

"Sorry I got you and Maggie involved, Benny Boy," Nick said. "I thought this was a simple sting operation. INTERPOL was going to handle it all."

"But we haven't exactly been dealing with INTERPOL, have we?" Ben sighed. "This is why we split up, Nicky. You never did your research. Every new game was going to be the Big One, the game that set us up for life and made us legends. But that never happened."

"Yeah, I know," Nick said. "But this is different. You gotta believe me."

"Do I?" Ben asked. "Why would I?"

Nick looked at Tony's men again. "I'm sorry, man. I truly am."

"My daughter's life is at stake, Nicky," Ben said. "Sorry will not cut it."

"Let's get a move on!" one of the men shouted.

"You better go," Nick said. "It's going to get dicey when I open the side door. The water is rough and getting rougher."

"Do you know what you're looking for?" Ben asked.

"He doesn't need to know," the other man snapped. "He just needs to drive the boat."

"Chill, dickhead," Nick said. "Same with you, dickhead junior."

"Mikey," the first man said. "You call me Mikey or I jam my hand down your throat and pull your asshole out your mouth."

"Mikey it is," Nick replied. "And this is...?"

"Chip," the other man said.

"Chip," Nick echoed. "Well, Chip and Mikey, you want to give me an idea of what we'll be doing on that ship?"

"No," Mikey said.

"I'm dying to know as well," Niya said as she hopped onto the speedboat. She was dressed in thick jeans and a heavy sweater with a knit cap pulled down over her hair. She had two shoulder holsters and the .45s were tucked securely in them. "That's why I'm coming with."

"Mr. Giraldi said you were only coming down here to see us off," Mikey said.

"Change of plans," Niya said, her arms folded across her chest. To an average observer, the simple gesture would look like she was just impatient. To a trained eye, it was obvious she was half a second from drawing her pistols. "Care to argue with me?"

"I'll make sure Mr. Giraldi knows," Ben said as he jumped off the boat and back onto the platform. He gave Nick a brief smile. "Try not to die."

"That's always my plan," Nick said as he started up the boat and the engines roared to life.

Ben hurried out of the hold and watched the hull slide open from behind the protection of a very thick door and heavy duty porthole. Nick gave a brief wave as water poured into the yacht and slammed against the speedboat. The boat was quickly lowered into the rising water. Once it was free of its lift, Nick took it out into the open ocean and the large waves that were pounding the ship.

As soon as the speedboat was out, the hull closed and the bilge pump went to work on the water in the hold. Ben started to turn away, but something caught his eye. A movement in the water. Something more substantial than just a heavy wave. He stared through the porthole until the water was completely pumped out then shook his head. Nothing there.

"Keep it together," he muttered to himself. "Don't start seeing things."

32.

The towel was dark red with blood, the color continuing to deepen as the flow refused to stop.

"He's going to bleed out," Lane said as the last of Giraldi's men looked on from the game room doorway. Lane's hand was pressed against Manny's belly as the wounded man lay on the poker table. "Bar towels can only do so much, mate. How about you go find us a first aid kit? Or better yet, how about a doctor?"

"If he dies, he dies," the man replied.

"What's your name?" Carlos asked from behind the bar. He poured a healthy amount of vodka over ice and tossed in a single olive. "I like to know who's pointing a gun at me."

"None of your business," the guard replied.

"You know what, None Of Your Business?" Carlos smirked as he took a sip of his drink. "I'm not sure I like your attitude."

"I don't care," the guard said.

"But does your boss?" Carlos asked. "This is all happening pretty damn fast and I have a gut feeling it wasn't supposed to go down this way." He took another sip. "In fact, my gut is also telling me that maybe this was a rush job. None of you seemed quite prepared to handle the difficulties of pulling off a heist at high seas."

"Ain't a heist," the guard replied. "It's a... Good try. I ain't saying nothing."

"It was a good try," Lane said. "Now, if this isn't a heist then what is it? Not exactly a hostage situation when you let your hostages die."

"Lane's right. That guy is dying," Carlos agreed. "Look at him."

"He's INTERPOL," the guard responded. "Let him die. No one cares about some corrupt cop."

"Corrupt?" Lane asked. "Interesting."

Manny convulsed and fresh blood flowed from under the bar towel, staining the poker felt around him almost black. Carlos grabbed a couple of fresh towels and tossed them at Lane who caught them easily.

"You know you're missing someone, right?" Carlos asked the guard. "Haven't seen Niya in a while."

"She went with Sheeran," the guard said.

"Did she?" Carlos asked. "Huh. From what I overheard, that isn't part of the plan either. You want to tell us why your boss seems to be making this up as he goes along?"

"All I'm going to tell you is to be quiet," the guard said.

"No need to get hostile, mate," Lane said. "But my friend here may have miscounted."

"I did?" Carlos asked.

"You did, mate," Lane said "There was another woman playing here. A different woman than Niya. Remember her? Jessica Holstein?"

"Don't forget the blogger's girl," Carlos said. "Who miscounted now?"

"True, true, but she wasn't playing," Lane said.

"Good call," Carlos responded, sipping again at his drink. He smiled at the guard. "Now, the girlfriend was pretty wasted, so she's probably not a problem. But what about Ms. Holstein? You've heard of her, yes? You know she's a tough cookie and could present quite the problem to your boss if she's loose on this ship."

"Tough cookie?" Lane laughed. "You sound like a twenties gangster."

"Cool," Carlos said. "That's what I was going for. I should probably be drinking rot gut gin, though." He raised his glass. "But as long as we have the good stuff then I'm drinking the good stuff."

The guard looked from Lane to Carlos to the bleeding and dying Manny. His grip on his rifle tightened and he shifted from foot to foot.

"Our babysitter looks nervous, Carlos," Lane said. "I think you may have confused him."

"Did I confuse you, None Of Your Business?" Carlos asked.

"Stop calling me None Of Your Business," the guard replied. "It's Joey. My name is Joey."

"Was that so hard, Joey?" Carlos asked. "That didn't seem hard to me."

"Me neither," Lane said.

"You know what else wouldn't be hard?" Carlos asked. "Getting on that radio of yours and seeing if your boss wants you to track down the stray player."

"Jessica," Lane said.

"Jessica," Carlos agreed. "I know from personal experience that she is wicked good with a pistol in her hand."

"Not bad with a knife, either, mate," Lane added.

"Is she?" Carlos asked.

"She is," Lane said. "I'd show you the scar, but it's in a personal place."

"Ouch," Carlos chuckled.

"Ouch, indeed," Lane said.

The two men watched Joey as the guard's confusion grew.

"Jesus," Carlos muttered. "We've got a bright one here."

"The radio," Lane said to Joey. "Get on the radio and report to your boss that you have one person not accounted for."

Joey hesitated then started to reach for the radio on his belt. His rifle dipped and Carlos's eyes shifted to the weapon. Joey instantly lifted the rifle and put it to his shoulder, taking aim at Carlos.

"I'm going to call Mr. Giraldi," Joey said. "From out in the hall. Don't try a damn thing."

"What can we try?" Carlos asked. "We're in a poker room with a bar. It's where we'd planned to be all night anyway, just with more poker going on."

"I try anything and this bloke is dead," Lane said, nodding his chin at the bone white Manny. "Not that he isn't heading that direction anyway."

"Poor guy," Carlos said, topping off his glass and throwing another olive in.

"You ever eat those olives?" Lane asked.

"I let them soak," Carlos said. "Save them for last."

"I'm not an olive fan," Lane said.

"Stay put," Joey said as he reached back and opened the game room doors. "I'll be back as soon as I speak to Mr. Giraldi."

"Good plan," Lane said.

"Best plan I've heard all night," Carlos said.

They watched the man move slowly out of the room and both sighed as the door closed behind him and the distinct sound of the lock being engaged clicked loudly.

"Is it that hard to hire men that aren't functionally retarded?" Lane asked.

"Tsk tsk," Carlos replied. "That is not a nice word."

"What word?" Lane asked.

"Retarded," Carlos said.

"Don't care," Lane said. "Fix me a drink."

"What would you like?" Carlos asked.

"I think I'm actually in the mood for gin," Lane said. "Make it a triple, neat."

"Certainly," Carlos said.

Lane let go of Manny's belly and the man moaned.

"Hush," Lane said as he climbed off the table and stretched.

"Giving up?" Carlos asked as he handed Lane his drink.

"Never really cared," Lane said. "Just playing the part." He sipped his drink and glanced at the doors. "You think he'll go after Jessie?"

"I think so," Carlos said. "We're locked in and I doubt Giraldi wants Ms. Holstein wandering around the ship."

"Are we locked in?" Lane asked.

"I heard it lock," Carlos said.

"Either of us could pick it and get us out of here," Lane said.

"True, true," Carlos agreed. "But good booze."

"Right," Lane said and nodded. "Good booze."

"Let everyone else sort it all out?" Carlos suggested and raised his glass.

"Let everyone else sort it all out," Lane agreed and clinked his glass against Carlos's. "Don't need Giraldi calling his people to hurt our families, do we?"

"We do not," Carlos said then nodded at the stack of unopened decks of cards at the end of the bar. "You want to play a few hands of gin? Penny a point?"

"I'd love to, mate," Lane said. "Better than standing here and watching Agent Bartender slowly die."

33.

"I thought you had them all in there?" Tony snarled into his radio. "You and Mikey were supposed to make sure they were secured before he left with Chip on that speedboat. Was I not clear on that?"

"Yes, Mr. Giraldi, you were clear," Joey replied over the radio as Ben stepped onto the bridge.

Tony gestured with his pistol for Ben to take a seat on the long leather bench against the back wall. Ben didn't even hesitate. He made his way to the bench and sat down, his hands on his thighs in plain sight.

"Are the doors locked?" Tony asked.

"Yes, sir," Joey responded. "I have a trip charge I can put outside them, if you want."

"Explosives? That would not be wise," Captain Staggs said.

"Not powerful enough to put a hole in your boat, Cap," Tony said then returned his attention to the radio. "Forget the charge and go find Ms. Holstein. I want her and the blogger's girlfriend locked up in that game room ASAP. Either of them give you any trouble and you have my permission to do whatever you need to convince them."

"Maggie is probably still passed out," Ben said, but shut up as Tony shot him a harsh glare.

"I want to hear from you in ten minutes," Tony said. "You got that, Joey? Ten minutes whether you have the women or not. We clear?"

"Yes, sir," Joey replied. "Ten minutes."

Tony tossed the radio onto the instrument panel in front of him and rubbed his forehead with the heel of his hand. He took a deep breath, let it out, picked up a different radio and double clicked the transmitter button.

"Mikey? Where you at?" Tony asked.

There was a squeal of static before a crackling voice responded.

"Getting the speedboat tied up to the ship," Mikey replied, his voice sounding muffled and far off.

"They'll need to watch that speedboat closely," Captain Staggs said. "That ship is still shifting around a lot. Won't take much for it to crush the speedboat."

"Mikey? Make sure Sheeran knows how to tie up that speedboat, okay? That's your way back," Tony said. "And keep an eye on Ms. Romanski."

Mikey started to respond then cried out.

"Don't worry about me, Tony," Niya said, having obviously taken the radio from Mikey. "I can handle myself just fine."

"That's not what I meant," Tony said. "And give the radio back to my guy, will ya?"

There was some muffled scuffling and Ben could hear Nick in the background snapping at someone.

"We're tied up and Sheeran is bitching about the waves," Mikey said. "I'll radio back as soon as we have confirmation of the cargo."

"You do that," Tony said. The second radio was tossed onto the instrument panel and Tony turned his full attention to the darkness outside the bridge's windows. "This thing have any floodlights? Shine them over at the other ship, Cap."

"This thing does not have floodlights like that," Captain Staggs said. "Not accessible from the bridge. There are some auxiliary lights down on the main deck, but they are small and meant to illuminate approaching vessels, not a ship as far off as the one we are following."

"Sixty-five million dollars and this stupid boat don't have floodlights," Tony said. "What a gyp."

"You know that's a racist saying," Ben said. "Gyp. It's short for gypsy and comes from…" He trailed off as he saw the look Tony was giving him. "Never mind."

"You know why I want you up here, Blogger Boy?" Tony asked as he walked over and sat down right next to Ben so their hips were touching. "You know why I want you on the bridge with me instead of locked in that game room with the others?"

"Others minus Jessica and Maggie, you mean," Ben said.

"You want to get shot?" Tony asked.

"No, sorry," Ben said.

"I have you up here because I respect you," Tony said. "May not seem like it, but I do. I watched you play cards and you are as good as they say. But I know you've been around, seen some things, know some people, and you aren't exactly a virgin to this life."

"You want me up here because you're worried I'll pull something and figure out how to take you down," Ben said.

"What?" Tony laughed. "No. Not even close. Don't make me second guess my choice, Blogger Boy."

"Then why do you want me here with you?" Ben asked. "I'm too tired and stressed to figure it out on my own."

"Because I know the others below will try something," Tony said. "I need you to convince them not to when the time comes. To remind them that they have family members that are far from safe. You are persuasive with words." Tony waved his pistol back and forth. "I'm persuasive with this. I'd like to get through the next few hours without using this. I know I got some corrupt part of INTERPOL up my butt already. I don't need any of our poker friends' associates deciding a vendetta needs paying if harm comes to them."

"But you don't mind harming their families? Or mine?" Ben asked.

"I mind," Tony said. "I honestly do. I have family of my own."

"Then why not let us go?" Ben asked. "We could take the speedboats and get out of here."

"I wouldn't advise that in this weather," Captain Staggs said.

"He wouldn't advise that," Tony said and rolled his eyes. "But I don't care about the weather. Let's just say I'm keeping all of you around as insurance. I have some associates I recently met coming to take the ship off my hands once I confirm it holds what it is supposed to."

"But you trust those associates less than you trust me or the others below," Ben said. "Things go wrong and we're all forced to help you because of our family members. We're your back up."

"Something like that," Tony said.

"Answer me one question," Ben said. "Why did you need to do any of this? You come from a pretty big organization. Why not just keep it all in house and handle this on your own? I'm calculating the variables and you have increased your risk potential by infinity when you decided to use Nick and this poker game to make your play."

"You get along with everyone in your family, Blogger Boy?" Tony asked.

"Is that a serious question?" Ben responded.

"That's what I thought," Tony said and smiled. "Yeah, my organization is pretty damn big. It's also just like a family. More so than Garfield's organization or Whittier's or Holstein's. Closer to Romanski's, but even the Russians don't do family business like we do."

"You aren't supposed to be doing any of this, are you?" Ben laughed. "If this goes wrong then you'll have your whole family on your ass."

"Again, something like that," Tony said. "Did things get out of hand tonight? Yes. I'll admit that. But as long as the outcome ends up the way I want then you and the others have nothing to worry about. In fact, I may compensate you all for your troubles. My new associates may not be handing me a blank check, but it's pretty damn close, Blogger Boy. Pretty damn close."

"Boss? You there?" Mikey called out from the radio.

"Showtime," Tony said then frowned. He looked at Ben. "That too much? I've been reading some business blogs and they say you need to build a brand to be successful, no matter what your business is. Catch phrases and slogans are one way to do that. You think 'It's showtime' is good or too cliché?"

"If your brand is as an eighties movie villain then it's perfect," Ben said.

Tony laughed and shook a finger at him. "You do have balls, Blogger Boy. I'd cut them off and shove them in your smart mouth, but I did ask for your opinion."

"I like my balls where they are," Ben said.

"Don't we all," Tony said as he picked up the radio. "What you got, Mikey?"

34.

"We're in the ship, boss," Mikey said into the radio as he waved his rifle at Nick. "Get a move on, Sheeran. You're going first."

"What was that?" Tony asked over the radio.

"Nothing, boss," Mikey said. "Just telling Sheeran to hurry his ass up."

"It's dark as hell in here," Nick said as he opened a hatch and peered down into the deep blackness of the ship. "Anyone bring a flashlight?"

Chip stepped up and smacked one against his shoulder.

"Get going," Chip snarled and gave Nick a nudge with the barrel of his rifle. He glanced back at Niya. "Then you, lady. No way I'm moving around in the dark with you at my back."

"I don't have to be at your back to kill you," Niya said, but didn't argue as she stepped behind Nick.

The four of them descended the stairs to the next deck. Nick shone the light around and stumbled a little at the shock of what was before him.

"Is that blood?" Nick whispered. "Am I looking at blood? Because that's a lot of blood."

"Hey, boss?" Mikey called out. "Things already ain't right here."

"Didn't expect them to be," Tony said. "I was told the ship might be in some distress when we find it. Just follow the instructions I gave you and work your way to the fifth deck down. There should be a vault there. If we're lucky, someone will be there to meet you. Don't matter if they are or not. You know what you need to confirm, so confirm it and I'll make the call."

"Okay, boss," Mikey replied. "I'll call ya back when I know more."

"You do that," Tony said and the radio went silent.

Mikey tucked the radio into his belt then put both hands on his rifle. "Keep moving, Sheeran. This ain't the first time you've seen blood."

"Not this much blood, man," Nick said as he took a deep breath through his nose then shook his head. "Oh, man, that stinks. Is blood supposed to smell like that?"

"That's not just blood," Niya replied, her .45s out and in both hands. "That's death. I can smell piss and shit."

"Something else," Chip said.

Niya looked over her shoulder at the man and gave him a sweet smile.

"Yes, there is something else," Niya said. "What is it?"

"Pussy," Chip said. "Smells like pussy."

"Dude," Nick said. "Not the thing you say to a lady like Ms. Romanski."

"No, Mr. Sheeran, it's not," Niya said. "But I'm not going to faint because of it. I am well aware of what pussy smells like and Chip here is very wrong. You are smelling sea life. The fact you attributed it to female genitalia tells me that you probably don't have a serious girlfriend."

"That ain't true," Chip said. "I got a couple of them."

"Then my condolences to the women in your life," Niya said. Chip started to respond, but Niya held up one of the .45s. "Don't. We need to be quiet and pay attention."

"Yeah," Nick said as he swallowed hard and aimed the flashlight at the end of the blood-coated passageway. "Paying attention is good because I see a foot up ahead."

The four of them made their way slowly down the passageway, their shoes making loud squelching sounds in the sticky blood that had coagulated on the floor. With every step closer, Nick visibly stiffened until he was moving like a wooden robot.

"Let me take point," Niya said and moved in front of Nick. "But keep that flashlight aimed ahead. Can you handle that, Mr. Sheeran?"

"Yeah, yeah, I can handle that," Nick said.

Nick aimed the flashlight's beam directly at the foot that was clad in a heavy black boot. Niya approached the corner cautiously then swung around fast, both pistols up and ready. She shook her head and kicked at the foot. It rolled across the floor. Alone. Unconnected to a leg or a body.

"If you are upset by the blood in that passageway then I would advise you prepare to suck it up, boys," Niya said as she nodded at the passageway she faced. "It's about to get a lot worse."

Nick stopped where he stood, but a hard jab by Mikey's rifle got him moving again and he staggered around the corner, almost bumping into Niya. He lifted the flashlight, stared at the scene before him, then turned and threw up.

"That is not being prepared," Niya said.

Chip and Mikey came around the corner, rifles to their shoulders, faces set like granite. They both turned around and puked, adding their sick to Nick's pile. Niya grumbled then elbowed Nick in the ribs.

"Stand up and keep moving," Niya said. "We have three decks to cover."

"Great," Nick said, wiping his mouth with the back of his hand.

The passageway was littered with severed body parts. Boot-clad feet, bare feet, glove-clad hands, bare hands. Arms, full and partial; legs in the same shape. A head here, a dismembered torso there. And enough blood to keep a vampire happy for eternity.

"More stairs down that way," Mikey said, spitting on the floor again and again. "Get moving."

"Are none of you worried by any of this?" Nick asked. "These bodies were ripped apart, man. Ripped the fuck apart! How?"

"Not our problem," Chip said.

"Seriously, dude?" Nick snapped. "Not our problem is your answer? I'm thinking maybe you aren't appreciating exactly what we're seeing here!"

"Whoever did this might still be on board," Niya said to Nick. "You want to keep yelling and letting them know our position?"

"Well, no," Nick said. "But, still…" He waved the flashlight around.

"I see your point," Niya sighed. "But Mr. Giraldi is under the impression that we were to expect this. We keep moving and find this vault."

"Better be nothing but gold in that vault," Nick muttered as he carefully worked his way through the body parts, following directly behind Niya as the woman led the way. "And my yacht sale better be real when this is all done. Tony can't go back on that, right?"

"You are nothing if not single minded, Mr. Sheeran," Niya said. "You are also annoying. Quiet for the rest of the time or I slice your tongue out."

Nick almost replied, but clamped his mouth closed instead.

"Very good," Niya said. "Here are the stairs."

The flashlight showed a set of stairs just as bloody as the passageways behind them. No body parts, though, so other than the occasional slip of the heel, the way down to the next deck was uneventful.

They made their way through the next passageway and then the next before they came to something that made even Niya pull up short and gasp.

"What are they doing?" Chip asked. "Why are they like that?"

Niya kept her pistols up and trained on the eight bodies arranged on the passageway floor. They were seated in a circle and facing each other, their hands in their laps and their legs crossed. The problem was that none of the legs or arms matched the bodies they were attached to. None of the heads did either as facial skin tone clashed with the skin tone of the necks the heads were precariously perched on.

"Is this some serial killer cruise ship or what?" Nick asked.

Niya inched closer and closer then waved Nick forward. "I need light."

Reluctantly, Nick followed her until they both stood directly next to the macabre-looking tea party. Niya knelt down and studied the first body closely. She sniffed it and drew her head back quickly.

"There's something on them," Niya said.

She placed one of her pistols in its holster then reached out and ran her fingers across the jagged edges where the body's neck and head were joined together. She held up her fingers to the light, rubbing her thumb and forefinger together.

"More blood," Nick said.

"No, it's not blood," Niya replied.

"It looks like blood," Nick said.

"Is blood black?" Niya asked.

"What?" Nick replied and bent closer. "Oh. Yeah, I see what you mean. Not blood."

"What is it?" Mikey asked from the spot where he and Chip stood, several feet back and away from the circle of corpses.

"Ink," Niya said. "That pussy that you smelled? It's ink."

"Ink?" Nick asked. "Why the hell would there be ink on these bodies? Who would do that?"

"*What* would do that is a better question," Niya said, standing up. She held out her free hand. "Give me the radio."

"Can't do that," Mikey said. "You got something to say then you say it to me and I say it to Mr. Giraldi."

"Never mind," Niya said. "I have an idea of what is going on. I heard the same rumors as Mr. Giraldi, I just didn't act on them. Looks like my reticence didn't matter in the end."

"Want to fill me in?" Nick asked.

"No," Niya said. "But I suggest we retreat back to the speedboat and get away from this ship as soon as possible."

"That's not happening," Mikey said. He and Chip raised their rifles and took aim at Niya. They pretty much ignored Nick. "We keep going. I have been given a job to confirm the package for Mr. Giraldi. That's what we are going to do."

"Can't really confirm anything if you are dead," Niya said.

"We've been told the package is contained," Mikey said. "If I return without confirmation then Mr. Giraldi will gut me and toss me overboard." He waved his rifle at the bodies. "I don't know what did this, but it don't scare me as much as Mr. Giraldi."

Chip nodded in agreement.

"Contained?" Niya laughed. "Does this look contained?"

"Something bad happened, I ain't denying that," Mikey said. "But if Mr. Giraldi tells me the package is contained then the package is contained. You didn't have to come along, but you did, so that means you do what Mr. Giraldi wants."

"That's not what that means, but I'll keep playing along," Niya said. "Mr. Sheeran? You can stop shining the light on these poor men. They are dead. That has been confirmed. Let's go confirm that the package is contained like Mr. Giraldi believes it to be. Because confirmation will keep us safe according to the genius over here."

"This package, it's not gold, is it?" Nick asked. "And it likes to play with ink? Are we talking about a cyborg printing press or something?"

"You are a funny man," Niya said. "A complete coward, but funny nonetheless. If you live through all this, we may have to get drinks. I like funny men. We can work on the cowardice part."

"Drinks are good," Nick said. "Would now be a good time?"

"Shut up and walk," Mikey ordered.

"Right. Maybe later," Nick said. "We have to confirm that the ghost of Gutenberg the Ripper is still locked in his vault. Gotcha."

35.

Joey knocked a second time, waited for thirty seconds, then stepped away from the cabin door and kicked out hard, his foot hitting the spot right below the handle. The doorframe cracked and the door swung inward. Joey rushed inside, his rifle covering the cabin with a fast sweep to the right then back to the left.

"Nice," he said to himself as he saw Maggie lying on top of her bed, half naked in only her underwear and her butt up in the air. "I've had worse jobs to do."

Maggie snored loudly and there was a large pool of drool under her face. She mumbled something in her sleep then let out a small fart and giggled. Joey grimaced and took a step back.

"Gross," he said. "Chicks shouldn't fart."

"That so?" Jessica asked from behind him.

He swung around quickly enough to knock the pistol from Jessica's hand, but not fast enough to block Jessica's elbow as it hit him square in the jaw, sending him spinning further into the cabin and slamming against a dresser hard enough to put a dent in the very expensive wood. He kept hold of his rifle, but couldn't get it up in time to ward off the oncoming woman.

Jessica knocked the rifle to the side with her left hand then kept her momentum going, clocking Joey in the temple with her right elbow. Joey had a good foot in height and at least a hundred pounds on Jessica, but there was not much the man could do against a well-placed elbow shot. He rolled along the edge of dresser then fell to a knee, his rifle slipping from his stunned grasp and sliding away across the smooth carpet.

A heavy boot came at his face, but he dodged to the side, his shoulder catching the heel instead of his cheek. He collapsed with his back against the dresser and barely managed to cross his arms in front of him and stop the next kick aimed right for his throat. Joey twisted his hands around from their crossed position and grabbed Jessica by the leg. He threw himself to the side, using all his weight to take Jessica with him.

Her leg firmly in Joey's grasp, Jessica had no choice but to tuck her shoulder and go into the roll as the large man spun her about. As her shoulder hit the ground, Joey got his legs up underneath him and launched himself upright. He still had Jessica's leg and he yanked on it hard as he walked backwards towards the cabin door.

Maggie grumbled and farted again and Joey gave her a harsh look.

"I'll teach you how to be a lady when I'm done with this bitch," Joey said as he reached the doorway.

That was as far as he got before he was forced to his knees after Jessica's other boot landed right in his crotch. Joey's face went green as he grunted and involuntarily grabbed for his badly bruised nuts. Two more elbows to the face and he was on his back out in the passageway.

Joey gasped for breath and struggled to keep from throwing up. The woman wasn't big, by any stretch of the imagination, but she was pissed off and knew exactly how to land a kick to the balls. Joey reluctantly flipped himself over onto his stomach and crawled as far and fast as he could manage. Which was about four feet before Jessica came out into the passageway with Joey's rifle to her shoulder.

"Shit!" Joey cried as he rolled to the side, bullets tearing up the floor where he'd just been.

"Did you say you were going to teach that woman how to be a lady?" Jessica shouted as she fired again.

Joey was able to roll out of the line of fire once more and landed with his back against the wall. He reached inside his suit jacket and pulled out his .45, but he didn't get a shot off as pain exploded in his legs. He screamed as slug after slug tore into his thighs. He screamed a second time as a burning hot muzzle was shoved against his scalp, the metal singing his hair and scorching his skin.

"Did Giraldi send you down here to rape innocent women?" Jessica asked. "Or was that you taking your own initiative?"

Joey grimaced and gritted his teeth as he watched his blood flow from his wounds and pool under his legs.

"I asked you a question!" Jessica shouted.

"Shit, okay, okay!" Joey yelled. "I thought that was a rhetorical question!"

"Do I seem like I'm in a rhetorical mood, asshole?" Jessica snarled, pressing the rifle harder into Joey's scalp. "Does the sound of me squeezing this trigger sound at all rhetorical to you?"

Joey pissed himself when he heard the dry click of the rifle's trigger. Then the fact he wasn't dead sunk in and he lifted his .45 at Jessica.

"Shit," she said as she threw herself backwards.

Joey fired six shots at her, but missed every one as they went too high and ended up just ripping hunks of wood from the ceiling. He adjusted his aim as Jessica scrambled on hands and feet towards the open cabin.

"You want to play word games, bitch?" Joey snarled as he fired and Jessica screamed. "I'll play word games."

The woman was lost from his sight as she crawled into Maggie's cabin. Joey had counted eight shots and knew he only had three left in the pistol, one in the chamber and two in the magazine. He ejected the magazine and grabbed a fresh one from his belt, but fumbled and dropped it as pain rolled through the gunshot wounds in his legs.

Joey took a couple of deep breaths and reached for the magazine which was lying in the massive pool of blood that had formed underneath him. He almost had the magazine when it was snatched away from him.

"What the hell?" he whispered as he tried to make sense of what had just happened. "That was a... What was that?"

He craned his neck and his eyes went wide as he watched a long, thick tentacle pull the magazine into the cracked open air vent above him in the ceiling. The tentacle was lost from sight and all Joey could do was stare at the spot where it had been, his mind refusing to admit he saw what he saw.

"That ain't right," he said as he grabbed at the last magazine on his belt.

He had a hard time getting it free and looked down quickly. When he got it and slapped it into the waiting pistol, he turned his attention back to the vent and nearly screamed as he saw a huge eyeball watching him. Everything around the eyeball was pitch black, but a kind of black that didn't quite fit the shadows of the vent.

Slowly, hoping not to draw attention to what he was doing, Joey brought his pistol up and aimed it at the eyeball. He never got a shot off as two tentacles came shooting down at him. One grabbed his wrist and snapped it, while the other snagged the pistol and threw it down the passageway so that it clattered against the wall at the far end, well out of reach.

"Oh shit, oh shit, oh shit, oh shit," Joey said.

The tentacles hovered around him then darted down and rolled their tips in his blood. They withdrew instantly and Joey heard a soft slurping noise. If he hadn't already pissed himself, he would have then as three tentacles came for him.

He screamed and screamed and screamed as he was lifted into the air. Four other tentacles whipped past him and coated themselves in the pool of blood on the floor. They withdrew when not an inch of their rubbery skin was visible. Joey hung there in the passageway, suspended in air by three tentacles, screaming his head off as the slurping sound above increased and intensified.

Then his left leg was gone. Gone. Torn right from his hip with a wet popping noise that made him throw up more than the pain of getting kicked in the balls ever could. Not that the pain of losing his leg wasn't enough to turn his stomach, but he'd heard a lot of things in his career and the popping of a leg out of a pelvis was a new one. Especially since it was his own leg.

His hands went to the gushing wound where his left leg had been and he pressed his palms against the opening, some part of his brain telling him that if he just stopped the bleeding he'd be alright. That part of his brain shorted out when his right leg met the same fate as his left.

He flailed at the tentacles that were tearing into him. He slapped at their strange skin, clawed at the suckers that opened and closed while they tasted his blood. He tried to dig his fingernails into one, but he couldn't find any purchase as the tentacle just warped and collapsed under his grip without any damage done.

When his left arm was yanked free from his shoulder, Joey's conscious mind decided that a vacation was in order. All rational thought left him and for some reason the image of the huge elm tree that was in the front yard of his childhood home burst into his mind. He could see that tree as plain as if it was right there in the passageway with him. Its green leaves fluttering in the summer breeze. He could smell freshly mowed grass and the hint of honeysuckle.

Then his right arm was torn off and he was brought painfully back to reality. His head slumped as the strength began to leave his body. Joey's chin met his chest and he could feel his heart slowing, slowing, stuttering. A small movement caught the last of his attention and he shifted his gaze to his right.

Jessica was peeking from around the doorway of Maggie's cabin, her eyes wide with horrified disbelief, her pistol limp in her hand.

Then everything went dark as his limbless body was pulled up through the vent in the ceiling. Of course, his body was too big for the opening, so a good part of him was crushed and mangled as the incredible strength of the creature in the ceiling continued to pull and pull until he was finally up inside duct work, his torso reunited with his severed limbs.

36.

Every single inch of the passageway's floor outside the vault was covered by body parts. Not in a haphazard way, but in a deliberate, jigsaw puzzle complexity where each part was nestled perfectly against the next.

Nick, Niya, Mikey, and Chip stood at the end of the passageway, none of them brave enough to set foot off the stairs onto the floor, and stared with open mouths at the scene. The vault was only a few yards away, but may have been miles distant for all the observers cared.

"The package is in there?" Nick asked. "In that vault? The vault that's standing open in the middle of Jeffrey Dahmer's personal game of Tetris? Well, I wish you all good luck. I'm getting the fuck out of here now."

"You're staying right here, Sheeran," Mikey said and pressed the barrel of his rifle into the small of Nick's back. "In fact, you get to go first."

"Ms. Romanski called point," Nick said. "And I have always been a ladies first kind of gentlemen. It's not exactly fashionable in the Pacific Northwest; in fact, you can get your ass handed to you for it, but I guess I'm old fashioned when it comes to manners."

"That pussy smell is now you, Mr. Sheeran," Niya said as she knelt on the stairs and plucked a small flashlight from the grip of a severed hand.

Flashlight on, she placed one foot down on a split open torso and tested its stability. The torso held her weight and she took another step, her other foot coming down on a thigh. Cautiously, placing every step with careful planning, Niya made it halfway to the vault before she turned around and gave the three men a reproachful look.

"You will be joining me," Niya said. "Or I explain to Mr. Giraldi that the men he has hired are spineless and weak."

"I'll totally own up to those names," Nick said. "Even if I don't work for Giraldi. Spineless and weak I can live with." He flapped his hands at the horror puzzle before him. "This shit? Nope. Big, fat nope. Not living with this."

"Then you can die," Mikey said as the barrel of the rifle moved from the small of Nick's back to the depression at the base of his skull.

"Not if you want to get off this ship," Nick said and slowly raised his hand. "Only one that can pilot the speedboat, remember?"

"We'll figure it out," Mikey said.

"Yeah, we'll figure it out," Chip echoed.

"Get your goddamn asses off those stairs and over here," Niya snarled as she pointed her flashlight and a .45 at the men. "All three of you or I drop you right here and you can become part of this morbid art installation."

Nick grumbled and mumbled obscenities as he stepped onto the bodies, trying to follow the path Niya had already taken. His left foot slipped in a rib cage and he pulled it out quickly, but ended up losing his balance and tumbling over into an elaborate arrangement of forearms and middle fingers.

Coated in blood and gore, Nick started crawling his way across the bodies until he was resting against the open door of the vault.

"I win," he gasped as he tried to wipe congealed blood from his face, but only ended up smearing it around and making it worse. "Oh, Jesus Christ, this is nasty. So nasty."

Mikey and Chip were a little more capable in their journey, but both still ended up taking a fall or two and were nearly as gore splattered as Nick when they reached the vault. Niya shook her head and gracefully walked past them all into the vault, her .45 up, with flashlight held underneath, both pointed ahead of her.

"Watch above," she said as the stepped into the cavernous space. "There's a hatch over that tank."

"Tank?" Nick asked as he followed her inside. "All of this is over a tank? Shit, I could of found you guys a tank. I know a guy in Israel that has like three on hand right now." He stopped talking as he saw the huge tank of bloody saltwater that occupied a good amount of the vault's space. "Oh, that kind of tank."

"I am not surprised to see this here," Niya said. "Not after finding the ink."

"The tank is open!" Mikey exclaimed and he spun around in a slow circle, his rifle jerking this way and that. "The package is loose! The package is loose!"

He fumbled his radio from his belt, but ended up dropping it into a thick pool of blood at his feet.

"Are you serious?" Niya asked as she walked back to him and retrieved the radio from the blood. She wiped it on her tights then clicked the transmitter button three times.

"What do you have for me, Mikey?" Tony's voice asked.

"It's Niya," Niya replied. "And we have an empty saltwater tank. Your package is not here."

"I wouldn't call that tank empty," Nick said. "There's certainly something floating in there." He walked towards the tank while Niya continued on with the radio conversation.

"I assume the package was some type of octopus?" Niya asked. "And not your usual sushi menu variety?"

"To be honest, I wasn't sure," Tony responded. "Yeah, I was told it was some genetic engineering project that was hijacked, making it that much easier for me to boost, but I never was told what kind of animal they were playing with. All I was told was to wait for the signal."

"You didn't think that was important?" Niya mocked. "That perhaps knowing that you were acquiring a creature with incredible intelligence, physical strength and dexterity, and camouflage ability might be good info to have?"

"I know it's worth nine figures," Tony said.

Niya had been following behind Nick, but the mention of nine figures stopped her in her tracks.

"High or low?" Niya asked.

"Very high," Tony said. "Almost ten figures."

"That's high," Nick said over his shoulder as he approached the tank. He stopped a few feet from it and shone his flashlight against the glass, but the beam only reflected back at him. "Crap. Gonna have to climb that ladder."

"You've been shitting bricks for the past hour, but now you're going to climb right up in that tank?" Mikey asked. "There is something wrong with you."

"I have been told that on more than a dozen occasions," Nick said as he took a deep breath and walked to the ladder on the side of the tank.

"Be careful," Niya called after him.

"The tank is empty, right?" Nick replied. "I mean, something big enough to take out a ship filled with heavily armed men would be easy to spot hanging out in its aquarium, yeah?"

"Did you not hear me say that an octopus is a master at camouflage?" Niya responded.

Nick paused halfway up the ladder.

"So it could still be in there?" Nick asked. "Just waiting for me to grab onto whatever this big thing floating in here is?"

"Yes," Niya replied.

"Okay then," Nick said and started to climb back down.

"Tell him I have Blogger Boy with me. He keeps climbing or I shoot his friend," Tony announced from the radio. "What was he doing?"

"He was about to fish out a corpse from the tank," Niya said.

Nick took a second look at the thing floating in the saltwater and shivered. "That's a corpse? Shit. I didn't think it was a corpse."

"What did you think it was?" Niya asked.

"I don't know," Nick said. "Not a corpse."

"Grab it," Mikey ordered. "You heard what the boss said, grab it or the blogger gets a bullet."

"He's not that good of a blogger to keep calling him that," Nick said. "He's great at cards, but is a barely passable writer."

There was a garbled response on the radio.

"What was that?" Niya asked.

"The blogger heard that and says for Nicholas to go suck his own dick," Tony laughed. The laugh stopped quickly. "But, yes, get the corpse out of the water. Now."

"Shit," Nick said as he reached the top of the ladder and leaned over the tank. "This is gonna suck."

The body floating in the water was draped in a white lab coat, but that was about all the detail Nick could make out. It was no wonder he didn't recognize it as a corpse considering how warped and twisted it was. It almost looked like something had tied the limbs together. But that wouldn't be possible without pulverizing the bones inside each.

Nick felt like he was quite the hero for not throwing up again as he snagged the lab coat and pulled the body to the edge of the tank. He was also fairly proud of himself for not falling into the bloody water either.

"Gonna need some help," Nick said as he yanked and yanked at the corpse, but couldn't get the leverage to get it out of the saltwater.

"Leave…it…"

"Oh my shit!" Nick yelled as he nearly fell from the ladder. He grabbed onto the top rung and spun around. "Did you guys hear that?"

"Yes," Niya said as she moved quickly over to a pile of bodies stacked against the wall. She stared at the bodies until one of the heads blinked back at her. "Here!"

Mikey and Chip hurried over and helped pull the man from the pile. None of them looked surprised to see him missing his legs from below the knees. They did look surprised when they spotted the makeshift tourniquets on the man's thighs.

"Who are you?" Niya asked, kneeling next to the man as she eased him onto the floor. "What happened here?"

"Wagner," Wagner replied. "Leave…the…body… The thing…won't…like you…touching it."

"Good enough reason for me," Nick said and jumped down from the ladder. "I really don't want to be here when whatever it is comes back." He looked at Wagner. "The thing is gone, right?"

"Yes," Wagner whispered. "Up."

They all looked up at the closed hatch above the tank.

"Up where?" Nick asked. "Because there's no up here."

"It…closed…the hatch," Wagner said. "Put…Glouster in its…cave…then left."

"Put Glouster in its cave then left," Nick said. "Yep. Totally makes sense."

"Shut up," Niya snapped and her .45 centered on Nick's chest without her turning her attention from Wagner. "Who made it?"

"O…A…S…" Wagner replied.

"You're OAS?" Niya asked. "You don't look OAS."

"What's OAS?" Nick asked.

"Shut the hell up," Mikey ordered, his rifle joining Niya's pistol in the pointing at Nick's chest.

Nick held up his hands and took a couple of steps back.

"N…C…D…C…" Wagner said. "I… Stole…creature…"

"Now we're getting somewhere," Niya said. "This very much looks like NCDC's style. Too much blood for OAS."

"At the risk of getting shot, would someone please tell me what's going on?" Nick asked.

Before anyone could respond or shoot him, a loud clanging and thud from far above echoed down through the ship to them.

Niya looked at Nick. "What was that?"

"How should I know?" Nick asked.

"Go check it out," Niya said to Mikey and Chip. "I think we're being boarded."

"We don't answer to you," Mikey said.

"Mr. Giraldi?" Niya asked into the radio.

"Yes?" Tony replied. "What did you find?"

"OAS project stolen by NCDC," Niya said.

"I don't know what any of that means," Tony replied. "But sounds expensive."

Niya shook her head and let loose with several long phrases in Ukrainian that didn't sound like she was praising Tony's intelligence. "What do you see? I believe we have company, so some eyes would be helpful."

"We don't see anything," Tony responded. "No, wait. Hold on. What is that? Let me get back to you."

"No, I need you to tell your men to listen to me and go check it out," Niya said. She waited for a response, but none came. "Giraldi? Giraldi!"

"See? We don't work for you," Mikey said.

Niya dropped the radio on top of Wagner's chest and pulled her other .45. Mikey didn't even come close to getting his rifle swung around before a slug went sailing past his cheek.

"I don't miss," Niya said. "Go see what's up on deck or you are useless to me."

"I'm going," Chip said, backing out the vault quickly.

"Smart man," Niya said. "Mikey? Are you a smart man?"

"You and me, babe," Mikey said as he followed Chip. "When this is over, it's you and me."

"Looking forward to it," Niya said. She waited until they were out of the vault then relaxed and put her pistol back in its holster. She looked up at Nick.

"Hi," Nick said, giving her a short wave. "Mind if I stay down here?"

"Not at all," Niya said. "You can help me search this vault."

"For what?" Nick asked.

"For the real treasure," Niya said. "Research. Look for files or computers. Maybe USB drives or a tablet or something."

"Fun," he said as he stared at the gore that coated everything. He nudged a stray hand with his foot. "Super fun."

He continued nudging things with his foot, refusing to dig his hands in the gore for a real search. He pushed a hacked apart thigh to the side and blinked a few times as he looked at the USB drive that just sat there. Nick knelt and snatched up the drive, jamming it in his pocket.

"Hey!" Niya called out, causing Nick to jump a foot in the air. "I found something."

She held up a tablet and grinned. The grin slipped slightly.

"What?" Niya asked. "Did you find something as well? What is it?"

"I found that no matter how beautiful the company, I can still embarrass myself by nearly pissing my pants," Nick said. "Warn a guy before you call out like that."

Niya sighed and shook her head. "Weak," she muttered as she pulled out a USB drive of her own and plugged it into the tablet. "This will only take a minute then we leave."

"What about Giraldi's men?" Nick asked.

There were some loud shouts and couple of gunshots.

"I do not believe they are our problem any longer," Niya said, grinning from ear to ear.

37.

Jessica pressed herself up against the wall of the shower, her hand to her arm as blood flowed from the gunshot wound. With every creak and groan of the ship, she jumped a little and had to bite down on the inside of her cheek in order to not cry out in fear and pain.

She looked past the glass door at the underwear glad rump of Maggie. Jessica had dragged the unconscious woman into the bathroom, gotten her into the bathtub, and locked the bathroom door before hiding herself in the shower. Maggie hadn't made a peep the entire time, only rolled onto her stomach and pushed her butt in the air. Every passed out drunk was different. Jessica had learned that in her many years navigating an underworld run by idiots and men. She barely distinguished between the two.

She shifted her weight, trying to find a comfortable position, but each movement sent waves of pain through her. She knew she needed to tie off the wound, but she was afraid the pain would be too much and she'd pass out. Getting Maggie into the bathroom was a product of the adrenaline that had been pumping through her. But that adrenaline was gone, or the strength part was, at least. Instead, she felt a heaviness caused by fear and shock start to overtake her.

There was a creak from above and Jessica's eyes instantly went to the air vent in the center of the bathroom's ceiling. She watched closely, waiting for the vent to be shoved open and one of those hideous tentacles to come out at her. Or at Maggie. Jessica realized she could put herself in the idiot category. She'd left the woman out there unprotected.

Hell, she wasn't even protected. The thing was in the ventilation system. How could anyone hide from that?

Jessica forced herself to think through the terror she felt overcoming her. She'd been in worse situations. Nearly beaten to death by Somali pirates. Tortured by a Columbian drug lord. Physically violated for days by a woman that never did tell her her name. Left to be sold as a sex slave in Malaysia. Even buried alive in the African savannah.

She'd lived and fought her way back to the top each and every time.

So, what, she'd let some mutant calamari freak her out?

Jessica pressed her back harder against the shower stall and then pushed up with her legs, carefully coming to a standing position as her eyes stayed locked on the vent, her pistol held at her side.

Another creak, louder than before, and Jessica froze. She counted to ten, counted to ten again, then slowly pushed open the shower door. Being of the quality it was, the shower door swung open like it was made of air; not a hint of a hinge squeak.

She set one foot out onto the bathroom floor, waited, counted to ten twice more, then set the other foot out. Jessica held her breath, her ears trying to parse what was the thing and what was just the boat's normal noises as it rocked in the ocean's waves.

Waves that seemed to be getting stronger by the minute, Jessica discovered as she had to brace her pistol hand against the ornately decorated wood paneling of the bathroom's wall. A part of her was sort of pissed that the blogger and his girlfriend, that couldn't handle her drinks, were given a better cabin than she was. Her bathroom wasn't nearly as nice.

Jessica smiled to herself as the thoughts flitted away. Some of her old strength was returning if she could waste a moment's thought on trivialities like whose bathroom was better.

A creak and heavy groan, but not above her.

In the wall.

Jessica turned slowly, her eyes tracking where her ears thought the sounds came from. By the linen closet then over the sink. Under the sink, under the floor, in the wall behind her.

"Too big," she thought to herself. "It's too big to be in the walls."

A cabinet exploded open and two tentacles shot at her from her left. Jessica dove to the side, her pistol falling from her weak grip, and screamed as she felt one of the tentacles grab her around the ankle. She twisted in its grasp, kicking at it with her free leg. But that free leg was quickly grabbed and she found herself being yanked towards the shattered cabinet and what looked like a huge parrot's beak.

Instinct kicked in and Jessica's hands scrambled about for anything she could use as a weapon. Her right hand closed around a hunk of wood, thick on one end, sharp and pointed on the other. She was glad for her almost religious need to work out, and bent up at the waist, jamming the giant splinter into the tentacle that had her right leg.

Blue blood spilled out across the floor and the tentacle darted out of sight, withdrawn almost faster than Jessica could track. The other tentacle tightened its grip and there was nothing Jessica could do since her makeshift weapon had been yanked away from her by the wounded tentacle.

Her body reached the cabinet and she braced her free leg on the frame. She pushed as hard as she could, but the tentacle that had her was so much stronger than her fatigued leg. Still bent at the waist, she clawed at the tentacle around her ankle, her nails digging deep furrows in the rubbery skin.

Before her eyes, she watched as those furrows filled in with fresh tissue then disappeared completely as the thing healed in less than a couple of seconds. The shock of watching that happen sapped her of her remaining strength and she screamed as her body was bent in ways it wasn't meant to be bent.

She was pulled inside the cabinet and towards the huge parrot beak. Her screams continued for several minutes until the blood loss was too much and she passed out, her life slipping away in a flow of dark red across the expensive marble-tiled floor.

38.

Tony pointed out into the dark night with one hand while the other gripped Captain Staggs's shoulder like a vice.

"You get us closer," Tony ordered. "I saw something land on that ship and I want to know what it is."

"I cannot get us any closer without risking a collision," Captain Staggs said. "I don't know if you have noticed or not, Mr. Giraldi, but we are not being blessed with calm seas. These waves are at least six feet and growing stronger."

"Do I seem like a man that cares about your excuses?" Tony snarled. "Do you think I didn't do my homework on you too, Cap? One phone call and everyone you care about gets their throats slit."

Captain Staggs, hands firmly grasping the ship's wheel, turned and gave Tony a stern look. It was the look of an angry school teacher or football coach. It was the look of a person that was used to having authority over his small domain.

"I have a brother and he is currently doing five years in prison for embezzlement," Captain Staggs said. "I haven't spoken to him in two years. If he dies, I will assume it is you, but it is not like I wouldn't be expecting the call. He stole money from bad people and his clock has been ticking down for a long time now."

"Look at you, Cap," Tony laughed. "I never thought you'd have brass balls so big."

"It's a nice yacht," Captain Staggs said. "Everything is brass and everything is big."

Ben snorted from his spot on the bench then tried to act casual as Tony turned on him.

"Something to add?" Tony asked.

"No," Ben said. "Sorry."

Tony pressed his thumb to his radio's transmitter. He started to speak, but a squeal of static roared from the radio and Tony quickly let it drop from his hand onto the dash before him.

"What the hell?" he muttered as he picked the radio back up. He turned down the volume and tried again, but the static was still there only quieter. "Radio is dead."

"Probably jammed," Ben said, nodding out the window. "If that was a helicopter that you saw landing on the ship then it wasn't a sightseeing tour. No lights, able to fly in this weather, and landing on a ship that is holding some special killer project? I'm thinking black ops. CIA? NSA? Something like that."

"That what you're thinking, Blogger Boy?" Tony asked. "Based on what? All your years of experience in covert intelligence?"

"No," Ben said and shrugged. "I watch a lot of History Channel programs."

Tony's lip curled up in a vicious-looking snarl and he shook his head.

"You are a strange man," Tony said. "Hard to get a read on. You seem soft then you talk shit. You act hard then fold the second things get violent. Back and forth, back and forth."

"I'm a mystery," Ben said. "So my ex-wife has said a trillion times."

"You said the Guillotine had your daughter, yes?" Tony asked.

"Yeah," Ben said. "Agent Mulgrew said he was your man."

"Not my man," Tony said. "Which means he's someone else's man." Tony pointed out the window in the direction of the NCDC ship. "I'm betting he's whoever just landed's man. Why?"

"What? How should I know?" Ben asked.

"Because you are the key to all of this," Tony said, spreading his arms wide. "I needed a ride out here to find this ship without arousing suspicion. Your friend Nicholas had this yacht available and I suddenly get an invitation. Nicholas set up a poker game with you as the draw and several power players in the underworld came to play cards with you. One of the most deadly assassins in the business has been sent to watch your daughter."

"To kill my daughter if I get out of line," Ben said.

"Is that so?" Tony asked. "The man isn't working for the rogue INTERPOL agents, he's not working for me, and I can guarantee you he's not working for Garfield, Whittier, or Holstein."

"Maybe Niya," Ben suggested.

"No, I doubt that even more than the others," Tony said. "Ms. Romanski does not deal with men like the Guillotine. She prefers to keep things in house, as do I. As do the others, from what I know of their reputations. The Guillotine has been hired by someone else, Mr. Clow. And I will wager everything I have that that someone else is connected to that helicopter that landed on that ship."

"I feel like we're in an eighties detective show," Ben said. "All the wild guesses are being thrown out there before the big reveal. Care to make another guess as to what the reveal is?"

"No," Tony said. "I'm done guessing. It's time you started talking."

Tony slid a very large knife from inside his suit jacket. He made sure Ben saw the fine edge it held.

"Hey, hey, hey!" Ben yelled. "I have no idea what's going on! I swear to fucking God, man!"

"I actually believe you," Tony said. "But I also still believe you are at the center of all of this somehow. You're an asset whether you know it or not. And in my experience? Assets are never left alone without a handler."

"You're crazy, dude," Ben said as he looked around the bridge for an escape. But Tony's body language showed him that no matter how fast he thought he was, the big man was faster. His eyes lit on Captain Staggs. "Captain? A little help?"

"I let go of this wheel and we all die," Captain Staggs said. "Get yourself out of your own mess, Mr. Clow."

"Great," Ben grumbled. "Just great. Nice attitude, asshole."

39.

In the bathtub, butt still at full attention, Maggie stirred.

The voices in her ear told her Ben was in serious trouble, but the heavy smell of blood told her she wasn't exactly out of the woods, either. Slowly, still acting as if she was completely shitfaced, she rolled onto her side and cracked one eye open. From the sound of how everything went down, Maggie knew what she would see.

The bathroom was a shambles, destroyed. Mirrors cracked, cabinets broken, blood everywhere.

She eased her hand to her head, making it look like she was nursing a brutal headache, and carefully pressed her finger to her ear, muting the shouting she heard coming from Giraldi and Ben. It broke her heart that Ben was being harmed for something he knew nothing about, but that was the risk of the job she'd taken. She'd known she was putting a good man in a bad situation.

With the shouting muted, Maggie listened hard for sounds of the creature's movements. After a couple of very long minutes, she guessed it had left to go find new prey, leaving her alone for some reason. Probably because she'd made sure she was doused in the stink of alcohol and piss. The piss part hadn't been fun and she cringed at the yellow puddle that was underneath her in the tub, but she knew it had probably saved her life.

Unlike Giraldi, Maggie had known exactly what she would encounter during the operation. She just hadn't known Giraldi would make things so difficult for her.

Her eyes watching the blood-covered, shattered cabinet carefully, Maggie pushed up into a sitting position. Again, she listened and waited a couple of minutes for tentacles to come flying out at her. When they didn't, she pressed her fingers on a hard spot just above the inside of her left ankle. She held it for three seconds, let go, held it for three more seconds, then let go again.

After three seconds, the hard spot under her skin vibrated for five full seconds then stopped.

They'd arrived. Her team was in place.

She started to unmute her earpiece to hear how bad things were for Ben, but she didn't get the chance as a tentacle burst from the air vent in the ceiling and grabbed her about the wrist. Maggie screamed and lurched back, her butt hitting the huge faucet on the side of the bathtub. Scalding hot water came pouring out instantly and she screamed again as the water hit the bare skin on her legs.

White hot pain ripped through her like an electric jolt causing her to pull hard against the tentacle and jump back from the faucet as fast as possible. The angle of her body brought the tentacle directly under the stream of boiling water and there was a clicking hiss from above. The tentacle detached itself immediately and withdrew back into the vent.

Maggie bit down on her lower lip as she endured the agony of the water, her eyes locked onto the vent. After almost thirty seconds, she couldn't take the pain anymore and shut the water off. Maggie waited with her hand gripping the faucet's hot water handle, ready to turn it back on the second even a hint of an octopus body part showed itself.

Twenty seconds, forty, a full minute went by before she dared to stand up and take a cautious step out of the tub. When nothing came for her, she hurried from the bathroom and into the cabin. She grabbed her suitcase out of the closet, tossed it onto the bed, and started ripping the bottom seam open.

With the material gone, she placed her hand against the cold metal of the suitcase's bottom and a hatch popped open. She pulled out a Browning 9mm pistol, a small metal box, and a thin wire with a black circle attached. Maggie put the wire around her neck with the circle directly over her voice box. She pressed her earpiece, but instead of the sounds of Ben screaming, she heard the chatter of gruff voices.

"This is Hoedown," Maggie said out loud. "Do you copy?"

"We copy, Hoedown," a voice replied in her ear. "This is Tumbler. We are in place on the NCDC vessel."

"Get off there," Maggie said. "The creature is no longer in place. It is active and on the Lucky Sucker."

"Shit, seriously?" Tumbler responded. "You okay?"

"Not sure," Maggie said. "It's already killed two people and came close to grabbing me. I need you and the rest to get over here and help me with containment as soon as you are done there."

"We're leaving right now," Tumbler responded.

"Negative," Maggie said. "The mission is to obtain the creature as well as all pertinent research files. You search that ship first, find those files, then come get me."

"Come on, Hoedown," Tumbler said. "All we need is the creature. We'll let the lab geeks study it. We're coming to get you."

"No!" Maggie snapped as she pulled a large combat knife from the compartment under the suitcase and set it on the bed. She flipped the suitcase upright and pulled out a pair of jeans. "I am giving you an order, Tumbler. You find the files then torch the ship before you even think of coming to get me."

"Roger that, Hoedown," Tumbler replied. "We'll move fast and be there shortly. Stay safe and keep the thing occupied until we can contain it."

Maggie slid on her jeans and glanced up at the vent in the cabin ceiling. She fumbled around and found a t-shirt then slipped that over her head.

"I don't think keeping it occupied is a problem," Maggie responded. "As long as someone is alive on this yacht, it's going to stay right here."

"Copy that," Tumbler said. "We'll be in contact. Tumbler out."

There was an audible click and the earpiece instantly switched back to its original channel. Ben's screams filled Maggie's ears and she winced.

"I am so sorry, Benjamin," she whispered as she strapped the knife to her thigh and looked around the room for her shoe bag. She found it, yanked it open, and pulled out a pair of heavy duty black sneakers.

Shoes on, knife on her thigh, pistol in her hand, Maggie moved slowly to the cabin door, which was wide open and smeared with blood. She peeked into the passageway, confirmed it was clear, then started moving in the direction of the bridge and Ben's pleading voice.

40.

"You hear that?" Carlos asked Lane. "Is that someone yelling?"

Lane cocked his head and listened. "No, that's someone screaming."

He laid down his hand and gave Carlos a huge grin.

"Gin, mate," Lane announced as he reached across the bar and grabbed a bottle of Bombay Sapphire. "And more gin."

"You have to be cheating," Carlos said as he laid his cards down and separated out the ones that he didn't have a set for. "But even when cheating you only get six points off me."

"I don't cheat," Lane said. "Not at cards." He wiggled his fingers. "Don't have the dexterity to stack the deck. I tried once and had all kinds of hell beat out of me."

"Lucky you didn't get killed," Carlos said. "Where I come from, cards are a very serious business."

"Yeah, well, my mum stepped in before my dad could do some real damage," Lane replied. "Learned a valuable lesson, though."

"Don't cheat at cards?" Carlos laughed.

"Not to play cards with my dad unless I had a can of pepper spray on me," Lane said. "Cheating or not, the man hated to lose."

Carlos laughed again and picked up the cards, splitting them into two piles. As his hands tensed to shuffle, a loud scraping noise came from directly below the bar.

"You hear that?" Carlos asked.

"How much have you had to drink, mate?" Lane asked. "Because you just asked me that question."

"No, not the screaming, the other noise," Carlos said.

"Lots of noises on this yacht," Lane replied as he poured Carlos half a glass of vodka then reached back over the bar for ice. "Dammit. The bucket's empty."

"Shhh," Carlos said, setting the cards down.

"Don't shhh me," Lane snapped as he got up to walk around the bar. "Bucket's out of ice, mate. This is an emergency."

There was a thump directly under Carlos's bar stool and he jumped to his feet, taking several steps back from the bar as he looked around. His eyes fell on Manny's body, who was miraculously hanging on to life by a thread. He dismissed the nearly dead man and kept searching the room.

"Something spook you?" Lane asked as he scooped ice from a small maker behind the bar into the empty silver bucket he had in hand. "You need a hug, mate? A shoulder to cry on while we piss away our time out on this scary, scary ocean?"

"Fuck you," Carlos said, nodding at the bar. "I felt something. There any knives back there?"

Lane held up a paring knife.

"Yes," Lane said. "It has already killed three limes and is about to slaughter another one."

The thump came again and the smirk on Lane's face faltered.

"Ha!" Carlos exclaimed. "You felt that, didn't you?"

"Yes," Lane said and slowly walked out from behind the bar, bucket of ice in one hand, paring knife in the other. "What was that?"

"Give me the knife," Carlos said.

"Like bloody hell I will," Lane replied. "This little guy could save my life."

They both stood there, next to the poker table with the nearly dead INTERPOL agent slowly bleeding to death on it, and stared at the bar.

A third thump and one of the bar stools fell over.

"Time to pick the lock," Lane said. "Odds or evens?"

"What?" Carlos asked.

"Odds or evens?" Lane said again. "To see who picks the lock."

"Odds," Carlos replied.

Lane looked at his occupied hands and set the ice bucket on the card table next to Manny's head. He held up a clenched fist and Carlos did the same. They shook their fists down three times then each extended a single finger.

"Evens," Lane said and grinned. "You go pick the lock."

"No, no, no," Carlos said. "I said odds. If we'd shook odds then I would pick the lock."

"Bullshit," Lane argued. "The winner gets to choose. I won with evens, so you pick the lock."

A fourth thump and another bar stool fell to the ground. The two men watched as the floor under the stools started to bow and bend upward.

"We both do it," Carlos said and sprinted to the closed game room doors.

He slid off his shoe, fished around inside, and pulled out a small packet. Lane had started to do the same, but stopped when he saw Carlos had beaten him to it. Instead, he spun about and held the paring knife out in front of him, aiming the tip at the still-bending floorboards.

"Come on, mate," Lane said.

"I am," Carlos replied as he slid a pick and hook into the lock. He wiggled it about then yanked out the pick. "I need a C rake."

"Then pull one out," Lane said.

"Mine's busted," Carlos said. "You have one?"

"Of course," Lane said as he hopped on one foot while he pulled off his shoe. He handed it back to Carlos, his eyes and paring knife still focused on the bowing floor boards that had started to splinter. "Grab it and hurry your arse."

Carlos pulled out the kit from inside Lane's shoe and found the C rake. He slid it into the lock over the hook and twisted it to the right.

"Come on, come on," Lane said as splinters popped into the air. "This is freaking me out, mate! Let's go!"

"Shut up," Carlos snapped as he wiggled the pick a couple of times, twisted it to the right while twisting the hook to the left. There was an audible click and Carlos sighed. "Done."

He stood up and yanked open the door. He was instantly greeted by the muzzle of a .45.

"Get back in there," the guard said.

"Where the hell did he come from?" Lane asked, looking back over his shoulder. He lifted his fingers and counted. "How many of you are there?"

"Enough," the guard said. "Now, get back in there. You stay alive if you stay put."

"I'm not so sure about that," Carlos said as he pointed at the floorboards that were busy popping loose and cracking before their eyes. "Whatever is happening there isn't good. We're coming out."

"No," the guard said.

"No? To hell with your bloody no," Lane said as he turned and started to shove past Carlos.

The gunshot was loud and sudden and Carlos threw himself to the floor before a second one rang out. He looked up and saw Lane standing there, his eyes wide, his hands patting at his body. The guard fell to the floor, collapsing inside the game room doorway and Carlos had to roll out of the way to keep from getting crushed.

"What the bloody hell?" Lane said as Maggie shoved him back.

"Are you shot?" Maggie asked, one hand on Lane's chest, the other holding her 9mm. "Did the guard get a shot off?"

"What? No," Lane said.

"What just happened?" Carlos asked, getting to his feet. He started towards Maggie and Lane, but stopped as Maggie's 9mm was turned on him. His hands went up and he shook his head. "We're cool, lady. We're cool."

Maggie looked past Lane at Manny's body and frowned.

"He dead yet?" she asked.

"Uh, no," Lane replied. His facial features went through several incarnations before settling on plain old confused. "Who the hell are you?"

"I'm Benjamin's girlfriend," Maggie said. "That's all you need to know."

"Yeah, right," Lane said, nodding his chin at Maggie's neck. "That a new necklace he gave you?"

"The less questions you ask, the less lies I have to tell," Maggie said. "The less lies, the less worried I am you are becoming a liability. Would either of you like to know what happens to liabilities?"

"Military," Carlos said as if that settled everything. "Special ops or something."

"Or something," Maggie said. "Now shut up and get back. You two are staying here so I don't have to deal with variables."

She pulled her hand on Lane's chest back and turned it palm up.

"Pick sets now," Maggie said.

"You can have the picks," Lane said. "But we aren't staying here."

Two floorboards cracked in half and splinters flew up into the air. Maggie shoved Lane out of the way and fired three shots into the tentacle that started to push through. It disappeared and the floor rippled across the room right at the doorway. Right at where Maggie and Lane were standing.

"Move!" Maggie yelled as she yanked Lane by the collar and pulled him out into the passageway just as the floor exploded upward and six tentacles started whipping about in every direction.

Maggie opened fire, nailing two of the tentacles before her pistol clicked empty. She ejected the spent magazine and slapped in a fresh one as three tentacles came shooting towards her. She threw herself up against the passageway's wall and the tentacles darted past her.

Lane screamed again as he was pulled off his feet and yanked back to the game room. Maggie took aim, but couldn't get a shot without hitting Lane.

"Shit," she swore as she pulled her knife free from her hip and dove at the tentacles.

Lane thrashed next to her, his face turning blue as a tentacle tightened around his throat. Maggie slashed at it, sending blue blood splattering everywhere. But instead of letting go, the tentacle tightened more and Lane's eyes started to bulge.

"HEY!" Carlos shouted as he lifted a bar stool over his head. "Let him go!"

He brought the bar stool down on as many tentacles as he could, smashing them over and over again as he roared German curse words.

Half the tentacles shrunk back from the attack, withdrawing into the hole in the game room floor. The other half whipped around and grabbed Carlos by the legs, lifting him high into the air before he could attack again with the bar stool.

Maggie pressed her pistol against the tentacle that had Lane by the throat and fired. It split apart and started flopping wildly about, coating her in blue blood. Lane scrambled back out of the game room, his fingers clawing at the part of the tentacle that still had him.

Getting to her feet, and firing down into the hole, Maggie emptied another magazine. She ejected that one and smacked in a fresh one then started firing again until the third magazine was empty.

The tentacles that held Carlos tossed him across the game room. There was a loud crack as he impacted with the bar and he cried out then was silent as his body tumbled over the side and out of sight.

Lane struggled and gasped behind Maggie and she whirled around in time to see his face turn dark, dark purple just as his throat was completely crushed. The tentacle around his neck continued to constrict, tightening even more until it severed Lane's vertebrae and his head popped off. It fell to the ground and rolled across the passageway, coming to rest at Maggie's feet.

She kicked it away and spun back around, pistol trained on the jagged hole in the floor. She could see pipes and cables below and was amazed that a creature as big as the one she was dealing with could fit down in such a tight space. Amazed, but not surprised. Octopi had no bones and could squeeze into almost anything as long as it was big enough for the beak to fit.

Maggie hurried across the game room and glanced behind the bar. She didn't need to check Carlos's pulse to know he was dead. The angle of his head and limbs told her that.

She moved to the poker table and placed a finger to Manny's neck. His pulse was almost nonexistent. But it was still there. Despite the man's less than honorable intentions, he was still INTERPOL. Maggie sighed and put her finger to her ear.

"Tumbler, come in," Maggie called. Two clicks in response told her Tumbler and the rest of her team were otherwise occupied. "Shit."

She looked at Manny and shook her head.

"Sorry, Agent Ruiz," she said as she carefully made her way around the hole and out of the game room. "I'll have to come back for you. Try to live, if you can."

She was down the passageway and around the corner when tentacles reappeared at the hole. One went for Lane's headless body, one went for Carlos behind the bar, and another reached up and grabbed Manny by the ankles. All three bodies were pulled down into the hole and the sound of slurping and munching started echoing up out of it immediately.

41.

Tony stepped back from the bench, blood coating the knife in his hand, as he cocked his head and listened.

"Those were gunshots," Tony said.

"I believe so," Captain Staggs responded.

Tony walked to the dash and picked up his radio.

"Report," he said. "Who's shooting?"

Only quiet static came from the radio.

"I said to report," Tony snapped.

"It's jammed," Captain Staggs said.

"No, the radios over there are," Tony said, nodding towards the bridge windows. "Whoever landed on that ship is jamming from there, not here." He clicked the button several times. "Hear the difference? Do you?"

"Yes, sir," Captain Staggs replied.

"Good," Tony said as he set the radio aside. He looked at the doors to the bridge. "How secure are these doors?"

"The locks can be shot open," Captain Staggs said. "So not as secure as they should be considering the issues with piracy these days." He gave Tony a quick glance. "And other dangers."

"You're lucky you're needed, Cap," Tony said, but didn't elaborate.

Instead, he walked back to the bench and knelt down. Ben lay there, bleeding and shivering, his left hand clutched to his chest. Two fingers were missing from the hand and blood soaked the bench's leather upholstery, dripping down to create a pool on the floor.

"That was two fingers," Tony said. "Just two. I can keep going for a while before I have to switch to your toes. Your handler is moving slow."

"I don't have a handler," Ben gasped. "I write a poker blog and have two daughters and an ex-wife. But no handler."

"Most men would be crying and begging for me to stop," Tony said. "You aren't. Yeah, you're a mess with snot coming out your nose, but you aren't acting like a little baby. I admire that."

"Not the first time I've been manhandled," Ben said. He looked down at his bleeding hand. "You can keep taking fingers, but you won't get anything from me because I don't know anything."

"Now I see shock is getting to you," Tony said. "I already told you I know you don't know anything. What I'm doing is getting your handler's attention. You scream loud enough and someone is going to have to come running."

"What if my handler was that Ashley woman?" Ben asked. "She's already dead so you're torturing me for nothing."

"She's not it," Tony said. "I have a good idea who it is and I'm waiting for her to show her innocent looking face."

"What? Who?" Ben asked. "She? What do you mean by she? One of the crew?"

"No, not the crew, you idiot," Tony said. "That sweet piece of Asian Latina you brought with you."

"Maggie? You have got to be kidding," Ben said. He started to laugh, but it came out more like a pained wheeze. "Maggie is a school teacher."

"That doesn't mean a thing to me," Tony said. "I have a hunch and my hunches are always right."

"Not this time," Ben said. "This time you are drawing to a dead hand."

Tony flicked his fingers against Ben's bleeding nubs eliciting a shriek of pain.

"You're about to have the dead hand," Tony said. "I guess we need to get started again. Try to scream louder, will ya? I really need your voice to echo through the boat."

"Yacht," Ben said as he spat in Tony's face.

Tony only laughed as he wiped the spit away then brought the knife up to Ben's face.

"Now, that was rude," Tony snarled. "I'm going to make you see how rude that was."

42.

The galley doors kicked open and Maggie rushed in, sweeping her pistol to the left then to the right. The place was empty. She waited, listening hard, then moved slowly down the cook line. She ducked her head over and over as she looked under the make table that split the galley in half. She didn't expect the creature to be there, it was far too large, but she needed to make sure no one was cowering amidst the pots and pans. Even though she hadn't seen a single one of them, she knew the yacht had a cook staff somewhere.

"Hello?" she called out. "If you are in here, show yourself."

There was no response and she stopped as she reached the end of the line. She quickly assessed her surroundings and saw several tactical advantages to the room, which is why she'd changed her mind and gone to the galley instead of going directly to the bridge above.

Metal walls, metal floors, heavy equipment, and two six burner gas ranges with four gas ovens underneath. It would be the perfect trap if she could lure the creature to it.

She tried her earpiece again, but she didn't even receive any acknowledging clicks. That was bad. Either her team was still too busy or they had been taken out. She doubted Tony's men could do it, but she'd seen Niya's dossier and knew the woman was not someone to mess with.

"Can't worry about that now," Maggie said to herself. "I have work of my own."

She began to take an inventory of all the heavy equipment. The huge floor mixer, the dough proofer, the boil kettle. She made note of the distance between the two exits, one that led into the passageway and one that led into the main dining room. She started to turn on one of the burners when a clang behind her had her spinning about with her 9mm up before her fingertips touched the numbered plastic dial.

Maggie waited. She felt like most of her time was spent waiting, watching, listening, then filled with bursts of action and violence. She wasn't thinking of just that moment, but her whole life. A tiny voice needled at her that she chose the life, not the other way around, and that a whole lot of nothing followed by a whole lot of everything was just how it went.

She took a few steps towards the latched door of the walk-in cooler. Just like the rest of the galley, the walk-in was much larger than it should have been, even for a yacht that size. But the former owner of the Lucky Sucker had loved to eat, so he'd spared no expense on the facilities that prepared his food. Maggie had done her homework on the yacht, not just the guests.

Her 9mm gripped tightly in one hand, Maggie reached out with the other and grasped the handle of the walk-in's latch. She popped it free and yanked hard, sending the door flying out and back. She moved in fast and had her pistol sweeping the misty space as her eyes did the same.

"Don't shoot!" a man cried, his hands out and in front of his face, warding Maggie off. "Please!"

"Chef Bermeto?" Maggie asked.

"Yes?" the man replied, his hands lowering as confusion filled his features.

"Get up," Maggie ordered. "I need your help."

"You what?" Chef Bermeto asked.

He was an average man, not heavy or fat as many chefs his age would have become. Life at sea had kept him in decent shape. Maggie waited for him to move, but he only cowered against a shelf filled with vegetables and cheeses.

"Get. Up," Maggie ordered again, her voice cold and deadly.

Chef Bermeto scrambled to his feet, his hands held high, and shivered as Maggie kept the pistol pointed at him.

"What do you need?" the chef asked.

"I need you to fill every pot you have with water and get it boiling," Maggie said. "Then I need those pots loaded onto serving carts and ready for me to use."

The man stood there, his brow knitted together.

"Did you hear me?" Maggie asked.

"Yes, I heard you," Chef Bermeto replied. "I just don't know why you want me to boil water."

"You don't need to know why, you just need to boil water," Maggie said, stepping out of the walk-in. She gestured with her pistol for him to follow then lowered it as he hesitated. "I'm not going to shoot you. I'm low on rounds and need to conserve ammo. You're more valuable alive."

"Thank you?" Chef Bermeto replied as he moved past her, hands still up.

"Put your hands down," Maggie said and he did. "Before you start boiling, help me move the equipment in front of the passageway door. I want only one way in and one way out."

The chef nodded his head and followed her to the heavy floor mixer. It took them a while, and the chef stopped each time they heard Ben's far-off screams, but they managed to get the door to the passageway blocked.

"Are you clear on what I want?" Maggie asked.

"Yes," Chef Bermeto replied, nodding vigorously.

"And what happens if the thing comes here before I'm ready?" Maggie asked.

"I lock myself in the walk-in and wait," Chef Bermeto replied.

"That's exactly what you do," Maggie said. "Do not get anywhere near this thing, understood?"

The chef nodded again then shook his head. "What is it again?"

"Giant Pacific Octopus," Maggie said. "But it's not like the ones you've seen in the aquariums."

"I suppose not if it has killed all those people you say it has killed," the chef responded.

"I hear doubt in your voice," Maggie said. "If you want to live through this then I advise you kill that doubt right the hell now."

Ben screamed again and Maggie flinched. She looked at the burners that Chef Bermeto had started to light up and gave the man a serious look.

"Have those pots ready," Maggie said. "I may need them very soon."

43.

The bullet burst from the heavy suppressor. There was barely even a flash and only a loud cough as the round flew down the passageway and impacted squarely between Mikey's eyes. The back of his head exploded into a thousand fragments of bone, chunks of brain, and a massive spray of blood. His body collapsed onto the mosaic of corpse parts that filled the floor outside the vault.

"Clear!" Tumbler called out. "Balls?"

"Clear here!" a man above called. "Just the two of them, it looks like."

"I doubt that," Tumbler said as he came out from his hide at the corner of the passageway behind the set of stairs that loomed over the bloody scene. "That son of a bitch just wouldn't give up."

"He had some solid training," Balls said as he stepped onto the stairs.

"No shit, Balls," Tumbler replied. He pressed his finger to his throat. "Tweety?"

"Yeah?" a man replied into his earpiece

"Hoedown was trying to call me during that fun little firefight," Tumbler said. "Get in touch with her ASAP and confirm she's alright."

"Gotcha," Tweety responded. "And heads up, weather is going to be shit in about forty-five minutes. We need to secure the package and lift off before that."

"Copy that," Tumbler replied. "We're at the vault now."

"Forty-five minutes?" Balls asked, coming down the stairs and moving alongside Tumbler as they stepped onto the jigsaw of body parts. "Can we make it in that timeframe?"

"Do we have a choice?" Tumbler replied.

"I guess not," Balls said.

Again, Tumbler pressed his fingers to the disc on his throat. "Skanks? Dipstick? Status."

"Clear," Skanks replied in his ear.

"Clear also," Dipstick said just after.

"On me now," Tumbler said. "We're at the vault and about to go in."

"On the way."

"Roger that."

"This is so not cool," Balls said as he looked down at the mess under his feet. "Are you telling me some eight-legged fish did this?"

"Mollusk," Tumbler corrected. "Not a fish."

"Fucked up," Balls replied. "Not giving a shit about the difference."

Both large men dressed in black combat gear and body armor, the two were almost indistinguishable. Except Tumbler held a heavily modified MK14 while Balls held an HK416.

The men moved slowly towards the open vault, pausing when they reached the edge. Tumbler pulled a small canister from a clip on his vest and yanked the pin free. He tossed the canister into the vault and turned his back to it, his hands clamped over his ears and eyes squinted shut. Balls mimicked the same motions and they crouched low as the flash bang went off, blinding and deafening anyone inside.

"Go!" Tumbler shouted as he sprang into motion and hurried inside the vault with Balls right behind him.

The two men swung their weapons back and forth, their highly trained senses searching for any and all threats. After they were halfway inside, and no one had fired on them or stepped into the open, Tumbler pulled up and lowered his MK14.

"Shit," he said. "Asset is not here. No sign of any more hostiles either."

"We better search for files," Balls said. "Fast."

"Get started," Tumbler said, his hand going to his throat. "Skanks? Dipstick? The vault is empty. Sheeran isn't here."

"We're on it," Skanks replied.

"Any sign of Romanski?" Dipstick asked.

"Negative," Tumbler replied. "So keep your eyes open. She is not to be taken for granted."

"Aye aye," Dipstick responded.

"Hey, T?" Balls said as he walked up to Tumbler with a tablet in hand. "Check this out."

"Is that what's holding the files?" Tumbler asked.

"My guess is it *was* holding the files," Balls answered as he turned on the tablet and swiped to the right. "But it's been wiped. Full factory reset. I'm surprised it wasn't smashed."

"We probably surprised Romanski," Tumbler said. "She got her info and took off. She had time to set it to reset, but couldn't risk smashing it before that process was done or our techs would be able to retrieve the data."

"Keep it?" Balls asked.

"Yeah," Tumbler said. "Just in case."

He sighed and held his throat.

"Hoedown, come in," Tumbler said.

"This is Hoedown," Maggie whispered. "But I really can't talk right now."

"I'll do the talking," Tumbler said. "Files have been purged from a tablet. We're bringing it with, but be advised that Romanski and the asset are not here. Either they're on the ship hiding or they're on their way back to you. You'll want to keep eyes open and alert because if she has the files then she's going to kill to keep them."

"Copy that," Maggie replied in his ear. "She can try to kill me, but she'll have to get in line. The creature is still at large and I'm putting something in place to flush it out."

"Flush it out? Shit, Hoedown, be careful," Tumbler said. "We're supposed to retrieve it alive if possible."

"That part of the mission has been altered," Maggie said. "Because I really do not think it is possible. This thing is huge, hungry, and homicidal."

"She's so good with alliteration," Balls said as he tapped at the tablet. "Dammit. Thing froze up on me."

"Stop messing with it," Tumbler snapped. "Put it in your pack and let's get going."

"Hurry over," Maggie said. "I could use as many boots as possible. This thing has eight arms, I only have two."

"Copy that and heading your way," Tumbler said.

44.

The wind and rain pelted Niya and Nick as they stepped up onto the main deck. The ship rocked back and forth, rising up over the growing waves then crashing down the other side. Nick slipped on the wet metal deck and fell hard on his ass. Niya growled and grabbed him by the wrist, yanking him to his feet hard enough to make him cry out.

"Jesus," he swore as he pulled his arm free. "Don't break me trying to help me."

"I'm not trying to help you," Niya said. "I need you to get the speedboat back to the yacht. You do me no good if you go sliding across the deck and fall into the ocean."

"There's a thing called a gunwale," Nick said. "It has this other thing called a railing on top of it. Been pretty effective for hundreds of years of nautical exploration at keeping people from falling overboard."

A huge wave crashed up over the side of the ship and soaked both Niya and Nick.

"There are also things called waves that have been more effective at taking egotistical morons like you over the railings and gunwales," Niya snapped. "Which way is the speedboat?"

"This way," Nick said, pointing to port. "But I don't think we're going anywhere."

"Why is that?" Niya asked.

"Because of those waves you pointed out," Nick said. "The boat isn't designed to handle these kinds of rough seas."

"We get to the boat and see," Niya said.

"If we can get to the boat," Nick argued. "It was a lot easier before, climbing up, but getting down in this? Good flippin' luck."

"Shut up and move," Niya said as she shoved him in the back.

Nick shook his head and carefully made his way across the deck to the port side railing. He grabbed ahold as the ship canted in their direction, using all his strength not to go tumbling over the side. As soon as the ship righted itself, he pushed away from the railing and hurried over to a hatch, grabbing onto the handle as he shook his head.

"What are you doing?" Niya shouted at him as she grabbed onto the handle as well.

"The boat's gone!" Nick yelled. "It's not tied up to the ship anymore!"

"What do you mean it's gone?" Niya shouted. "How can it be gone?"

"I don't know!" Nick yelled. "But it is! It may have been crushed by the ship when a big wave came or it broke loose! I didn't tie the damn thing off, Giraldi's men did!"

A string of Ukrainian curses flowed from Niya's mouth as she pounded a fist against her thigh. She grabbed Nick by the shirt and almost lifted him off his feet.

"How do we get off this ship?" she snarled in his face.

"Well, we ain't swimming!" Nick snarled back. "So, unless you can fly, we're stuck here with whoever the new peeps are!"

Niya cocked a fist and almost sent it flying into Nick's face, but she hesitated. Then she smiled. Nick looked from the fist to the smile and back, not sure which looked more dangerous.

"You just had a thought," Nick said. "What is it?"

"We fly," Niya said. "I do not know boats, but I do know aircraft. All aircraft. Including helicopters."

"Helicopter? The thing we saw parked on the foredeck with the soldier-looking guy sitting in it?" Nick exclaimed. "That's your solution?" He looked about and spat rain from his mouth. "Oh, yeah, what could go wrong with flying in this shit!"

"I trusted you with that boat, you will trust me with the helicopter," Niya said. She pulled a .45 and jammed it up under Nick's chin. "Or you can argue with me some more."

"Done arguing," Nick said. "Let's fly these friendly skies."

"Good," Niya said. She wiped water from her face with the back of her hand, but it was instantly replaced by more. "Stay close to me and try not to be swept overboard."

"Why bother?" Nick asked then held up his hands. "Not arguing, just wondering. Why have you kept me alive?"

"I need you to corroborate my story with Giraldi," Niya said. "I despise the man and would rather put two bullets in his face, but he is powerful and has even more powerful friends. You will make sure he understands that his men did not die because of me."

"What if he doesn't believe me?" Nick asked.

"Then you are dead and I will be forced to kill him or run," Niya said. "Neither of those choices are acceptable since they will both result in his friends coming for me."

"Man, I need to find a different circle to run in," Nick said. "Benny Boy always said this world would kill me."

"Pray he is wrong for a little while longer," Niya said, giving him a hard shove towards the fore end of the ship. "Move."

Nick moved. He crept along the deck, making sure his footing was secure before he took a step. It was painfully slow, but Niya was doing the exact same thing so Nick didn't worry about getting smacked upside the head for taking too long.

They wound their way around the superstructure then stopped as Niya held up her hand and pointed at the long, sleek shadow of the helicopter sitting on the deck before them.

"I need you to go talk to the pilot," Niya said.

"Come again?" Nick laughed. "What happened to you needing me alive?"

"He won't shoot you," Niya said. "He'll point a gun at you and probably knock you to the deck so he can restrain you, but he won't shoot you. This mission is about intelligence gathering, not assassination."

"How can you be so sure about that?" Nick asked, seriously thinking of making a break for it. Where he would go, he had no clue, but it was better than getting shot right then and there.

"Because they would have blown the ship up by now," Niya said. "And you heard the flash bang down below. That is nonlethal."

"Yeah, I'm not completely buying that," Nick replied. "But you're the one with the pistols, so I'm just going to go along and pray you are right."

"Are you really a praying man, Mr. Sheeran?" Niya asked.

"I am now," Nick said as he took a deep breath then stepped away from the cover the superstructure provided.

Once he was fully out in the open, and knew he was within sight of the helicopter pilot, he waved his hands over his head. He was almost to the helicopter when he was finally noticed.

"Down! Down now!" Tweety yelled as he jumped from his seat and aimed his M4 at Nick. "Get on your knees! Hands behind your goddamn head!"

"Getting on my knees!" Nick responded, dropping to the deck slowly, his hands coming up even slower behind his head. "Hands are up! I'm unarmed!"

Tweety, a lanky man with a heavy black helmet on his head and a scruff of grey beard on his chin, moved towards Nick, his M4 sweeping the area. He was five yards from Nick's position when he stopped and swung the carbine to the left and started firing.

There was a high-pitched scream and Nick hit the deck, pressing his belly against the wet metal as more shots were fired. He squeezed his eyes shut and his body jumped with every report. Even with the weather raging around him, the shots were incredibly loud and he gritted his teeth and held his breath until they were finally over.

He waited a few seconds then lifted his head.

Lying on the deck, his blood being washed away by the rain, lay Tweety. Half of the man's face was gone, leaving a gaping, bloody hole below the visor of the helmet he still wore.

"Shit," Nick said as he pushed up to his feet.

"He was good," Niya said as she limped over to Nick. "Not as good as me."

"You're hit," Nick said, pointing to the wound on Niya's right thigh.

"Superficial," Niya replied. "In and out, just hit flesh and muscle, no bone. I will live."

"Well, that's good since you're my ride," Nick said. "Speaking of, can we go now?"

"Get in," Niya said, pointing to the helicopter with the .45 in her hand. "You will watch for the other men while I begin the startup procedure."

"Right. Watch for other men that now want to shoot us because we killed their buddy," Nick said. "How long is the startup procedure?"

"A minute or two," Niya said. "This is not a BMW that you can turn a key in and it goes vroom."

"Beemers all have push buttons now," Nick said then frowned and hurried to the helicopter. "But that's not the point."

45.

Maggie stared at the bullet holes in the bridge door and guessed that Manny was the recipient considering the man's state the last time she saw him. She'd left him alive, but had no allusions that he was still breathing. Either his wounds finally got him or the creature did.

She gripped her 9mm and lifted her foot to kick the door in.

The door opened before she could nail it and Tony stood there, a knife to Ben's throat, and a wide grin on his face.

"The girlfriend," Tony said. "It's always the innocent-looking ones. My uncle taught me that, so the second I saw you I made note to keep my eye on you."

Maggie's pistol was aimed directly at Tony's head, but the man knew how to handle a hostage, making sure Ben was in the way enough to make her shot close to impossible. Maggie liked close to impossible. But she still needed Tony alive.

"Let him go, Giraldi, and you get to walk away from this," Maggie said. "Hurt him anymore and I drop you."

"I don't think so," Tony said. "I have no idea what organization you are with, but if you had wanted me dead then you would have killed me before this mess even got started. So I think I will ask you to put down your pistol or I slit your boyfriend's throat."

Ben only stared at her. With his one eye. The other was gone, replaced by a bloody rag that was packed in the empty socket. A quick glance and Maggie saw that Tony had also taken more than a couple of Ben's fingers.

"Why?" Maggie asked.

"You will need to be more specific," Tony replied. "I have many motivations to do many things, Ms… What do I call you?"

"You don't," Maggie said. "Why did you torture Benjamin?"

"I wanted to see who would show up," Tony said. "I wasn't exactly surprised it was you. Perfect placement, really. Put the handler in a romantic relationship with the asset so she can watch over him day and night. Was it hard? Faking your feelings for this man? Sleeping with him like a common whore? Pretending to like his children and care for them?"

"I didn't have to pretend anything," Maggie said. "Benjamin is not my asset."

Tony's grin faltered and a surge of joy rushed through Maggie as she watched the man try to puzzle out what she'd said.

"I don't believe you," Tony said. He fished something out of his pocket, making sure the hand with the knife stayed in place. He held up a small disc and shook his head. "This is a subcutaneous bug. You were monitoring Blogger Boy."

"Big word for such a small brain," Maggie said. "That doesn't make Benjamin my asset."

"Then why would you put fifty thousand dollars worth of tech under his skin?" Tony shouted.

"Because I love him," Maggie said. "Have since the day I met him. You see, Giraldi, here is your problem. You don't know how to trust. I understand that. I'm in a line of work where trust can get you killed. We have that in common. Except sometimes life slaps you in the face, kicks you in the ass, and shoves your nose in the deepest, darkest horrors all so you can be ready for the good that waits on the other side."

"You've lost me," Tony admitted. He tossed the bug at her. "This doesn't make sense."

"I met Benjamin because of my cover," Maggie said. "His youngest daughter was a student of mine. I liked him. We talked way too long for a parent/teacher conference and neither of us wanted to stop talking. That is why we are together. Everything else came out of this. But not because I wanted it to. He had that bug on him so I could keep him safe from the dangers out there he has no idea exist. I just didn't know I'd be the one forcing him into the danger."

"No," Tony said. "Still doesn't make sense. You are black ops for some organization. Government? Deep government? Coalition? Corporate? I am guessing very deep government. So far off the books that even those that are in the know don't know about you. It would explain the Guillotine."

Maggie snorted at the name. "Hal? Please," she laughed. "It cracks us up how the underworld is so scared of him. Did you know he collects Christmas stamps each year? He also raises racing pigeons."

"Many killers have hobbies," Tony said. "Don't try to tell me a man with hobbies can't be a stone cold butcher."

"Oh, Hal is a lethal killer," Maggie said. "So good that his victims are rarely ever found. Just a lot of blood, a severed appendage left behind, perhaps an ear, maybe some pieces of scalp with hair still attached. Any normal investigator would assume the victim was dead."

Tony narrowed his eyes. "More assets. Rats and snitches that have served their purpose and are brought in. Deaths faked."

"You catch on fast for being such an imbecile," Maggie said. "Hal is an expert at asset retrieval and obfuscation. He can fool the best of us, if he wants."

"Tanni…?" Ben whispered.

"She's quite possibly the safest teenage girl on this planet," Maggie said. "All threats have already been removed from the equation. She will get to Bobbi's house safe and sound and not even an Israeli strike force could get in there and harm her."

"Hoedown? Hoedown, come in!" Tumbler yelled into her earpiece. "We have a problem! Tweety is not responding and we're hearing chopper rotors starting up! Can you get eyes on our bird? We need to know what is going down up on deck!"

"Copy that, Tumbler," Maggie said. "In the middle of a situation, but it's about to be resolved. I will get you those eyes in two seconds."

"Make it one," Tumbler responded. "Sheeran's boat was lost when we landed. There's no way off this ship without that bird. You copy?"

"I copy," Maggie said. "Tell me one thing, T. How pissed will brass be if Giraldi catches friendly fire?" Tony's eyes went wide.

"Pissed as hell, you know that," Tumbler replied. "But people die. It's a fact of life."

"Yes, people do die," Maggie said. "Getting you eyes now."

She cleared her throat and her finger tensed on the 9mm's trigger.

"Knife gets dropped now," Maggie said. "No countdown. Now."

"You can't just—" Tony started, but never finished as the bullet from Maggie's pistol entered his right eye and blew out the back of his skull.

Maggie rushed forward and kicked Ben in the stomach, moving his body back just enough so as Tony's corpse fell, the knife in his hand didn't slice a gash through Ben's throat.

"Sit down," Maggie ordered, taking Ben by the arm and shoving him onto the bloody bench. She nearly jumped as she saw Captain Staggs standing at the wheel, his hands bone white around the grip. "What the hell? You were in here the entire time and did nothing?"

She brought her 9mm up.

"I should put you down for that," Maggie snarled.

"My duty is to the ship and everyone on it," Captain Staggs said. "I let go of this wheel and we are lost. Put me down or whatever it is you do, but I am keeping you, me, and Mr. Clow alive by doing exactly what it is I am doing."

Maggie hesitated then lowered her pistol. She hurried to the bridge's windows and stared out at the water, her eyes searching for the NCDC ship.

"Where is it?" she barked. "Where is the other ship?"

"Behind us," Captain Staggs said. "I could not stay close to it any longer."

"Shit," Maggie growled as she hurried to the outside door. She yanked it open and wind and rain blew in at her, ripping at her clothes. "Shit."

She rushed into the storm, yanking the door closed behind her. The world was nothing but water. Water coming down in sheets from the sky, water rushing up in waves from the ocean. Water was everywhere. She squinted into the deluge and hunted for a sign of the NCDC ship. But she couldn't see it. Without running lights, or a visible horizon to frame it against, the ship was a shadow on a black canvass.

"Tumbler? This is Hoedown, come in," Maggie called.

"What do you have for me Hoedown?" Tumbler asked.

"I do not have eyes," Maggie said. "Not on the bird or on the ship. I can't see you anywhere."

"Great," Tumbler said. "We'll figure it out. If the bird is gone then I need your authorization to call in another ride."

"I'll do it," Maggie said. "I think we'll need it anyway. The creature is a lot larger than we thought and our containment equipment will not hold it, dead or alive."

"This won't go over well," Tumbler said.

"Calling in a second bird is the least of my worries right now," Maggie said. "Giraldi accidentally caught a bullet to the head. Couldn't be helped."

"It probably could have, but I understand," Tumbler said. "Call that bird so we can get the hell out of here."

"Roger that," Maggie said. "Stay put and I'll…"

"Hoedown? You there? I think I lost you," Tumbler said.

"Can't talk," Maggie whispered and cut the com connection.

She couldn't see the other ship, but she could see something else. Something very large as it crawled its way across the main deck below, its tentacles acting as legs. Maggie lifted her pistol and the creature stopped. What little illumination came from the yacht's running lights glinted off the thing's eye as it rolled to stare up at Maggie.

She took aim and fired, her finger squeezing the trigger six times. Before her finger was done with the last shot, the thing was rushing at her. Maggie couldn't tell if she hit it or not, but if she did, the thing didn't care.

Maggie scrambled back to the bridge door and yanked it open as a tentacle shot out and wrapped itself around her thigh. She didn't even think as she pressed her pistol to the tentacle and fired. The pain was intense as the bullet ripped through the soft tissue of the creature and tore into her quadriceps. Maggie angled her body so she fell inside the bridge. As her back slammed onto the floor, she emptied her magazine and was grateful to see the creature's tentacle withdraw.

"A little help," Maggie grunted as she dragged herself into the bridge. She looked back at Captain Staggs and he just stared at her. "Asshole."

The wind and rain whipped about the bridge as Maggie ejected her magazine and put in a new one. White hot pain burned through her leg as she crawled over and grabbed the door's handle, nearly collapsing from the effort as she yanked it shut and closed off the bridge to the maelstrom that brewed outside.

"We're going to have a talk when this is done," Maggie said to Captain Staggs. She crawled over to the bench where Ben was laid out and leaned her back against the leather cushions that stuck out. "You'll get points for keeping us alive, but I don't think you'll have much future as a ship's captain."

"I feared that was my fate the day Mr. Sheeran took possession of the Lucky Sucker," Captain Staggs replied. "I have a backup plan."

"So do I," Maggie said. "You have a first aid kit?"

Captain Staggs pointed at a blue and red box hanging from the wall a few feet away.

"Really?" Maggie said.

"I let go, we die," Captain Staggs replied.

Maggie painfully made her way over to the wall and pulled herself upright. She yanked the first aid kit off the wall and threw it onto the dash next to her. She found what she needed inside, tore open her pants, and got to work.

Blood spilled everywhere as she sliced into her leg and extracted the bullet. Pain filled her mind as she did a hatchet job of suturing the wound. Even with the stitches, the gunshot still leaked more blood than Maggie was happy with.

"Flare gun?" Maggie asked.

That time Captain Staggs reached out and popped open a small drawer. He pulled out a bright red flare gun and tossed it to her. Maggie cracked it open and extracted the flare. She sliced through the plastic shell and poured a very small amount of the calcium phosphide into the wound. As soon as the powder hit the moisture of her blood, it began to burn, searing her skin and cauterizing the wound in less than a second.

Maggie was not too proud to scream as the wound flared white hot, matching the pain that ripped through her. She almost collapsed, but kept it together enough to hobble back to the bench and plop down next to a dazed and traumatized Ben. She still held the flare shell and wiggled it in front of Ben's face.

"Your turn," she said. "We need to stop those nubs from bleeding."

"Yeah," Ben said, his eye barely focusing on Maggie. "I guess we do."

"I'm so sorry," Maggie said and kissed him on the cheek. "For all of this."

"Me too," Ben whispered and then closed his one eye. "Do it."

Maggie did it. Ben screamed then passed out.

"I really hope you've turned this thing around and we are heading back in to shore," Maggie said to Captain Staggs.

"This isn't a Mazda Miata," Captain Staggs replied. "I can't pull a u-turn and just head the other direction. But, yes, I have been in the process of reversing course for the past three hours."

"Keep on doing that," Maggie said as she leaned her head back and closed her eyes.

There was a scream from below and Maggie's eyes shot back open.

"The chef," Maggie said. "Shit. I forgot about my plan."

She heaved herself up to her feet and walked over to Captain Staggs, handing him back his flare gun and flares.

"You'll need this," Maggie said. "If anything tries to come through one of the vents, shoot it with a flare."

"That could set the entire ship on fire," Captain Staggs exclaimed.

"Fires can be put out," Maggie shrugged. "Heads can't be reattached. Think on that."

Captain Staggs gave her a look like that was the very last thing he wanted to think on.

Maggie double checked her pistol, looked at the door, and limped her way off the bridge.

"Tumbler? I'm going to engage the package," Maggie called over the com. "Wish me luck."

There was no response, but she didn't necessarily expect one.

46.

Tumbler heard Maggie's words in his ear, but he was too busy at that moment to respond.

"That side!" he shouted at Balls. "Get around the cockpit!"

"I have a bead on her, T!" Dipstick shouted from his position on the deck. "Want me to take it?"

"Hold!" Tumbler yelled, as much over the roaring wind as the helicopter's whirring rotors. "Let's try to salvage something from this mess! She may have the files!"

"I have eyes on the asset!" Balls called.

"Me too!" Skanks added.

The four men held their position of a rough circle around the helicopter, all eyes locked onto the furious form of Niya Romanski.

"Romanski!" Tumbler shouted. "There is no way out of this! Put your hands over your head and exit the chopper slowly! If you cooperate, you get to live! Twitch a tit and we end you now!"

"Do you know what happens if you kill me?" Niya shouted at him. "You will declare war! Whoever is paying you will be found out and my people will hunt every last one of them down and butcher not just them, but their families and their friends! Yours too!"

"No," Tumbler responded.

"Excuse me?" Niya laughed. "You should have more faith in what I say!"

"I have faith in who I work for," Tumbler said. "Your people will not survive a war with us. The second I report your death, your entire operation, and the operations of anyone associated with you, will be wiped from the earth! This isn't our first go round!"

Niya started to move and Tumbler tensed, ready to pull the trigger.

"Hold on! Hold on!" Nick shouted, waving his arms. "Do not shoot! She can get us out of here! Do any of you know how to pilot this thing?"

Balls, Skanks, and Dipstick raised a hand.

"Oh," Nick said. He smiled at Niya. "Well, I tried. You are on your own."

Niya glared at him then looked back to Tumbler.

"I give you the files and you let me live?" she shouted.

"You give me the files, I verify they are the files, you don't try anything stupid, and I let you live," Tumbler said. "But only while you are in my custody. I have no authority over what happens when we return to land."

"That is not much of a deal," Niya said.

"I'm not in much of a deal-making mood," Tumbler responded. "Live or die, your choice."

"Live," Niya said and held up her hands.

She struggled to get out of the pilot's seat and fell out onto the deck as her wounded leg gave out on her. She looked up as Tumbler and Dipstick rushed her, the latter planting a heavy boot in the middle of her back. Tumbler yanked her arms behind her and zip-tied her wrists together.

Dipstick yanked Niya to her feet and shoved her towards the body of Tweety.

"If you think they'll let you live after that then you are kidding yourself," he snarled in her ear.

"Dip!" Tumbler shouted. "Put her in the bird! We've got to go!"

Dipstick lifted Niya by her arms, bending them high up behind her back, and the woman screamed as she was shoved back to the helicopter.

Balls climbed into the pilot's seat and checked the instruments.

"We are good to go!" he yelled. "But we've lost a lot of time! Tweety was right, we may not be getting out of this storm!"

"Just get us to the yacht!" Tumbler ordered, climbing into the co-pilot's seat as he shoved Nick out of the way.

Nick climbed in back and plopped down next to Niya while Dipstick and Skanks flanked them.

"You guys twins?" Nick joked as he pointed at their matching clothes and body armor. He laughed weakly then let it fade out. "Yeah. Right. Just a little kidding to lighten the mood."

Tumbler spun about in his seat as Balls lifted the helicopter off the ship.

"The asset will shut the holy fuck up or the asset will learn to fly. Are we understood?" he snapped at Nick. Nick nodded. "No, I want to hear it from the asset."

"Yes, we are understood," Nick replied. "Loud and clear."

"Coward," Niya muttered.

"Says the bitch playing white trash bondage games," Nick said. "You can act superior when you're out of those zip ties."

"Strap in and hold on!" Balls said as he took the helicopter out away from the ship and over open water. "I can't get too high because of the wind or too low because of the waves. I'm threading a weather needle, gentlemen!"

Everyone strapped in and held on.

47.

Maggie pulled out a small tablet from a pouch on her leg. She felt lucky it wasn't the leg she ended up shooting or her cobbled-together plan was over before it began.

She checked the plans of the yacht, swiping away unneeded information and leaving only a basic framework of the rooms and the schematics of the ventilation system. It was designed the way she had hoped it would be. She knew that if she timed things just right, she could trap the creature and keep it contained until backup arrived.

But, as the yacht canted to port and she nearly dropped the tablet trying to keep her balance, she had a sinking feeling backup wasn't coming anytime soon.

She also had a sinking feeling that her help wasn't going to be much help as she rushed through the main dining room and saw the pool of blood spreading out from under the galley's double doors.

"Shit," she muttered, her pistol up and pointed at the round windows in the doors.

Slowly, and painfully, she stepped to the doors and nudged them open. Just inside was half the body of Chef Bermeto, the top half, the man's eyes wide with fear and blank with death. The bottom half was hanging from the pot rack over the make table, blood spilling out of the severed pelvis into a large stock pot.

Maggie's shoulders sagged as she saw that the ranges' burners were all dark, not one was lit and boiling the pots of water that Chef Bermeto had put there on Maggie's orders. The disappointment Maggie felt wasn't so much that her plan to flush the creature from the ventilation system and into the walk-in cooler had failed before it had started, but from the realization the chef hadn't been the one to turn off the burners.

The creature had.

It was obvious from the smears of blood, both red and blue, and the black ink that trailed from the forced-open galley door to the ranges. Maggie stared at the floor mixer that easily weighed several hundred pounds as it lay on its side, broken and useless. The other pieces of heavy equipment were a few feet from the galley door, deep gouges in the metal floor from being shoved out of the way as well.

A crunch and thump made Maggie spin about and she ducked just in time. The tentacle sailed over her head as she dove into a forward roll, biting her cheek from the pain in her thigh, and came to rest with her back against the make table. Three tentacles shot in at her from the dining room and she fired over and over, nailing one of them before the other two wrapped about her ankles and started pulling her from the galley.

She let go of her pistol, pulled her knife free and slashed at the tentacle grabbing onto her left ankle. It let go as blue blood spurted high into the air. Maggie started to slash the other one, but the wounded tentacle smacked her knife from her hand and wrapped about her arm instead while the second tentacle, still firmly attached to her right ankle, continued to pull her to the dining room.

Maggie struggled to pry the tentacle from her arm, but it was like grabbing onto a rubber hose with the strength of a hundred men. Her foot hit the torso of Chef Bermeto and she looked down as she was pulled by. There, on his hip, was his chef's knife tucked safely into its sheath. She had a friend that had worked KP when she was in basic training and said a kitchen was a daily battle zone and a chef always stayed armed.

Maggie yanked the chef's knife free and stabbed the tentacle that had her ankle, pinning it to the floor. She was amazed at how sharp the knife was, able to slice into the metal floor like it was a thick cut of meat. Subconsciously, she found a new respect for chefs. Consciously, she found something new to fear as the tentacle let go of her ankle and pulled away, slicing itself in half at the tip as it withdrew around the blade.

Her whole world spun into a new direction as the tentacle that had her arm took over and pulled her sideways out of the galley doors and into the dining room.

She gasped at the sight of the massive creature that filled the entire dining room, its mantle resting on the thick wooden table, its tentacles flailing about in a way that could only be interpreted as rage. Up close, and fully visible, the thing was nothing like the docile octopi she'd studied before planning the mission.

The front of its mantle was thick and grey, no longer a rosy pink. The skin almost looked plated, like it had folded in upon itself again and again to create a heavy armor. Its tentacles pulsed with blue blood, the skin of the creature going from translucent to opaque and back again, changing colors instantly as they came in contact with a new surface.

Maggie could barely breathe as she looked up at the creature. She almost completely stopped when the thing lifted its mantle off the table to show her its huge sharp beak.

Sharp beak…

Maggie's training kicked back in and she assessed her predicament. No blades, no pistols, no weapons of any kind. Just her fingernails and teeth.

Beak. Teeth.

Maggie lunged for the tentacle that had her arm, sinking her teeth into the rubbery flesh. She shook her head back and forth, her mouth filling with the strangest tasting blood she'd ever experienced. Not coppery like human blood, which she had tasted too many times for her liking, but organic, loamy; salty yet vegetable like.

Her teeth sawed through the tentacle and the monster raged from the dining table, its beak clacking and tentacles slapping the wood paneled walls. Instead of just letting go, the giant octopus threw her back into the galley, tossing her as far away as possible. It was a genetically modified killing machine, but at its core it was still a cautious being that thousands and thousands of years of evolution had programmed to flee when a dangerous predator was near.

But then there was the ever-present elephant in the room of nurture versus nature. The creature shook its wounded tentacle about, splattering everything with blue blood, and slowly slid down from the table. Its fear was gone, Maggie could see that easily as she tried to crawl further back into the galley, and the thing's body language said playtime was all over.

Maggie grabbed up a sauté pan that lay on the rubber safety mat in front of the make table. She held it up, swinging it back and forth, trying to use it to divert the monster's attention. For a second, she thought it had worked as the octopus paused in mid-crawl. She kept swinging then realized it had paused not because of her feeble sauté pan diversion, but because there was a very distinct sound fighting through the noise of the storm outside.

The helicopter.

With a speed that made Maggie tighten her bladder to keep it from loosing, the octopus was gone and out of the dining room, leaving only a swinging door and a long trail of blue blood behind it.

"Shit," Maggie said and pressed her throat "Tumbler! Do you copy? You have incoming hostile now! The package is moving fast and coming right for you!"

"Roger," Tumbler replied. "We have weapons hot and eyes wide open! Balls is trying to land this bird without us punching through the deck and into the bridge, but the winds are not cooperating!"

"Set that bird down fast and get the hell away from it!" Maggie shouted.

"That's the plan!" Tumbler responded.

Maggie sighed and leaned back against the make table. Her body felt broken and crushed, but as far as she could tell, she was only wounded in her thigh. Which had opened back up.

"Shit," she whispered as she took a deep breath and pulled herself back to her feet. "Gotta be a first aid kit in this place. Kitchens are battle zones."

48.

"Get us down, Balls!" Tumbler yelled as the helicopter was buffeted by the wind. "We have a hostile incoming!"

"I'm trying!" Balls yelled back. "But I have to keep the rotor power up to fight the wind which is making it hard to set down without crashing! Do you want down in one piece or down in many pieces? Make the call, T!"

"I want us down now!" Tumbler said as he looked out the windshield at the yacht below.

The door to the bridge burst open and Captain Staggs came fleeing out, his head tucked low against the wind and rain, his legs pumping as fast as possible. Tumbler tracked the man's progress as Balls swung the helicopter around, angling it towards the helipad on the upper deck.

"What the hell is he doing?" Tumbler shouted.

Then everyone saw as the bridge door, as well as most of the structure around it, exploded outward and the giant octopus came bursting out on deck, its tentacles flapping and flailing around it. Two shot out at the captain, snagging him about the waist, bending him in half as it pulled the screaming man back. It may have pulled too hard as Captain Staggs's soft middle seemed to disintegrate from the attack and blood began to fly about the deck from the wind and rotor wash.

The octopus threw the broken man aside and pushed up to its full height on its legs, bringing its mantle almost level with the open doors of the helicopter.

"Holy fucking kraken!" Nick yelled as he tried to scramble away from the door. "Fly away! Fly away!"

Balls had started to do just that, but the helicopter's engines began to whine and protest as he pushed the throttle hard. They weren't going anywhere. The helicopter was stuck in place and as all eyes turned to the monster they knew why.

Tumbler made a split-second decision and raised his MK14. He opened fire just as the rest of the team came to the exact same decision and began firing as well. Nick slapped his hands over his ears and screamed, unable to join in the battle. Niya only stared at the thing that held them in place midair.

A tentacle burst up through the floor of the helicopter and wrapped around Dipstick's left leg. It yanked down and the man screamed as part of him was pulled through the jagged hole, metal tearing into his calf, his thigh, then up into his pelvis, while the rest of him was stuck inside the helicopter. He had an HK416 like Balls, but that fell from his grip as he reached out, desperate for any handhold he could get.

He found Niya's leg and she smiled down at him. Then she pulled free and smashed her boot down on his hand, crushing the bones with a loud enough snap to overcome the roar of the helicopter, shouting of the men, and the firing of the rifles and carbines. Dipstick looked up at her with terrified eyes then he was gone as his body folded in on itself and was pulled through the hole, sending a spray of blood and flutter of black material shooting up into the air.

As the blood of his former teammate splattered against his face, Skanks turned his attention on Niya. But he wasn't fast enough as she kicked out and her boot caught him across the chin. He lost his balance and tumbled from his seat and onto the floor, sliding towards the wide open door.

The monster didn't waste a breath and plucked him from the helicopter in the blink of an eye.

"God dammit!" Tumbler yelled as he turned in his seat and put two shots in Niya's chest.

The woman slumped over against Nick. Nick, in turn, screamed louder and fumbled at the buckle of his safety harness.

"We're going in!" Balls said. "I can't keep this thing up!"

Both Tumbler and Nick looked at the free buckle of the safety harness that flopped useless against Nick's chest.

"Son of a bitch," Nick said just as the helicopter started to flip to the side and the rotors began to slice into the helipad below.

The octopus let go of the machine and easily scrambled out of the way, leaping down to the next deck and tearing open the first hatch it found, lost from sight inside the ship once again as the men inside the helicopter screamed and screamed until everything came to a dead stop in a pile of flames and shearing metal.

49.

The entire ship rocked and shook from the impact. Maggie didn't need confirmation of what had happened, but she pressed her throat anyway.

"Tumbler?" she called out. No response except the ominous hiss of empty static. "Balls?" Still nothing. "Skanks? Dipstick?"

Maggie's hand fell away from her throat and she forced herself to keep moving. She leaned heavily against the wood paneling of the passageway, her eyes locked onto the stairs ahead of her that would take her back up to the bridge. She was halfway there when the ship suddenly began to list heavily and she found herself thrown against the opposite wall.

"Staggs," she muttered, realizing something must have happened to the captain with the way the ship felt out of control.

The yacht continued to list then suddenly it angled hard and Maggie fell to the floor. She began to slide down the passageway, going the wrong direction from the stairs she needed to get to. However, that was quickly rectified as the ship leveled out then started angling the complete opposite direction than before.

She rolled onto her stomach and reached out as she slid towards the stairs. As soon as she reached them, she clamped her hands on the bottom of the spiral banister, locking her fingers in place as the ship leveled out and returned to the previous angle.

Waves. They were climbing and falling over waves. The storm was in full force and they were right in the middle of it. There was no way a second helicopter was going to get to her, to them, in time before the yacht went down, especially with whatever damage happened when the helicopter above crashed.

But Maggie shoved those thoughts from her mind. The mission was over. The package was not going to be retrieved, that was plainly, and belatedly, apparent. Even under ideal conditions, she doubted her team would have been able to take down and capture the creature. It was enormous. Much larger and considerably more intelligent than the reports she had been given. It was a doomed mission from the start and she and her team found that out the hard way.

When the yacht leveled out once more, Maggie pulled herself up and started climbing the stairs. As the angle changed again, she let herself half fall "down" the stairs until she reached the landing that should have been above, but was suddenly below. Again the yacht leveled and Maggie hurried down the short passageway to the open bridge door where water poured in from outside.

She threw herself inside the bridge, her hands grabbing onto the brass railing by the dash, as the yacht started climbing the next wave. That time she could see what the ship was battling and her mouth hung open at the sight of the massive wave in front of her. The view became nothing but pitch black water then pitch black sky as the yacht climbed and climbed until it crested the wave.

Rain streamed in on top of her and she realized that half the roof was missing, most likely sheared off by the helicopter crash. As the yacht began to descend the other side of the wave, Maggie braced herself against the dash. Something slammed into her, almost knocking her legs out from under her, and she looked down to see an unconscious Ben crammed against the backs of her calves.

When the yacht hit the valley of the wave, Maggie let go of the rail, knelt, undid her belt, then strapped it through one of Ben's belt loops before she slid it back through hers and buckled it tight, cinching them together.

"Hang on," she yelled as the yacht started to climb again.

She held Ben about the waist and closed her eyes as they reached the summit of the wave and the yacht balanced precariously then dove over the other side.

It was the most terrifying drop she'd ever experienced and she'd trained extensively in airborne extraction techniques, so for her stomach to suddenly visit her throat was no small thing.

Ben groaned against her as she held them both to the railing. Water rushed up to meet the bow of the yacht and then washed over them, nearly filling the bridge before it drained back out.

"Hold on, babe," Maggie whispered in Ben's ear. "Just hold on. It's gonna be over soon."

Another climb and Maggie was about to close her eyes when she saw something out on the main deck. It could have been debris, equipment that had come loose, anything, but Maggie's brain refused to put it in any of those categories.

Then she saw the something lift its bloody head as it slid down the deck to slam into the yacht's superstructure.

Nick.

The son of a bitch was alive and trying to survive the nightmare of the storm.

Several thoughts raced through Maggie's mind, but she finally landed on one: he was her asset, she was his handler, and if she lived she could at least return with him in hand. It was small comfort considering the failure she'd endured, but it was better than nothing. That and he was her boyfriend's best friend.

She kissed the top of Ben's head then reached up and slapped him hard.

"Uh…" Ben muttered.

Maggie slapped him again.

"Whaaaaaa?" he groaned as his one eye flickered open.

"Babe, we need to move," Maggie said. "Nick needs us."

"Screw…him…" Ben sighed and his eye fluttered closed.

Maggie took a deep breath then squeezed Ben's hand where his fingers had been. His eye shot open and he screamed.

"Jesus!" he shouted, his eye wide with pain. "What? Why?"

"I need you to walk with me," Maggie said, gripping his chin so he looked right at her. "We have to get Nick and then get below. If the yacht doesn't fall apart, or sink, we may live through this."

"Yeah, yeah, live," Ben said. "Great."

"Hey!" Maggie shouted in his face. "Are you folding, Blogger Boy? Did you just quit this hand and cash in all your chips?"

"No," Ben said.

"Good," Maggie replied. "Then let's get moving."

"I meant no as in don't use poker metaphors to motivate me," Ben said and smirked. "You just can't pull them off."

"Shut up," Maggie said and kissed his cheek as she helped him with a half drag of a walk to the bridge door. "And hang on tight. Shit's gonna get weird out here."

50.

The wheel in the middle of the hatch door was slippery as shit, but Nick managed to hang on by looping his arms inside and hooking his elbows around the metal. As the yacht dropped again, he knew what was coming and he took a deep breath just as the ship reached the valley and half the ocean slammed into him, crushing him up against the hatch.

He coughed and gagged, spitting seawater from his mouth as the yacht began another climb. He knew he had maybe seconds to do what needed to be done and he started yanking at the wheel, using all his strength to turn it to the left and get the hatch open.

But there was one problem, the yacht was a very expensive craft and had a hundred safety features built into it. One of those features was an emergency lockdown of all hatches if the ship's sensors picked up on any type of breach. Such as half the bridge being sheared off.

As long as the yacht had power, which it still did due to its exceptional, duel Caterpillar 3512C DITA-SCAC engines and the backup diesel generators that were designed to survive hurricane conditions.

In essence, Nick found the features that were designed to keep him alive and safe inside the yacht were going to kill him since he was stuck outside the yacht.

He screamed at the hatch, pounded his fists against it, and then started crying as the yacht crested the wave and began to fall again. He looped his arms back through and waited in midair, his feet dangling below him as the ship dropped at a near ninety-degree angle.

"I'm dead," he said to himself. "I am so dead and I lived a shitty life."

Everything went dark as the yacht hit the bottom of the wave and Nick found himself almost completely submerged for about two seconds. Then the ship righted itself, because for sixty-five million dollars it sure as hell better, and Nick was once again gagging and coughing up seawater.

He let out a string of curses and tried the wheel one more time. It moved. He was so surprised that he let go. But the wheel continued to move and he couldn't figure out why until he saw the face peering at him through the porthole. Maggie's face.

"Open up!" Nick screamed. "Get me inside!"

Maggie yelled something back at him, but he couldn't hear a word of it. Then the hatch bucked under him and he realized what she wanted.

Nick rolled to the side and the hatch was pushed up and open. Maggie reached for him and they grasped each other by the forearm so she could pull him inside. He almost tumbled down the passageway that loomed below him like an open shaft, but the yacht had reached its apex and was leveling out for another fall over another wave.

He was on his knees, gasping for breath, as Maggie tugged at his arm.

"Get up, idiot!" she yelled. "Help me get this hatch closed!"

Nick looked up at her then felt the yacht begin to tip and he pretty nearly pissed himself as he realized he was inside the ship, but so was half the ocean going to be if they didn't get the hatch closed. He forced himself to his feet and turned to the hatch, reaching outside with Maggie to grab the interior wheel and yank the opening closed.

That was the theory, at least. The actual practice was considerably flawed as Nick saw Ben strapped to Maggie's side, a rag jammed in his empty eye socket and his wounded hand clutched to his chest. Nick registered the missing fingers right away and he couldn't stop staring at the scorched and blistered stumps, no matter how much Maggie screamed at him to pay attention and move his ass.

Then they were plummeting down the wave and it was all he could do to brace himself against the wall and keep from falling out of the open hatch. Maggie was next to him, with Ben jammed between them, their backs pressed to the wall, their bodies supine as the yacht raced to the bottom.

"Your freezing up probably killed us," were the last words Nick heard before the ocean came inside the yacht and propelled them up the passageway and slammed them into the far wall, crushing them up against the paneling. Nick's lungs burned as the water filled the ship and he said every prayer from every religion he had ever learned but never believed in.

51.

Wedged into a corner of the passageway, Ben awoke to nothing but pain and panic. He rolled over and began to vomit, his body soaked with seawater. The same seawater that was coming out of his guts by the gallon. Between burps, he looked over and saw Nick doing the same thing, the man's arm twisted through the brass railing halfway up the wall.

"Get it all out," Maggie said next to him and pushed up onto her hands and knees. "Try to cough out as much as possible and press it from your lungs."

Ben tried to respond, but instead of words, saltwater spewed from between his lips. His body shuddered and shivered from the cold wind that whipped through the passageway, turning his soaking wet clothes into forms of torture that almost rivaled what he'd endured under the hands of Tony Giraldi. Almost.

His hand throbbed, but probably not as much if he'd been warm and toasty. His head was nothing but one dagger stab of agony after another. Just the simple act of letting his chin rest on his chest was excruciating.

"Storm's over," Maggie said as she stood up. She braced herself against the wall then leaned down and pulled Ben to his feet. "We need to assess the situation and make contact so they know we're alive."

"They?" Ben croaked, his eye a pleading beacon of confusion and distrust. "Who are they?" He stepped back from Maggie. "Who are you?"

"My handler," Nick said as he found his voice and struggled to his feet. His legs wobbled and he fell to his knees, saltwater splashing up from the puddles that pooled on the passageway's floor. "She handles me."

"I don't know what that means," Ben said. "How about you explain it to me?"

"Not now," Maggie said. "There's time for that later. First, we have to—"

"Assess and make contact, I heard you," Ben said. He took a few cautious steps and then stopped, his lungs protesting against the exertion. After a few gulps of fresh air, he kept moving. "It's morning."

Nick and Maggie followed behind him as he pushed open the broken hatch and moved out into the frigid air coming off the Pacific Ocean.

"We need to get up to the bridge," Maggie said, turning around as she got outside. "Oh."

Ben knew the tone in her voice. He reluctantly turned, his reluctance more because his body protested every single movement than honest reticence in fear of what he'd see, and stared up at the spot where the bridge should have been. What he saw was a half-collapsed wall and a bench covered in torn leather he would have rather forgotten about.

"No sign of the chopper or my team," Maggie sighed.

"The waves washed it all away as soon as we hit," Nick said. "I got thrown free against the bridge then bounced off the main deck." He clutched at his side. "Ow and yay."

"What now?" Ben asked.

"There are auxiliary controls in the engine room," Nick said. "Radio, navigation, stuff like that."

"Stuff like that?" Ben snapped. "Don't you even know what your own boat has?"

"Yacht," Nick said and tried to smile, but failed miserably when he looked Ben straight in the face. "Um, yeah, I know my own boat. We can call for help down there and sit tight until the Coast Guard gets here."

"There won't be any Coast Guard," Maggie said. "I'll make the call and my people will come get us. No other way to handle this."

"Whatever," Ben said. He stepped in a puddle of seawater and glanced at Nick. "Why aren't we sinking?"

"We could be," Nick said. "But we seem to still have power, so the bilge pumps must be working. Staggs always said he felt safer on this ship than he did on land. Now I see why. That storm could have sent us down to Davey Jones's locker, but it didn't. The gods have favored us."

Ben huffed derisively at Nick's flippant use of sea slang then moved slowly across the deck of the slightly listing yacht. He looked out at the waters and shook his head then regretted the movement instantly.

"Calm seas," Ben said. "Like glass."

"Weather is weird, Benny Boy," Nick said, putting a hand on Ben's shoulder.

Ben started to shrug it off, but stopped as he stared at a dark spot a few yards out in the water. Nick looked at him then followed his gaze.

"Oh, piss," Nick said. "Is it the thing? Oh, shit, it's the thing, isn't it?"

"What thing?" Ben asked.

"What thing? Have you lost your damn mind?" Nick exclaimed. "The giant freakin' octopus that killed everyone on this boat, I mean yacht, and nearly killed us except the storm tried harder, but we survived and…and…" He stopped talking and pointed, jabbing his finger at the shadow in the water.

"It's just kelp," Maggie said. "You can see the bladders bobbing up and down. The storm uprooted it and pushed it to the surface."

Nick nodded like he understood, but kept pointing. Ben grabbed his arm and shoved it down.

"Come on. Let's get below," Maggie said, her voice firm and uncompromising.

It was her teacher's voice. Ben knew it well. Except what he didn't know was the person using it. Not anymore. Not after what all had happened.

"Below," Maggie ordered and Nick hopped to and moved quickly to the hatch.

Ben stared at Maggie for a second. Maggie stared back.

"We don't have time," she said quietly. "Please, Benjamin."

"Sure, *Mags*," Ben replied and moved past her, his hand to his chest, his face on fire. "Since you said please."

It was slow going getting down to the auxiliary controls in the engine room. Many of the passageways were impassable, their walls bowed and blocking the way, or their floors destroyed and nothing but gaping holes to fall in. Nick had joked they could save time and just jump in one of the holes and probably land outside the engine room door, but no one laughed, not even Nick.

They kept moving until they finally reached the engine room.

"You know what's weird?" Nick asked.

"Are you fucking kidding me with that question?" Ben snapped.

"Where are all the Carls?" Nick asked. "I haven't seen a Carl in like forever. Those bastards had better not have taken the lifeboat."

"Forget the Carls," Maggie said. "I need to make that call right now."

"Radio," Nick said, pointing to a console in the engine room against the wall next to a row of dials and pressure gauges.

As Maggie moved quickly to pick up the handset and dial in the channel, Ben looked around the room.

"Shouldn't an engine room have engines in it?" he asked.

"This is the 21st century, man," Nick said. He stomped his foot on the floor. "The engines are below, sealed off and protected from the sea. This is called the engine room only because it has the controls in here."

"Huh," Ben said and found a metal chair in a corner he could collapse into.

His mind barely registered the words that Maggie was saying as she spoke to someone on the other end of the radio transmission. He caught a couple like "mission failure," "threat risk," and "international incident." None of that meant a damn thing to him. The world he thought he lived in with Maggie apparently was built on fiction and falsehoods, so he had no idea what *anything* meant anymore.

"Engines are at three-quarter power, but still holding steady," Nick said as he tapped a computer screen built into the wall. "At least I think that's what this means. It could mean the engines are three-quarters dead, but I think lights would be blinking if that was the case."

There was a thud and sloshing sound from directly above them. Ben and Nick looked up as the thud happened again. Maggie froze in mid-sentence, her thumb on the transmitter button of the radio handset.

"I need to call you back," Maggie said. "The operation may still be on."

"Oh, man," Nick said. "It didn't leave. It stayed and has been munching on bodies and doing whatever it is giant octopuses, or octopi, or octopussies, or whatever, do when they rip a ship apart and kill everyone on board."

"Octopus?" Ben asked.

"Yeah, dude, octopus!" Nick snapped. "Where the hell have you been these past few hours?"

"Getting tortured on the bridge," Ben said and held up his wounded hand then pointed at his face. "Where the hell were you when this was going down, *Nicholas*?"

"Quiet, both of you," Maggie hissed. She pointed up as they heard the distinct sound of heavy limbs slapping on the floor above. "What room is that?"

"I don't know," Nick whispered. When Maggie glared at him, he held up his hands and shrugged. "I don't. If it doesn't have a bar or a bed in it then I don't really care what room it is."

Maggie patted herself down and shook her head. "I have no weapons," she said. "Not that they would do much good."

"No weapons to fight a giant, bloodsucking octopus." Ben smirked. "My whatever she is girlfriend doesn't seem to have a weapon to fight a giant, bloodsucking octopus. You can't make this shit up, folks."

"Who are you talking to?" Nick asked.

"Myself, asshole," Ben said. "Because talking to you two is way too fucking confusing."

"Keep your voice down," Maggie snapped. "It may leave the ship if it thinks everyone is dead or gone."

"The giant fucking octopus? Is that what may leave the ship?" Ben said, his voice rising. "Hey! Doc Oc! We're down here! Come and get us, you big piece of sea shit!"

Maggie and Nick gaped at him.

"He's lost his mind," Nick said.

"Yeah," Maggie agreed and moved towards Ben. "Benjamin, listen to me very carefully, you have to calm down. I think you are going into shock and—"

"Shock? SHOCK!" Ben roared. "I am so past shock that I've entered an entirely new—"

His words were cut off as two tentacles punched a huge hole in the ceiling and started sweeping the room. Maggie grabbed Ben and threw him to the ground, covering his body with her own. Nick screamed and dove for the door, missing spectacularly and smacking his head into the base of the wall next to it.

Maggie grabbed Ben by his arm and yanked him out into the passageway as two more tentacles came shooting down into the room. Nick was crawling on his hands and knees right after them. The three stood quickly and started running down the passageway, heading deeper into the ship.

"Where are we going?" Ben cried.

"The hold!" Nick yelled. "There's a lifeboat in there we can use to get the hell off this boat! Yacht! Dammit!"

The ceiling behind them exploded into a thousand fragments of teak and oak and mahogany. Wooden shrapnel pelted their backs as they reached the next corner and hurried around. Ben felt blood trickling from his shoulder, but he didn't dare stop to inspect the wound. And after having his eye gouged out with a knife and his fingers sliced off, a big splinter wasn't exactly on his pain radar.

Nick led them down one more set of stairs, a set that was thankfully stable and not about to come unbolted from the wall, and shoved open a door that Ben recognized. It was the door that he and Maggie had come through from the other side when they'd first entered the yacht. Except now the hold held only one speedboat and it didn't look too sea worthy.

"Ouch," Nick said as he stared at the cracked and broken vessel. And what was strewn across it. Bodies. Dozens of them, their limbs twisted and tied together.

"Found the Carls," Nick said.

"That had better not be the lifeboat you were talking about," Ben said.

"What? Oh, hell no," Nick said, turning away from the grotesque sight. "The lifeboat is through here."

They walked along the hold's small platform and came to a wide hatch. Nick grabbed the wheel in the center of the hatch and struggled to turn it.

"You'd think they'd make this easy since it's for emergencies," Nick said.

"You'd think it would be kept up above since it's for emergencies," Ben mocked.

"That would be ugly," Nick replied. "Rich people hate ugly more than they hate death. Come on, man, you've met my mom. She'd rather slit her wrists than wear last season's outfits."

"Move," Maggie said as they heard the sound of shearing metal echo down from above. "No time for you two to blabber on."

She pushed Nick out of the way and yanked on the wheel. It protested, but then gave and turned freely. She yanked open the hatch and revealed a small space barely big enough for six people.

"I guess the crew has their own lifeboat?" Ben asked.

"The crew goes down with the ship, dude," Nick said. "Haven't you seen Titanic? Of course, the crew are all a bunch of bloody pretzels right now, so they aren't going anywhere except out a monster's asshole when it returns and eats them up. You think the thing will dip them in mustard?"

"You are not as funny as you think you are," Ben replied. "That is just bad taste, dude."

"I don't care," Nick said. "I'm scared shitless and just trying to keep going, man."

"Get in," Maggie ordered.

The two men complied and she followed them inside. The space was pure white with two long, red benches. The walls were covered in ocean survival gear, none of it looking like it had ever been touched except for maybe a yearly inspection. There were small portholes along the top of the walls with a single, small windshield at one end of the lifeboat just above a wheel and console of controls.

Nick pointed at the benches. "We strap in and I hit this button here and the lifeboat gets ejected out the ass end of the yacht. My ship poops safety."

"Where's the radio?" Maggie asked.

"There," Nick said, pointing to a panel by her head. "I think it only broadcasts on emergency channels."

"Which are wide open," Maggie said. "I can't use those. The helicopter will just have to be looking for us in the general area."

"Your people, the helicopter," Ben grumbled. "Handler, asset. Is James Bond going to pop out next and offer me a martini?"

There was a loud crash from somewhere in the yacht and Maggie turned around, facing back towards the hold. She glanced over her shoulder at Ben and Nick.

"You two get settled," she said. "I'm going to take care of something real quick."

"You do that," Ben said.

"Dude," Nick snapped at him. "Knock it off with the pouty dick thing. That is still Maggie out there and she still totally loves you. You gotta understand that. Whatever else there is going on, happened after she met you. All this shit is only because you and I are friends, man. Don't blame her, blame me."

"I'll do both," Ben said.

"Dick," Nick said. Then he started and began to pat his pockets. "Shit."

"What?" Ben asked.

"I had something for Maggie," Nick said. "Found it on that other ship. It's gone now."

"Whatever," Ben said as he turned his back on Nick while the man continued to search his pockets.

Ben took a deep breath then grunted and moved towards the hatch. He looked into the vehicle hold and saw Maggie messing with the damaged second speedboat working her way around the entangled bodies.

"What are you doing?" he asked.

"Cutting the fuel lines," Maggie said. "Emptying the diesel tanks into the hold." She looked back at him and frowned. "Get back in the lifeboat."

"Yeah, you're not my handler," Ben said.

There was a shudder and thump above. They both froze. When it didn't happen again, Maggie pointed to a coil of rope hanging on a hook by Ben.

"Hand that rope to me then," Maggie said. "Since you won't be smart and go sit your ass down."

"What do you need the rope for?" Ben asked, grabbing it and tossing it to her.

She caught it easily and then held it under the fuel lines she'd severed.

"I'm making a fuse," she replied. "It's not exactly safe since diesel-soaked nylon burns fast, but it'll have to do."

"You're gonna blow this whole ship up and kill the thing?" Ben asked.

"That's the plan," Maggie said. "You know of a better one?"

"I'd think you'd want the thing alive," Ben said. "Then your operation wouldn't be a complete failure. Why not try to trap it?"

"I don't think it can be trapped," Maggie said. "Not on a ship like this. It spent most of the time hiding in the ventilation system. Out of water for hours. That didn't kill it. I fired I don't know how many rounds into the thing and it wouldn't die. It wiped out an entire NCDC cruiser filled with men and women, many of whom had almost as much training as me. Still alive."

"I understood twenty-five percent of that," Ben said.

"The bottom line is that we are food and if it is still alive then it's going to just jump in the water and come pry that lifeboat open, eating us like anchovies straight from the can," Maggie said. "I don't want to die, I don't want Nick to die, and I especially don't want you to die. So I am going to blow this boat up with the monster on it."

"Yacht," Nick called from the lifeboat.

"Shut up!" Maggie and Ben yelled.

"Sorry," Nick said.

"Take this end and walk it back to the lifeboat," Maggie said as she held out the end of the fuel-soaked rope. "Don't take it through the hatch, we don't want diesel inside there."

"Yeah, I figured that out on my own," Ben said.

He took the end of the rope and walked back towards the hatch of the lifeboat, taking time to choose his steps carefully since his field of vision and depth perception were completely shot. It only took a few seconds to cross the hold, but even that exertion nearly wiped him out. Ben rested next to the hatch, his head leaning back on the cool metal of the hold's wall.

"You good?" Nick asked, leaning out to help Ben inside.

"No," Ben said. "But I can take care of myself, Mr. Asset."

"Screw you, dude," Nick said. "I wanted to tell you a million times. Maggie wanted to tell you a million times. Neither of us could, man. Everyone has a boss and her bosses are scary. Like send you to a hidden jail in Lithuania for the rest of your life scary."

The hold shook and the ship rocked to the side as the sound of chaos erupted around them.

"Shit!" Nick shouted. "What the hell is it doing?"

The ship rocked again and the noise got louder, making the pain in Ben's head quadruple in intensity.

"Get in there!" Maggie yelled at the two men as she jumped from the speedboat and rushed towards them. "Get strapped in and ready to—!"

Her sentence was cut off as the hold's outside door was ripped away. The massive octopus jammed all legs into the hold opening and pulled back, warping and peeling the ship's hull like it was an old tin can. It hesitated when it caught sight of them with its huge, black eyes.

"Maggie," Ben whispered as he saw the woman lying unconscious near the dock. Her body was draped across a pile of bumpers and heavy tarps. He started to move towards her, but Nick grabbed his shoulder.

"No," Nick said. "This shit is my fault. Get her inside the lifeboat. I'll take care of this."

"What are you talking about?" Ben asked.

He didn't have time to wait for an answer as a tentacle shot across the hold and slammed into the wall next to his head. He screamed and jumped out of the way, moving in the complete opposite direction of where he was supposed to go, adding distance between him and Maggie's prone form.

"Get her!" Nick yelled as he cracked a flare, sending a fiery burst shooting towards the octopus. "HEY! OVER HERE!"

The man sprinted towards the hatch leading back into the ship, but skidded to a stop as two tentacles slammed into the platform, crushing the heavy duty plastic boards only a foot in front of him. Nick pulled a second flare from his waistband and fired it into one of the monster's tentacles and it shrank back. The creature shuddered and the other tentacles flailed about before rocketing right at Nick.

But Nick was already through the hatch and yelling for the monster to follow him. The thing wavered, its tentacles undulating back and forth, then it took off, squeezing its body through an opening that was only a quarter of its size. The metal around the hatch warped and bent, but didn't tear as the boneless creature jammed its entire bulk through. Then was gone from sight.

Ben stumbled over to Maggie and rolled her over. She had a huge gash across her forehead and blood poured into her eyes. Ben wiped it away with the bandage on his hand then started to laugh.

"Look at us," he whispered. "Some vacation, huh? Blood and guns and a giant octopus."

"Yeah…" Maggie muttered. Her eyes blinked a few times then fell closed again.

Ben tried to lift her up, to get her arm around his shoulder so he could carry her to the lifeboat, but he barely had the strength to stand. There was a huge crash from inside the ship and he heard the distinct sound of Nick screaming every epithet in the book. But he pushed those sounds away and looked about the hold for a way to get Maggie from the pile of gear she was on and into the lifeboat.

He saw a gear cart pushed up against a wall and he limped over to it, grabbed the long handle, and swung it around. The wheels protested and stuck, but he was able to manhandle the cart over and rest it right near Maggie.

"Now what?" Ben said to himself. "You can barely lift your arm. How will you get her in there?"

There was a crashing sound and a scream so loud that Ben thought it was his own voice. A second later, he watched in horror as Nick fell into the water just outside the ripped-open hole that used to be the sliding hold door. Ben stared at where Nick had fallen into the water and counted. Fifteen seconds later the man came back to the surface, spitting and coughing.

Nick looked at Ben then looked up. He dove out of sight as a huge shadow darkened the water from above. The creature landed right where Nick had been and water rushed through the hole and into the hold, splashing up over Ben and nearly knocking him off the small platform. But the force of the wave also lifted the tarps and bumpers Maggie was on, rolling her right next to Ben and the cart.

He grabbed her under her arms and in one heave lifted her into the cart. That about sapped his strength, but he dug deep and wrapped his good hand around the cart's handle. He rolled it two feet before he had to rest. Another two feet, another rest.

The ocean outside the hold churned and the monster's massive mantle rose from the surface until its eyes were visible and locked on to where Ben sat with his chest heaving and strength all but sapped.

"No," Ben croaked as he took the cart's handle again and scooted back on his ass, taking Maggie with him.

Tentacles reached into the hold once more and the creature pulled itself slowly through the water, its black eyes never leaving Ben. Ben's eye never left the monster, either. The two beings were locked in a stare off that was considerably disproportionate.

Ben's back bumped against the wall next to the lifeboat hatch and he risked a glance behind. All he had to do was get Maggie inside and slam the hatch shut. Then strap them in, hit the button, and hope the octopus didn't decide to rip the lifeboat apart before Ben could eject it from the ship.

Easy.

Instead of pulling Maggie inside, Ben crawled around to the front of the cart, putting himself between Maggie and the creature, and leaned back, using his weight to push the cart right inside the lifeboat. Maggie moaned and Ben froze as the monster's tentacles jerked and twitched at the sound.

He didn't understand what it was waiting for, why it wasn't attacking. Then a tentacle slapped a small buoy that hung from one of the many hooks on the walls. The buoy rocked back and forth and the octopus waited until it stopped moving before slapping it again.

"Oh, shit," Ben thought as he kept pushing Maggie into the lifeboat. "It's playing with us. This is a game now."

Maggie's cart thumped over the hatch's threshold and rolled into the lifeboat, coming to a stop against one of the long, red benches. Ben crab walked backwards after the cart, his eye never leaving the monster that was inching its way closer and closer.

Ben couldn't help but think that the beast wanted him to close the hatch and eject the lifeboat. It wasn't a rational thought because why would a giant, mutant octopus want him to escape? But rational thought had left reality a long time ago.

"It wants to play before it kills," Ben thought again. "It knows we're the last and it wants to drag it out." He looked at the hatch then the big emergency button that would eject the lifeboat. "It wants to play chase."

He looked back outside the hatch and saw the end of the diesel rope lying harmlessly to the side of the dock, only a couple feet from the monster that was slowly closing the distance between it and the lifeboat.

He took a deep breath, which hurt like hell, and then said out loud, "This isn't a game. It never was."

Ben got to his feet, took a couple more deep breaths, and watched the creature. It watched him. He reached out and plucked an emergency kit from its spot on the wall next to the hatch. He opened it slowly and smiled when he saw three of the four flares gone. At least Nick had tried to think ahead, taking more than just one flare. The man had also thought enough to leave one flare behind. One very important flare.

Ben put the flare to his mouth and pulled off the cap with his teeth, revealing a long pull string at the end. He stared at the pull string dangling from the end of the red and yellow stick. He had no idea how he would pull it and ignite the flare with his other hand basically useless. If he yanked the string with his teeth, he'd end up with a face full of flare and he was pretty sure his face couldn't take much more trauma

"Shit," he mumbled around the cap still clenched between his teeth.

He looked around for some place to wedge the flare, so he could pull the string with his good hand. But the lifeboat was all smooth and textured heavy duty plastic. Even the screws holding things together had been sunk deep so they wouldn't pose a danger to anyone being tossed around inside. There was no place to hold the flare. Even if there was it would have to be a place that pointed out of the lifeboat

"Shit," he mumbled again and spat the cap to the floor.

The octopus grew closer and closer then stopped. Ben froze, his mind torn between slamming the hatch closed and hitting the eject button or continuing to find a way to ignite the flare. That time was all the creature needed to get right in front of the lifeboat's hatch. A tentacle reached in and plucked the flare from Ben's hand, withdrawing it from sight, gone forever.

"Hey," Ben managed to squeak out. "Uh… Octopus. Listen, okay? I'm just some guy that got caught up…"

He stopped talking as a tentacle slithered in and rose just in front of his face. Ben gulped hard as the tentacle hovered before his eye. Then it smacked him hard enough to send him flying against the wall. He fell to the ground, his hand clutching his cheek. He could feel blood trickling down and he tried to figure out how badly he was hurt when the same tentacle wiped its tip along his cheek. It withdrew with Ben's blood dripping from its end.

Ben shuddered as he watched the octopus's tentacle disappear into its beak while it closed its eye in what looked like ecstasy.

Another tentacle started to reach for him, but stopped as Nick's voice echoed from outside the lifeboat.

"Hey, fuck fish!" Nick shouted. "I hate sushi! I like my fish cooked!"

Ben didn't have time to groan over what Nick said as all the air was sucked from the lifeboat, and his lungs, as a massive WHUMP exploded from the hold. The creature shrank back from the lifeboat and Ben felt the intense heat that came from the rest of the ship.

Nick had lit the fuel.

Nick had lit the fuel…

"Nick's lit the fuel!" Ben shouted as he scrambled weakly to the hatch and jammed his shoulder between it and the wall.

He shoved the hatch closed, his eye registering the growing flames that spread across almost every surface of the hold. He couldn't see Nick, anywhere, but he could hear him. Hear him screaming in agony as the octopus's body was wrapped around him, chomping down with its beak. Blood geysered up into the air and that was the last thing Ben saw as he hurried to the emergency button.

He didn't have time to strap himself or Maggie in and just said a prayer that the ejection wouldn't be too violent.

He hit the button and his prayer was ignored.

He flew back, colliding with the far wall and the world became a swimming, swirling illusion. Only the sight of Maggie sprawled out on the lifeboat's floor kept him from passing out. He managed to get to her as the lifeboat sped through the water, thumping and bobbing along until its momentum finally slowed and the emergency vehicle came to a stop.

"Mags?" Ben asked as he pushed the woman's blood-matted hair from her face. "Mags?"

"Yeah," Maggie whispered, but didn't open her eyes. "I love you, Benjamin."

Then her breathing evened out and Ben knew she was completely unconscious. She probably had a concussion, which meant he needed to keep her awake, but he was struggling to keep his own eyelid open, let alone try to pry hers apart.

He wrapped an arm around her and was able to scoot her head onto his lap. The lifeboat bobbed and rocked and Ben looked up to see a view of the yacht, far off and smoking, through the small windshield.

The view was filled with a massive fireball that shot hundreds of feet into the air. The yacht exploded everywhere and Ben ducked instinctively as flaming debris rained down against the lifeboat. He was glad that it was a completely enclosed vessel as fiery shrapnel pelted the outside over and over for several seconds until the sky finally cleared of the falling wreckage.

Ben's throat constricted as he thought of what Nick had done for him and Maggie. He choked back tears, not just because he didn't want to lose control, but because the act of crying brought nothing but agony to the torn and mutilated tear duct in his empty eye socket.

"Thanks, dude," he whispered. "You stupid son of a bitch."

He leaned his head down, placing his forehead on Maggie's, and slowly let sleep take him.

52.

When Ben woke up, he wasn't at all surprised to find himself in a hospital bed, the sound of beeping machinery piercing his brain, fueling the excruciating headache that he assumed was the reason he was even awake. He glanced around, but all he saw was a small slit of a window along the top of the wall to his left. There was no cheesy hospital furniture, no faux wood dresser or convertible chair for visitors to sit or lie in.

Nothing but grey concrete and the constantly beeping machines.

"You are awake," a man said as a door opened to Ben's blindside. "I wasn't sure or not."

Ben rolled his head and cried out then tried to focus on the short, fat man that was carrying a folding chair up to Ben's bed and setting it down.

"Yeah, you'll be hurting for a long time," the man said as he sat down and offered his hand. "John Jones. Pleased to meet you, Mr. Clow. Or can I call you Ben? Whatever you prefer is fine."

Ben only blinked at the man.

"Yeah, I get that look a lot," Jones said. "I tell you what, I'm going to make this debriefing as short as possible so you can push that little button by your left hand and make the morphine train pull into the station. It's good stuff, believe me. I ask a couple questions, you give me a couple answers, to the best of your ability, of course, then you can nod off to Pain Management Land."

"Where am I?" Ben asked.

"That's not a question I can answer," Jones responded. He pulled out his phone and set it on the bed next to Ben. "Do you mind if I record this?"

"Where's Maggie?" Ben asked.

"You are full of questions, aren't you?" Jones chuckled. "None of which I am going to answer. Once we complete the debriefing, then an entire department of threat assessors will go over your answers and decide what you can and cannot know. But, let me warn you now, the stuff you can know will be very vague and very frustrating. The Devil is in the details and unfortunately you do not have clearance to meet the Devil."

Jones waited then shook his head.

"No one ever even cracks a smile at that," Jones said.

"I want to talk to Maggie," Ben said. "I need to know if my girls are okay. I want to talk to a lawyer. I want to get the hell out of here."

"But you don't even know where here is, Mr. Clow," Jones said. "Leaving here right now would not be in your best interest. The OAS and NCDC are a couple of angry wasps nests and they'd love nothing more than to pluck you off the street and put you somewhere that doesn't come close to the nice ambience that this room has."

Jones waited again and shook his head again.

"Still no smile?" Jones sighed. "Listen, Mr. Clow, your daughters are completely safe and secure. Their lives haven't been interrupted at all. As far as they and your ex-wife know, you are still on a happy holiday with your beautiful girlfriend. When we return you to them, which I can assure you we will do, they'll be informed that the yacht had an accident, it caught fire, and you were the only one to escape alive."

"And Maggie," Ben said. "Maggie escaped alive with me."

"Yes, Ms. Rodriguez-Kimura did escape alive, but that won't be part of the story," Jones replied. "Not yet, at least. We'll concern ourselves with your story first then decide whether or not there is a dramatic revelation and a miraculous deep sea rescue of another survivor found floating out in the open ocean. But that is not up to me, so we won't dwell on it."

"Won't dwell on it," Ben mumbled and rolled his head back so he could stare up at the ceiling. "Good idea."

"I think so," Jones said. "Now, how about we start from the beginning. Not the very beginning, but when you first stepped onto the Lucky Sucker. Tell me everything you can remember."

Ben coughed a sad laugh at the mention of the yacht's name then took a deep breath and began.

53.

A man wobbled precariously on a ladder as he struggled to free the Christmas and holiday decorations from the hooks over the supermarket's automatic doors. The ladder shook under the man's weight, which wasn't exactly in a healthy percentile, and Ben could see the feet starting to slip and then tip.

"I got you," Ben said as he grabbed the ladder and steadied it for the man.

A dagger of pain shot through his head as a slight rush of adrenaline coursed through his system, making his empty eye socket throb and pulse.

"Thanks, bud," the heavy man on the ladder said as he looked down at Ben. "You saved my bacon." He frowned as he saw Ben's eye patch and heavily bandaged hand. "Oh, Jesus, bud, I'm sorry. You shouldn't have to save anyone's bacon."

He let out a loud whistle and a skinny woman with scraggly hair and a distinct hint of meth head came shuffling from her post by the self-check register.

"Bess can hold the ladder for me," the heavy man said. "Thanks again, though."

"Damn," meth-head Bess said as she looked Ben up and down. "You a soldier or something? Lose your eye in Afghaniraq?"

"No," Ben said. "I lost it playing poker."

Ben grabbed onto his shopping cart laden with groceries and wheeled it past the ladder and out of the supermarket before meth-head Bess could recover from her slack-jawed confusion.

The cart's front wheel wobbled as Ben navigated through the ubiquitous puddles that filled the supermarket's parking lot. It was January in Seattle and the never-ending misty rain had fully set in. Nothing but cold, damp, and grey until spring hit.

He slowed the cart when he reached his minivan. He smacked the back hatch with his good hand and after a couple seconds it popped open, rising automatically at a pace almost as excruciating as the pain in Ben's head. He managed to get the bags of groceries into the minivan's cargo area without too much trouble, but he was exhausted when he finally plopped himself into the passenger's seat.

"Home, Jeeves," he muttered to Tanni who was sitting in the driver's seat, staring at something on her phone.

"I don't know who that is," Tanni said as she tossed her phone onto the dash and started the minivan up. "Where to now?"

"Just home," Ben said. "We need to put away the groceries and I need to take a nap."

"That's like the sixth nap this weekend," Tanni said. "Didn't the doctors say to let them know if you felt really sluggish? Should you call them?"

"No," was all Ben said.

"Okay. Whatever," Tanni replied, her face pinched with teenage indignation. "Go ahead and die then, but don't come bitching to me."

"I won't," Ben replied.

He rested his head against the cold glass of his window and looked past the trails of raindrops at the gloomy parking lot. Tanni backed them out then headed for the traffic light at the lot's entrance. Ben watched the busy shoppers try to stay warm and dry and failing miserably just like everyone else. He couldn't wait to get his damp clothes off and crawl into a warm bed. That was his favorite pastime, just curling up in bed and letting the world go on without him.

He knew it wasn't fair to the girls. They needed him. But after everything that had happened on the yacht, and the zero amount of information he got from that Jones guy before he was released to a normal hospital for the rest of his recovery, Ben just didn't have it in him to pretend the world was the same as before he'd stepped foot onto a speedboat with Nick and Maggie.

Maggie…

Maggie?

"Stop the van!" Ben shouted as he saw a figure in a hooded rain poncho duck into the bus shelter next to the parking lot's entrance. "Tanni! Stop!"

Ben shoved open his door, ignoring the honks from the cars stacking up behind them, and hurried as fast as his body could over to the bus shelter. He reached it and rested a hand against the metal and glass enclosure, his eye blinking over and over as he stared at nothing, at no one. The shelter was empty.

The honking was joined by angry shouts and Ben slowly backed away from the shelter and turned back to the minivan. Tanni's eyes were wide with fear and Ben tried to give her an apologetic smile, but he knew she wouldn't see it that way since anytime he smiled it scrunched up his eye patch, reminding the world he was not a whole man.

Ben got into the van and pointed at the light that had just turned yellow.

"Blow it," he said and Tanni hit the accelerator, hurrying the minivan through the intersection before the traffic light turned red.

Neither of them said a word on the drive home.

54.

The spring sun warmed Ben's skin as he lay on the plastic lounge chair, his face turned up to the sky, his eye patch off and next to his cold beer.

May. Early May. The threat of spring rain looming in the distance. But for that moment, the sun shone and Ben soaked it in, the feeling that his life may be moving forward for the first time since…

Since.

Everything around him related to that single word. Since. Most of his conversations began with that word. Most of his interactions with neighbors or even his girls began with that word. Damn he hated that word and as he breathed in the clean air, he vowed he would drop it, let it go, never utter the word again.

The new start he'd been promising his daughters needed to go ahead and start and he felt strong enough for that to happen right then. Too much time wasted, since…

"Dad?" Norma asked from the sliding patio door.

They had moved from his old place almost as soon as he could hold a pen to sign the papers. Too many memories. Too many good times that Ben knew had been complete and utter bullshit.

So he'd bought a cute bungalow, big enough for the girls to have their own rooms and for him to have a space large enough for a bed and a dresser. One bathroom, but he didn't care. He let the girls dominate it and they were perfectly happy with that.

Bobbi had tried to insinuate herself back into his life, coddling him, mothering him, doing everything she could to take over his daily affairs while he recuperated. But he'd had enough strength to shut that down almost before it began. Bobbi was not the answer to starting something new. Far from it.

"Dad?" Norma called again and Ben picked up the emotion in her voice.

He opened his eye and turned around in the lounge chair.

"Norma? What's wrong?" he asked. "Did you cut yourself in the kitchen or…"

There was no need to finish the sentence. He knew instantly why Norma sounded off. The woman standing in the doorway behind her was the reason.

"Hi, Benjamin," Maggie said.

"Tanni let her in," Norma said, her voice suddenly protective. "Then she told me to go get you and went back in her room."

"I'm sure she did," Ben said as he slowly got to his feet. "Thanks, sweetie. You can go back inside and watch Netflix or something."

"I was drawing," Norma said before she turned around and squeezed by Maggie.

"Guess what she was drawing?" Maggie smiled. "An octopus."

Ben glared.

"Too soon?" Maggie asked, her smile dropping away.

"*Never* would be too soon," Ben said. "What are you doing here, Maggie? Or is that actually your name?"

"It's my name," Maggie said. She looked at the lounge chair next to Ben's. "Can I sit down?"

"Really?" Ben snapped.

"I want to explain," she said. "Everything. Or everything I'm authorized to explain."

"Authorized," Ben replied, spitting the word back at Maggie. "Sure. Sit. Explain everything you're authorized to."

Maggie sat down in the lounge chair then looked at the one Ben stood next to. "Are you going to sit?"

"Oh, I think I'm going to stand," Ben said. "What the hell made you think coming here would be a good idea?"

"You don't want to see me?" Maggie asked.

Ben thought about the time at the supermarket and how he'd jumped out of the minivan without a thought. He'd wanted nothing more than to see Maggie right then. But now? With the new life promise he'd made to himself?

"I don't know," he answered honestly. "You really messed up my head, Maggie. I don't know how I feel about you."

"I know how I feel about you," Maggie said. "I love you."

Ben laughed.

"I know that's hard to believe, but it's true," she continued. "It's why I'm here. I needed to talk to you before tomorrow."

"What happens tomorrow?" Ben asked.

"Tomorrow there will be a quiet announcement of a survivor found at sea by a fishing boat," Maggie said. "Then I get to come back from the dead officially and start over."

"What does that have to do with me?" Ben asked.

"Everything," she replied. "If this conversation goes the way I want it to then it'll be a Canadian fishing boat that finds me just north of Victoria."

"If this doesn't go the way you want?" Ben asked.

"Then I'm found by an Alaskan fishing boat way up in the Bering Sea," Maggie said. "Far away from Seattle and far away from you."

"Ah," Ben said. "So you are here to see if I'm going to play the part of the relieved boyfriend and welcome you home or if you'll just be greeted by Eskimos and bush pilots."

"No," Maggie said. "You don't have to play a part. My return will be a back page event. A paragraph at the most. No one wants any eyes on me, so things are already in motion to make sure not even a hint of me gets mentioned on social media or in any way that can't be controlled."

"Yeah, you gotta control that flow of information," Ben said. "That's what this is all about? Will I talk out of turn if I don't agree to let you back in my life?"

"You've already been vetted," Maggie said. "No one thinks you'll ever tell what really happened. They've been monitoring your activity and all of your communications, which I'm sure a smart guy like you already knew."

"I assumed as much," Ben said.

"You are completely clear," Maggie said. "As of yesterday, your file has been closed and there isn't a single person assigned to watch you."

"Yay me," Ben said. "Free at last."

"It's the same for me, Benjamin," Maggie said. "As of yesterday, I became an independent person. I work for no one and no one will bother me again as long as I keep to my non-disclosure agreement and don't say anything stupid."

"I have too many comebacks for that one," Ben said.

"A joke," Maggie said. "That's a start."

"No, it's not," Ben said. He sighed and pointed at the sliding door. "I think you need to go, Maggie. You wanted an answer? That's it. There is no way I can do this."

"Let me talk first, please?" Maggie asked. "Then you can kick me out. But I want you to have all the facts before you do or say something that can't ever be taken back."

Ben almost pointed at the sliding glass door, but the way the sun hit Maggie's face, lighting up the hair that fell across his forehead, all the strength he'd been building up just left him. Poof. Gone. He sat down quickly before his legs buckled.

"Then talk," Ben said. "After that, you leave."

"Okay," Maggie agreed.

She wrung her hands together then placed them on her knees.

"You, me, it was real," she started and held up a hand immediately as Ben began to protest. "It was. I met you, fell for you, began a relationship with you, and it was completely authentic."

"Except for the you being a teacher part," Ben said.

"No, that's real too," Maggie said. "I have a Masters in education. I also have a few other skills. But I am a teacher. It made a perfect cover for my other job."

"Your real job," Ben said.

"My other job," Maggie insisted. "I met you, we were getting along great, I thought I had something that would be separate from my other job, something to keep me grounded and feeling like a person. But that all changed when the connection between you and Nick was discovered."

"You found out I had a past that wasn't so squeaky clean and you decided to use that for your own means," Ben said. "I get it. If I'd found out some info I could use against another card player then I'd have jumped on it too."

"No, you're misunderstanding me," Maggie said. "When I found out about your past, and about Nick, I didn't report it. I kept it quiet. It wasn't until those above me found out that it became an issue. I couldn't lie to them, so I was suddenly in deep shit for keeping back important, usable information. I could either call it off with you and disappear from your life, or I could exploit your connection to Nick and bring him in as an asset. You were my perfect cover and those above me made it very clear they were not going to be happy unless I utilized that."

"Awesome," Ben said.

"Not so much, no," Maggie said. "It tore me up, Benjamin. It racked my guts day and night and I nearly lost my mind for a bit there. Things were falling apart. Then Nick came to me with his idea to sell that damn boat of his."

"Yacht," Ben said and grinned in spite of himself.

Maggie grinned back. "Yacht. He needed to unload it and things fell in place. We knew some corrupt INTERPOL agents had come across info that Giraldi was planning something big, Nick had access to friends of friends of his, and the rest is sad history."

"Sad history that killed him, everyone else, nearly me, nearly you, and also put my daughters in danger," Ben said. "Don't just wipe it all away with a wave of your hand. People died. My best friend died. A crazy international crime lord had one of his men watching Tanni, ready to kill her on his order if I didn't play ball."

"She wasn't at risk," Maggie said. "I had the Guillotine on it. Giraldi's man wouldn't have even been able to hand Tanni a beer, let alone harm her."

"Is that argument supposed to make me feel better?" Ben asked.

"No, sorry, of course not," Maggie said. "But I need you to know that I love your girls and I take Tanni's wellbeing very serious."

"So do I, which is why you in our lives is not a good thing," Ben responded. "You kill people, Mags. You do whatever else it is you do, but that still includes killing people."

"Only bad people," Maggie said. "Very bad people. And that is over."

"Is it?" Ben asked. "Can it ever really be over for someone like you? Can it ever be over for someone like me? You think those days won't be sitting between us for the rest of our lives? Because you'd be stupid to think so."

"They don't have to be between us," Maggie said. "They can bring us closer."

"They can, but they won't," Ben said. "I'm sorry, Mags, but it ain't gonna happen. You need to leave. We can't get back what we had."

"Whatever," Tanni said from the sliding glass door.

Ben and Maggie turned their heads, surprised to see the teen standing there.

"I'm making stroganoff and veggie meatballs for dinner," Tanni said. "I'm making enough for Maggie to join us."

"Tanni, this isn't something you get to butt in on," Ben said.

"Bullshit it isn't," Tanni said and flipped him off. "You're better with her in our lives. We all are. And it sounds like she can keep us safe, so I'd rather she was hanging around than up in some Alaskan fishing village."

"You heard everything?" Maggie asked.

Tanni tapped at her nose. "Nothing gets by me, Magster. This sullen teenager pays attention to way more than you guys give me credit for." She sighed and looked at her father. "Do you really want Mom to be the only female role model in my life? Have I told you that she's thinking about starting a spiritual healing business for pets? Oh, and she wants to start a support group for pagans with gay daughters. Yeah, both of those things are happening."

"Jesus," Ben said and rubbed his forehead. "I am so screwed."

"She's staying for dinner," Tanni said. "You guys can talk more, you can yell and scream, throw things, just not each other, even though Maggie will win, and then maybe make up, do it like bunnies, and then start over in the morning."

"Jesus," Ben said again.

"Dinner will be ready in an hour," Tanni said. "Get another beer and keep chatting."

They watched Tanni walk away, a cocky swagger in her hips.

"I know some people that would recruit her in a heartbeat," Maggie said.

"Holy shit," Ben said. "Really?"

"What? Oh, sorry," Maggie said and frowned. "Old habits."

She looked at Ben's beer and stood up.

"You want another?" she asked. "I'm going to grab one. Teenager's orders. You want one more? When did you have your last pain meds? I don't want you OD'ing."

"I'm off the meds," Ben said. "It's easier to deal with the pain as it comes and goes than deal with the fog of hydrocodone."

"I get that," Maggie said. "So…beer or no beer?"

"Beer," Ben said finally after a couple seconds. "Go ahead and bring two. I'm going to need them."

"It's going to be one of those nights?" Maggie grinned.

"Could be," Ben said. "But either way, I'll need the beers."

"Two beers coming up," Maggie said and walked inside the house.

Ben watched her disappear into the shadows then turned his face back to the sun. He closed his eye and let out a long, slow breath.

Maybe, just maybe, what he needed wasn't a new life, but a new chapter to build on his old life.

He had no idea if that was the answer, but as he heard Maggie come back outside, the sound of a bottle cap being popped off a beer, he decided that the day was too nice to be rash. He'd have his couple beers, maybe a couple more, probably yell and scream at Maggie while she yelled and screamed at him, and then he'd let things sort themselves out.

"You can't always control the cards you're dealt, but you sure as hell can control what you do with them," Ben thought as he felt a warm hand on his face and a cold beer pressed into his hand.

Damn if he didn't like the feel of both.

55.

The doors opened and two of the most powerful CEOs in the defense world walked in at the same time.

"Mathias," Agnes Marion said, surprised. "I didn't know you would be here."

"Hello, Agnes," Mathias McDowell said. "OAS did develop this project, so why wouldn't I be here?"

"Well, I just assumed this was an exclusive offer," Marion said.

Both of the CEOs had heavily armed men flanking them. But the number doubled as a new man walked in, a wide smile on his face.

"Ah, I see this is to be a bidding war," the man said.

"Bidding war?" McDowell asked. "I think you are mistaken."

"No, he is not," a woman said as she was wheeled into the room from a side door.

The number of heavily armed men doubled once again.

"Ms. Romanski?" Ms. Marion gasped. "But you died."

"Did I?" Niya laughed from her wheelchair.

There was a blanket across her lap and she pulled it back to reveal only a left leg. She was wheeled closer and the room's light caught the right side of her face. A side that was nothing but mangled scar tissue with a dead, white eye staring out at everyone. The other eye was alive with intelligence and stared at the people gathered.

"As people always find out the hard way, I am extremely hard to kill," she said and laughed again. It was a harsh rasp of a sound and everyone except the hired guns shivered. "Let's get started."

"I don't understand," McDowell said. "Who is this man?"

"That doesn't matter," Niya said.

"How can he be here if he doesn't have the first part of the research?" Ms. Marion asked.

"Oh, he does have it," Niya replied, reaching into a pouch on her lap. She withdrew a USB drive. "Because I gave it to him. Well, I did not expressly give it to him, but he has the research in his possession."

She withdrew a second USB drive.

"Which brings us to tonight's proceedings," she continued. "The second part of the research. The secret part that Dr. Glouster created where the creature can be controlled. Once you make a new one, that is."

"I do not appreciate the deception," McDowell grumbled.

"Then leave," Niya replied.

He stayed where he was.

"That is what I thought," she said and grinned. The scar tissue on her face pulled tight and the others grimaced. "Now…how about we start the bidding at one billion? I think that's more than fair, don't you? Considering everything I went through to bring this drive to market."

McDowell glared but raised his hand.

"One billion? Excellent." Niya grinned wider, reveling in the reactions from those around her. "Do I perhaps hear two billion?"

THE END

Jake Bible, Bram Stoker Award nominated-novelist, short story writer, independent screenwriter, podcaster, and inventor of the Drabble Novel, has entertained thousands with his horror and sci/fi tales. He reaches audiences of all ages with his uncanny ability to write a wide range of characters and genres.

Jake is the author of the bestselling Z-Burbia series set in Asheville, NC, the Apex Trilogy (DEAD MECH, The Americans, Metal and Ash) and the Mega series for Severed Press, as well as the YA zombie novel, Little Dead Man, the Bram Stoker Award nominated Teen horror novel, Intentional Haunting, the ScareScapes series, and the Reign of Four series for Permuted Press.

Find Jake at jakebible.com. Join him on Twitter @jakebible and find him on Facebook.

CHECK OUT OTHER GREAT DEEP SEA THRILLERS

MEGA
by Jake Bible

There is something in the deep. Something large. Something hungry. Something prehistoric.
And Team Grendel must find it, fight it, and kill it.
Kinsey Thorne, the first female US Navy SEAL candidate has hit rock bottom. Having washed out of the Navy, she turned to every drink and drug she could get her hands on. Until her father and cousins, all ex-Navy SEALS themselves, offer her a way back into the life: as part of a private, elite combat Team being put together to find and hunt down an impossible monster in the Indian Ocean. Kinsey has a second chance, but can she live through it?

THE BLACK
by Paul E Cooley

Under 30,000 feet of water, the exploration rig Leaguer has discovered an oil field larger than Saudi Arabia, with oil so sweet and pure, nations would go to war for the rights to it. But as the team starts drilling exploration well after exploration well in their race to claim the sweet crude, a deep rumbling beneath the ocean floor shakes them all to their core. Something has been living in the oil and it's about to give birth to the greatest threat humanity has ever seen.

"The Black" is a techno/horror-thriller that puts the horror and action of movies such as Leviathan and The Thing right into readers' hands. Ocean exploration will never be the same."

CHECK OUT OTHER GREAT
DEEP SEA THRILLERS

PREDATOR X
by C.J Waller

When deep level oil fracking uncovers a vast subterranean sea, a crack team of cavers and scientists are sent down to investigate. Upon their arrival, they disappear without a trace. A second team, including sedimentologist Dr Megan Stoker, are ordered to seek out Alpha Team and report back their findings. But Alpha team are nowhere to be found – instead, they are faced with something unexpected in the depths. Something ancient. Something huge. Something dangerous. Predator X

DEAD BAIT
by Tim Curran

A husband hell-bent on revenge hunts a Wereshark...A Russian mail order bride with a fishy secret...Crabs with a collective consciousness...A vampire who transforms into a Candiru...Zombie piranha...Bait that will have you crawling out of your skin and more. Drawing on horror, humor with a helping of dark fantasy and a touch of deviance, these 19 contemporary stories pay homage to the monsters that lurk in the murky waters of our imaginations. If you thought it was safe to go back in the water...Think Again!

CHECK OUT OTHER GREAT
DEEP SEA THRILLERS

LAMPREYS
by Alan Spencer

A secret government tactical team is sent to perform a clean sweep of a private research installation. Horrible atrocities lurk within the abandoned corridors. Mutated sea creatures with insane killing abilities are waiting to suck the blood and meat from their prey.
Unemployed college professor Conrad Garfield is forced to assist and is soon separated from the team. Alone and afraid, Conrad must use his wits to battle mutated lampreys, infected scientists and go head-to-head with the biggest monstrosity of all.
Can Conrad survive, or will the deadly monsters suck the very life from his body?

DEEP DEVOTION
by M.C. Norris

Rising from the depths, a mind-bending monster unleashes a wave of terror across the American heartland. Kate Browning, a Kansas City EMT confronts her paralyzing fear of water when she traces the source of a deadly parasitic affliction to the Gulf of Mexico. Cooperating with a marine biologist, she travels to Florida in an effort to save the life of one very special patient, but the source of the epidemic happens to be the nest of a terrifying monster, one that last rose from the depths to annihilate the lost continent of Atlantis.

Leviathan, destroyer, devoted lifemate and parent, the abomination is not going to take the extermination of its brood well.

17857529R00150

Printed in Great Britain
by Amazon